TAILS OF LOVE

"Don't worry about it," Jenny said. "Listen, this woman, this Clara Kelly, you say she's all alone?"

"Well, she said she has kids, but they live out of state," Brad explained. "And she has a friend who brings in groceries. But she seemed awfully sorry to see Fido leaving."

Jenny glanced down at her Fido. "Yes," she said, "a dog can be a lot of company. If Mrs. Kelly lives on Denver Street, maybe I could go see her."

"That's a great idea!" Why hadn't he thought of that? Another chance to get to see Jenny. "I'll go too. We'll see to it that she has company."

"Well." Jenny looked away from him again. "I meant to go alone. But I guess we could go together sometimes."

Brad and Jenny stood there together, looking down. The dogs were curled up together, looking as if they'd known each other forever.

"Smart dogs," he said. "They know when they've got something good."

She sighed. "Life's a lot easier for them, I guess."

She sounded so wistful, so lost. He wished he was a dog so he could curl up with her, give her the comfort she so obviously needed. But he wasn't a dog. And neither was she. Besides, sniffing noses wouldn't be enough for him. She was a beautiful woman and he wanted to kiss her.

He wanted to, and the next thing he knew, he was.

It's A Dog's Life

NINA COOMBS

Man's Best Friend

LOVE SPELL  NEW YORK CITY

LOVE SPELL®

June 1997

Published by

Dorchester Publishing Co., Inc.
276 Fifth Avenue
New York, NY 10001

Printed in the United States of America.

For all those who have known the love of dogs.
And for those special dogs who have been
my friends on the journey through life.

Man's
Best
Friend

Chapter One

The October wind whistled down the street of the Cleveland suburb, scurried between the middle-class houses, and tugged at the long dark brown hair of the woman standing with her hand raised to knock. The big scruffy dog beside her whined and tugged at the leash. Jenny Carruthers hesitated. She looked down past two ragged ears into soulful brown eyes pleading through snarled hair. "Don't worry, boy. You'll be inside in a minute. You're home now." The dog whined again and pressed his cold nose against her fingers. She jerked her hand away, out of his reach. She hadn't petted a dog since . . . "None of that. You're not mine. I don't have a dog anymore. And I don't want one."

She felt the stinging behind her eyes, but there was no time for tears now.

She knocked, huddling down into her jacket. Should have worn her heavier coat. The wind was cold. The sooner this dog was returned to his owner the better. Being around dogs made her think of Torrie. And that hurt too much.

She knocked again. Come on. Answer the door. Still no one. Maybe the owner was out looking for the dog. Well, she'd knock once more, then leave a note. She raised her hand again. And the door swung open.

Her breath left her lungs in one great emptying whoosh. The hunk standing there could have posed for a *Cosmo* centerfold. Above his bare tanned feet, faded jeans looked like they'd been enameled to his thighs. His bare chest was a mini-jungle of golden furry hair that invited a woman's exploration.

In one of his big hands he gripped a bright red bath towel. Absently he rubbed his chest with it, hiding his body from her fascinated gaze. For a moment she wanted to reach out and brush the towel aside, to look some more.

"Sorry to keep you waiting. You caught me in the shower."

His voice was deep and sexy, reminding her of warm summer nights and parked cars on Sweetheart Hill and the feel of—She raised her gaze to his face. "I—ah—" He not only had a great chest, he was swallow-your-tongue handsome. Blond curls, still damp, clung around his face and brushed his neck. A mustache didn't conceal his strong, even teeth. Or lips that looked like he could kiss with the best of them. He had a bold nose, a chin that said he took no guff, and gray-green eyes that held a hint of mischief. Those eyes gazed down into hers and her stomach did a series of somersaults that landed it in her mouth.

"Yes?" he said in that deep sexy voice. "What is it?"

She struggled to find her wits and get her tongue to work. "I—ah—I saw your poster. I found your dog."

He glanced at the animal beside her, then back at her face. "My dog?"

"This *is* three-twenty-five Oak Street, isn't it?"

"Oh, yes," he said. "This is. But—"

"Good." She hurried on, afraid to stop talking for fear she wouldn't be able to start again. What was there about this man that interfered with her breathing? After all, she'd seen hunks before, even been engaged to one. And she'd sworn off men anyway, so what did she care *what* they thought. "I saw your notice on the telephone pole outside the grocery store. And then I found this dog hanging around in my backyard. He came right to me when I called out 'Fido.' So I knew he was yours and—"

"That?" the man exploded, opening his eyes wide. "That?" And he burst into loud laughter.

He had a nice laugh, but why was he laughing now? Well, some people did laugh when they were nervous. But why should he be nervous? A hunk like that had no reason to—

"That *thing's* not *my* dog."

The dog pressed against her thigh, almost as if he understood he was being insulted. Automatically she reached down to scratch behind his shaggy ears. It wasn't his fault this guy didn't have any manners.

She glared at the man. "The notice said big dog, bushy-tailed and bright-eyed, answers to the name Fido. Didn't it?"

The man nodded, his eyes still gleaming with laughter. "Yes, I guess it did."

"Well," she snapped, "he is and he did."

The man coughed, like he was swallowing another laugh. What was so funny anyway? She was sick and tired of—

"Maybe so," he said, "but he's not mine. My Fido is smaller. Cleaner. And a she."

She snorted in exasperation. "Well! You could have said so."

He shrugged those magnificent shoulders. And then he burst into laughter again.

Crim-in-ently! She didn't have to stand there and listen to some bozo laugh at her. Even if he *was* a hunk. Well, what could she expect? Men were like that. Lying so-and-sos like Hugh said they'd love you forever and then took off the minute some slinky blonde beckoned to them.

Dishonest bosses like Morris called your work their own and made piles of money for themselves. Men were all alike. No good. That's why she'd sworn off them.

She turned her back on this one, fleeing down the steps and out onto the leaf-covered sidewalk, his laughter echoing in her ears. Ignorant so-and-so! Let him find his own blasted dog!

She dragged the stray down the street, her sneakers making a satisfying splatting sound against the pavement in spite of the fallen leaves. She'd like to splat *him*—laughing at her like that. Too bad it wasn't his face down there she was stomping! Why hadn't he made his stupid poster more specific? Anyone with sense knew Fido was a male dog's name.

Suddenly, without warning, the stray dropped to his haunches. He was a big dog, and she wasn't expecting him to stop like that—so quickly. The leash jerked her off balance and she ended up on her behind, sitting right there on the sidewalk among the damp leaves, swallowing curses she'd rather scream out loud.

The dog came over and pressed itself against her, whining again. "I know," she said. "You didn't mean to make me fall. But nothing was hurt." She scowled. "Unless you count my dignity—and my bruised behind."

What was she doing with a stray on a leash anyway? "Guess there's no need to keep you on this now." She undid it from around his neck and waved him off.

"Calm down," she told herself. "Just forget the creep. So he laughed. So what? He's not worth getting all upset about. He's not."

It was good advice, but, like a lot of advice, hard to follow. And the dog still sitting there didn't help. "Get out of here," she told him, trying to shoo him away with her hand, out toward someone's yard. "I'm not looking for a dog. *My* dog's dead. My *only* dog."

He looked at her with those sorrowful eyes and whined. "Sorry, boy, I can't help you. I thought I was taking you home. But I guess you're lucky you don't belong to *him*. That man's a no-good—"

"I'm so sorry," the stranger said, coming up behind her.

She felt the blood flooding her cheeks. He *would* have to catch her like this! Sitting on her behind on cold, wet concrete, looking like a real fool.

"I'd have caught up with you sooner," he said, hurrying around in front of her, "but I had to put shoes on." He shivered dramatically. "It's cold out here, you know."

She had a fascinating glimpse of bare tanned ankles above well-worn sneakers. Then he slid his hands under her elbows and pulled her to her feet. Somehow she ended up against him and discovered that her hands were *inside* his unbuttoned jacket, on his bare chest, on that bare furry chest!

"I—ah—" She couldn't talk. She couldn't get her tongue to come unstuck from the roof of her mouth. All she could do was look up at that handsome face and remind herself that she'd sworn off men. Sworn off them forever.

"I'm really sorry," he said, little lines crinkling in a friendly way around his eyes, nice eyes peering at her with concern. "I shouldn't have laughed at you. Are you all right? I saw you go down." He patted her back, his hand soothing. "I hope you didn't hurt anything in that fall."

For one wild second she almost burrowed against him. His chest was warm under her fingers and his face was so close to hers. His lips were even with her eyes, those kissable lips that seemed to be pulling her toward him. If she stretched just a little, lifted herself the tiniest bit on her toes, she could reach—Enough already! Stop it! "I'm—I'm all right," she mumbled, feeling anything but.

He sighed, his green-gray eyes twinkling; then he shrugged. The motion made his flesh move invitingly under her hands. There she stood, her hands against a stranger's bare chest. She ought to take them out of his jacket; she ought to move away from him. She ought to, but she didn't.

"Well," he said, those wonderful warm eyes smiling down into hers, "I am really sorry."

Her hands were still inside his jacket, still resting against his flesh. She could feel his heart thumping under her fingers. She took them away, finally, regretfully, feeling their emptiness as they lost the feel of his skin.

"Listen," he said, smiling down at her, "it's awful cold out here. Why don't you come back to my place and have a cup of coffee? Please. Let me show you that I'm not such a bad guy after all."

"I—" she began. *No men*, she reminded herself. But she *was* cold. "Well, I guess I could use a cup of coffee."

From behind a nearby bush Fido watched the humans walk away together. Good job! he told himself. That laughing man human ought to make the woman human laugh, too. That's what she needed—lots of laughing. There was too much sadness in her. He could smell it a block away. Just like he could smell the goodness in the man. And the loneliness in them both.

He'd been a little rough on her, maybe, stopping so quickly like that, making her end up on her behind on the sidewalk. But he hadn't had much choice. Humans took a lot of training, and he hadn't had this one long enough to teach her anything. So, if he wanted to let the man human catch up to her, he had to resort to drastic measures. Do something to make her stay there till the man could get there.

He scratched at a persistent flea behind his ear. Time he had a bath. Well, no sense hanging around here. He'd better get back to the house and scout out a place to sleep. She wasn't convinced yet that she was *his* human, so he'd probably have to spend another night outside. But she'd get the idea before too long. He could tell she was smart. That's why he'd chosen her.

Chapter Two

"The name's Brad Ferris," Brad said, opening the front door for the woman and motioning her inside. "Ferris Studios, specializing in children's portraits."

Her eyebrows went up. "Children's?"

He shrugged. "What can I say? I like kids." He liked what he saw, too. The woman who'd been so angry was smiling at him now, her eyes deep brown, luminous, but, thank goodness, no longer reproachful, like the dog's. Her mahogany hair, blown by the wind, framed a delicate face that was even prettier now that she wasn't so ticked off at him. Her faded jeans clung to her long legs and a dark green jacket hugged her upper body. Neither one hid the fact that she was nicely put together. Very nicely.

Instead of pulling her back into his arms as he'd wanted to, he showed her into the kitchen and put the kettle on.

She opened her jacket, revealing a plaid flannel shirt. He smiled to himself—a down-to-earth woman. Just the kind he liked.

"How'd you lose your dog?" she asked, settling into a chair.

He made a rueful noise. "Sheer stupidity, I guess."

She gave him a questioning look, those brown eyes bright.

"I should've been more careful with her," he explained. "She's always been like that—open the door and she's gone. A real dog explorer."

She smiled at him and he felt his body growing warm. Of course that could be because he was still wearing his jacket. He took it off and reached for the shirt he'd left hanging over a chair. She was looking at his chest. Did she like it? If he could just pull her up and feel her touch him again . . . Good grief! He had to stop thinking like that. This woman was a stranger. He couldn't invite her to touch his chest! He shrugged into his shirt.

"We've only been in this house a few weeks." He buttoned the shirt with fingers that seemed to have become all thumbs. "I'd been real careful, too, watching the door and using a leash whenever I took her out. If a snotty little kid hadn't rattled me that day, sticking out her tongue just when I finally thought I'd gotten the shot her picky mother wanted, I wouldn't have been so ticked off when I got home. And I wouldn't have forgotten and opened the door too wide."

"Maybe she'll come back yet, Mr. Ferris." Her voice was comforting and warm, a cozy-blanket voice he could listen to for the rest of his life. Wow, where had that come from? He'd only just met the woman. But would he ever forget the feel of her hands on his chest?

"I hope she does." He set a cup in front of her, filled his own, and sank into a chair. "Call me Brad. What shall I call you?"

"Jenny."

"Just Jenny?" Why couldn't he think of something smart and snappy to say? He wanted to, but his body was still reacting to the feel of her hands. Her warm, tender hands on his chest. He wished they were there right now. He wished . . .

"Just Jenny."

Get with it, he told himself. You can't lose now. Get the necessary facts. "You live around here?"

She took a sip of coffee. "A couple of blocks away."

He swallowed a sigh of disappointment. Well, that was it. He couldn't push any further. He didn't know how to. He wasn't exactly Mr. Magic where women were concerned. He still didn't know how he'd managed to get her to come back to his place for coffee.

It was almost dark when Jenny opened her back door later that evening. "What are you doing here?" she demanded of Fido. "I thought you'd gone home. When I left Brad's I didn't see you anywhere around."

Fido sat up, wagging his tail and trying to look hungry. That wasn't hard. He *was* hungry. He peered with longing at the bag of garbage she was holding. Saliva formed at the sides of his muzzle, but he didn't move. Humans didn't like pushy dogs. He'd learned that long ago.

She went on out to the garbage can. She knew he was hungry. He could smell her distress at the knowledge. But she knew she shouldn't feed him. He could smell her indecision, too. The wind caught the edge of her jacket, blowing up under it. It was getting colder. Well, maybe she'd give him a good meal. She had a kind heart.

Jenny shivered in the cold wind. The stray was really hungry. Maybe she should give him a meal. Then, like all males, he'd be on his way.

She sighed. She was getting to be a real male-basher. Well, whose fault was that? Today Morris had told her Smithers & Company loved the new designs *she'd* come up with. And today she'd found out, not from Morris, of course, that Mr. Smithers himself had congratulated

Morris on *his* fine designs! Morris, who hadn't drawn a decent plan in the whole year she'd been working for Morris & Pleasant, Architects, had taken complete credit for the plans *she'd* slaved over.

She pitched the garbage in the can and slammed the lid back on. She'd like to stuff old Morris in there where he belonged, with the rest of the spoiled stuff. Brad now, he'd seemed nice. Nice to look at, too. But it was easy to be nice for a little while—and besides, she was through with men. They were too much trouble. And it was too easy for them to hurt you.

The dog was still sitting there, in front of the back door, his look hopeful. "All right," she said. "I think there's a can of dog food left in the cupboard. But after that, out you go."

Three blocks away, the door to 325 Oak Street opened for the tenth time in the last hour. Brad Ferris peered out into the growing darkness. Where on earth had the blamed dog gone to? "Fido," he yelled. "Come on in now. Supper's ready."

But no dog answered his call. He hadn't thought she would; not really. But calling her made him feel better. For a minute at least. He shut the door harder than he needed to. He should've been more careful with her. He knew she liked to roam. She'd always been like that—open the door and she was gone.

Of course, on Fenton Street she'd always come home. Eventually. But this was new territory. She hadn't had time to get to know it in a couple of weeks.

He went to the kitchen and got a can of pop from the fridge. Back in the living room, he threw himself into his favorite beat-up chair. Tilted back, he lay, staring at the ceiling. He didn't want to watch some mindless TV show. He didn't want to sit here worrying about Fido either. What he really wanted was—

He sat up with a start. He wanted to see Jenny, her mahogany hair blowing around her face, her expressive hands moving in the air as she talked. Why wouldn't she tell him where she lived? She'd been walking, and she'd said she lived a couple of blocks away.

He groaned. Fat lot of good knowing *that* did him. He couldn't go knocking on every door around asking if an angry woman lived there! Funny how clearly he remembered her—her eyes, deep brown, luminous, reproachful like the dog's, then smiling. Her mahogany hair, tangled by the wind, framing her delicate face. She had that long, leggy look he'd always admired in women. And a figure that even in a big flannel shirt heated his blood. Or was that just the memory of her hands on his chest?

He shouldn't have laughed at her the way he had. After all, she thought she was doing a good deed, returning his lost dog. He chuckled. If you could call that thing a dog. He looked like he'd been through a hurricane, his fur all matted and tangled. Been in more than one fight, too, from the looks of him. At least one of his ears had been torn. Probably a street dog, used to fending for himself.

Brad sighed. But his Fido wasn't. His Fido was a lady.

Maybe the move here hadn't been such a good idea. But he'd wanted a house of his own for such a long time. Renting didn't seem the thing to do anymore. His business was established; he could afford a place of his own. Not a classy bachelor pad or a mansion on the hill, but a nice house on a nice street, the kind of house a family might live in someday, a house where *he* was boss, where he could have a dog, keep a beat-up chair, pound nails in the wall if he wanted to. A place where he didn't have to answer to anyone—not to a landlord, not to the parents who never should have had him.

Funny, all his life he'd wanted this house, a home of his own. And now that he had it, it wasn't enough. It wasn't that he hadn't thought about settling down, finding a wife, starting a family. All the things most guys wanted. He'd been thinking about it for quite a while. But photographing kids all day didn't exactly put him in touch with the singles crowd. He hated bars; he wasn't good at approaching strange women. And the ones who approached him were usually not the sort he wanted. He'd had more than enough of women whose only interest in life was money and the things it could buy.

So he'd settled for a dog. And now he didn't even have *her.* He got up and went to the door again. Where the devil was she? And where did Jenny live?

Chapter Three

The next morning Jenny dragged herself wearily out of bed. It was getting harder and harder to go to work. If only that head hunter would come through with another job. Much as she'd like to, she couldn't just walk out on Morris & Pleasant, Architects. For one thing, she had this house to pay for. She couldn't go home again to live—not without a job—and there weren't many architects in the middle of Iowa farm country either.

That was one reason she'd come to Cleveland. Mom and Dad had enough to handle, with Sue and her girls coming home to live. They couldn't support their second daughter, too. And even if there hadn't been any of that to think about, Hugh was back there. She didn't want to be where Hugh was. Ever.

Showered and feeling somewhat better, Jenny slipped into her coat, grabbed her purse, and opened the back door. "Good grief! You again!"

The stray pushed himself to his feet. He cocked his head and barked at her once.

"Good morning to you, too," she said, fighting a smile. This was just a stray; she wasn't going to feel anything for him. No more feelings for dogs. "You might as well get out of here." She scowled at him, deliberately raising her voice. "I'll be gone all day. And I—don't—need—a—dog."

The dog wagged his tail and looked at her hopefully. Darn it! She didn't have time for this. She climbed in the car, looking back over her shoulder. He had settled down in front of the door again.

Just what she needed; something else to worry about. But no, she wasn't going to worry about this stray. He could look out for himself. She wasn't going to have any more dogs. Having them die on her hurt too much.

The office bustled with its usual pandemonium, everyone running around trying to look busy even if they weren't. She nodded to people and went into the cubicle Morris called her office. At least it had a door, which she shut behind her. Morris wasn't being considerate giving her this cubbyhole; he just knew that without it she wouldn't be able to create. And if she didn't create, *he* wouldn't have anything to steal.

She hung up her coat and reached for the phone book. Better call about the dog first or she wouldn't be able to concentrate.

But neither the animal shelter nor the dog pound had a report of such a lost dog. "You want us to come pick him up?" they asked at the pound.

"No, no. He's gone now. Just take my number and make a note that he was around here. In case someone asks."

She put the phone back in the cradle. She wasn't going to keep him, but that didn't mean he should be locked up. The way Brad had laughed at him yesterday . . . well, he didn't look like much. It wasn't likely anyone would pick him as a dog to take home.

A sudden picture of Brad, standing in his doorway in all his bare-chested glory, surfaced in her mind. He was really nice to look at. And he'd been kind to follow her down the street like that. Nuts! She didn't need to be thinking about him now. She didn't want to think about him at all. Not now. Not ever. No dogs. No men. And therefore no pain.

She turned to her computer. Time to get to work.

* * *

An hour after quitting time Jenny drove slowly toward home. Going home was the hardest part of the day, even harder than leaving in the morning. Torrie had always been there to say good-bye to her in the morning, and, waiting right inside the kitchen door, to welcome her home at night. Now the house was empty, except for the memories, memories that after three months still hurt like crazy.

Well, she'd get over it. She'd have to. Funny thing, Jenny thought as she swung into the driveway, losing Torrie had hurt a lot worse than losing Hugh. But then, Torrie had been worth ten of him. More even. Torrie'd been there to help her get through the loss of Hugh. Torrie had been her best friend for as long as she could remember, and now that she was gone there was no one to help with the pain of losing her.

Jenny turned off the motor and opened the door. And the stray came bounding down off the porch to greet her. "What are you still doing here?" she demanded in exasperation. "I'm not going to feed you again. I'm not. Now get out of here."

The dog wagged his tail and barked once, then paced beside her back up onto the porch. He stopped at one side of the door and sat there, his dirty tail brushing the porch floor. He didn't try to push past her, didn't try to go into the house. He just sat there, as if he was saying, "I don't expect anything from you. But I'm here if you want me."

Tears rose to her eyes, blinding her. "I can't!" she cried. "I can't have another dog!"

She rushed in and slammed the door.

At two A.M. Jenny was wakened by thunder and wind. Heavy wind. The dog was on the porch; he wouldn't get wet. She shivered in her warm bed. Sure, he was dry, but it was awful cold out there. And he probably hadn't eaten today. Confound it! Why had this had to happen to her? She was on her way to the top. She couldn't afford any baggage along the way. No dogs. No men. She'd left all that back in Iowa.

Jenny threw back the covers and reached for her robe, then shoved her feet into her slippers. Just once more. She'd feed him once more. Maybe then she could sleep.

Half an hour later Jenny was in the bathroom, on her knees, and Fido was in the tub. "This is crazy," Jenny told him. "I don't want a dog. I don't need a dog."

She could say that all she wanted, Fido told himself. But he knew better. She needed him bad, and he knew it. But give her time, she'd learn.

He barked once and sank down into the water. Ahhhh! Good. He'd been wanting this bath. Besides, when he was lying down she could reach him easier. He wasn't stupid—he knew how to train a human. Some were easier to train than others, of course, but they were all trainable in the end. It just took patience—and a lot of love. He loved his human. He wasn't sure why, except, maybe, that he'd chosen her, that he knew she needed him, needed to be loved. But he didn't need to know why he loved her. He'd lived long enough to know that he needed to love, that without someone to love there wasn't much use to anything.

"There," she said. "If you're going to sleep in the house, you have to be clean. I don't want the place infested with fleas."

He sank lower in the water. Let the pesky things get theirs!

When he was clean and toweled dry he felt like a different dog. He'd been on the street for a long time. Under his now silky coat she traced his ribs with gentle fingers. Well, he *was* on the lean side. "I guess I'd better bring some more food tomorrow," she said, scraping a can into a bowl for him. "In case you're still around."

Oh, he was going to be around. He was in this for the long haul. He'd found his human and he was going to make her happy, whether she wanted him to or not.

She led him to a clean rug near the back door. "You can sleep here," she said earnestly. "Right here. But tomorrow you go outside again."

He might as well humor her. He turned

around three times and lay down with a sigh of contentment. And she went back to bed.

In the morning Jenny woke and rolled over, and there was Fido, asleep on the rug beside the bed, his head resting on her slippers. A sob wrenched its way out of her throat. That was Torrie's spot!

Well, it didn't matter. She'd keep him till someone claimed him. She could do that much. It wouldn't be like having Torrie back. Nothing would be like that. But he *was* company.

Late the next afternoon a weary Brad reached home. He looked around the empty kitchen, put a frozen dinner in a slow oven, grabbed the leash, and headed out again. Fido had to be around somewhere. He just had to keep looking.

Maybe his folks were right about one thing—dogs *were* a lot of trouble. But he missed the dumb dog, and he was worried about her. Besides, he hated to think his folks were right about anything. A man needed *something* to love, even a man who'd been raised with hardly any love at all. It might be that a man like that needed more love than other people. Even if he had to get it from a dog.

He'd rather get it from Jenny, of course. He started off down the sidewalk, his mind a riot of churning thoughts. Why hadn't he insisted she tell him her name last night? Now he had about as much chance of finding her as he did of finding Fido. She was right about that, too; he should have put on the poster that Fido was female. But then he wouldn't have met *her*. He could see her almost as plainly as if she was standing right there in front of him, especially those reproachful brown eyes and that firm little mouth. He'd like to make her eyes light up, make her mouth smile.

There was nothing he could do about that, though, unless he put up another notice outside the grocery store. He grinned. LOST, it would say, ONE ANGRY WOMAN WITH SCRUFFY DOG. PLEASE RETURN TO 325 OAK STREET. Nice way to advertise himself in a new neighborhood!

He turned a corner. He'd gone this way night before last, but he might as well try it again. "Fido! Fido! Come on, girl!"

In the distance someone was walking a dog. A big dog. He couldn't see much more than that from this distance. But his heart gave a great leap. That jacket! That was the same color jacket Jenny'd been wearing. He walked faster. If only it was her. But if it was, would she speak to him? She'd seemed to have forgiven him last night, but maybe she was still mad that he'd laughed at her. He wouldn't be surprised if she told him to get lost—permanently lost. Well, a

Chapter Four

"I don't know why you had to come this far for a walk," Jenny complained to Fido. "There's plenty of yard at home. And," she said, glaring down at him, "if you go to the bathroom on somebody else's yard, I'm in deep trouble. I don't have a scooper, you know."

Fido looked up at her. Did she think he was some kind of pup? He had more sense than that. He wasn't out to make trouble for her. He wanted to make her happy. He sniffed at the air. Someone was coming. Someone who could make her happy. He slowed down.

"You sure do heel well," Jenny said. "Someone spent a lot of time training you. Well, I've been wanting to get some exercise. Walking you every night should do it."

Just what he wanted, more walking.

"I don't understand why you're running around loose. A good dog like you. Someone's got to be looking for you."

No one was looking. He was his own boss, had done his own training, too. But there was no way to tell her that. He reached up to touch her fingers with his nose. This time she didn't pull away; she patted his head. She was learning.

Jenny sighed. Fido's fur was silky now, nice and clean. At least when they came for him, he'd look good. And he wouldn't have to go hungry. He had a home, however temporary.

Fido slowed down and glanced back over his shoulder. There must be another dog around somewhere. If it hadn't been for the leash law, she'd have let him go loose. After all, if he wanted to run away, he'd already had every opportunity.

"Hello there!"

The call came from behind her.

"Wait a minute. Please!"

She swallowed. It couldn't be Brad. She'd deliberately avoided Oak Street. But that voice . . .

"Hello! Wait! Please."

She stopped. She couldn't outrun the man, so it looked like she'd have to put up with him. And really, would that be so hard? She'd given up men romantically, but she could still speak to them.

She turned as he came jogging up and panted to a halt beside her. "Thanks—for waiting. I wasn't—sure—I could—catch you."

She shrugged. "Well, you did." Even out of breath he was something to look at. No bare chest, of course. Not in this weather. Today he had on a jean jacket and under it a plaid flannel shirt. She could see the collar above his jacket collar where the curls from his pony tail didn't hide it. Enough of that. His clothes were no business of hers. Nor his hair. And certainly not his chest—his wonderful furry chest. "Have you found your dog?" she asked, pulling herself together.

"No." He took another deep breath and showed her the leash he was carrying. "Still looking."

"I'm sorry," she said. "I hoped she'd be back by now."

He sighed. "Me, too. I miss her."

He glanced down at Fido, then did a double take and looked again. "Don't tell me that's—"

She looked down. "Yes, this is the stray I had with me the last time I saw you."

"Wow!" Brad grinned. "He cleaned up real nice."

"I'm only taking care of him till someone claims him," she said. "I didn't mean to. I mean, I thought he'd run off. But he was awful thin and . . ." How stupid. Why was she babbling on like this? She wasn't interested in men, especially not in hunks.

"That's kind of you," he said. "Listen, I really am sorry I laughed at you the other night. I hope you've forgiven me. And I want to ask you: How about having dinner with me some night?" He looked like a little boy caught with his hand in the cookie jar; a lovable little boy, one you wanted to hug and give another cookie to instead of scolding.

But she shook her head and gave him her stock answer. "Sorry, I don't do dinner."

He stared at her, his eyebrows going up, his face a study in surprise. "You don't—"

"I don't date," she said flatly. "I don't have time for that nonsense. I want to get ahead with my career."

"I see. I think." He looked around as if he was embarrassed and changed the subject. "Wish I could find Fido. She's been gone almost a week now. And it's getting colder every darn night."

"I know," Jenny said, wondering why she felt vaguely disappointed that he hadn't pressed her about going out. "That's why this dog's so clean. The storm last night woke me and I was worried about him."

"So you brought him in the house."

She nodded. "And then he had to have a bath."

"And now you belong to him."

She gave him a quick glance. He knew more

about dogs than she thought. "Something like that. And he's taking me for a walk."

He grinned again. "Mind if I walk along with you, Miss . . ."

"Jenny." She wasn't going to give him her name. Maybe he could be pleasant at times, but he was still a man. "I suppose so. Wherever we've walked, we've been watching for other dogs, Fido and me. You say your Fido is smaller than this one?"

"Yeah. I've been walking the streets every night, calling for her. But no luck. I hope she wasn't hit by a car or something."

Jenny swallowed. She didn't want to think about something like that. "I hope so, too. It's hard losing your dog."

He looked at her, a question in his suddenly sober eyes. "You've lost one lately, haven't you?"

"Yes." She swallowed again. "I don't want to talk about it."

"I understand." He looked away. "Guess I ought to be calling the dog."

Half an hour later Brad looked at his watch. Wow, where had the time gone? Much as he wanted to, he couldn't stay with Jenny any longer. "Thanks for letting me walk along with you," he told her. "I've gotta run now. My dinner's in the oven. Don't want it to burn. Listen, will you please give me your name and address? I mean, if I find Fido, I want to let you know.

Don't want you to have any sleepless nights worrying about her."

She stared at him. Why that suspicious look? Did she think he was some kind of masher or something? What kind of a world was it where somebody as harmless as he could look suspicious?

The dog leaned against her thigh and she rubbed his head without looking at him. Then she sighed. "Jenny Carruthers, 515 Pine Street. I've got to go, too. I hope you find your Fido."

What was this thing about her not dating? A woman who looked like *that* didn't date?

He didn't want to leave her without touching her. He wasn't sure why, but there was an awful yearning inside him just to touch her. He could still feel her fingers on his bare chest—tender, warm fingers. He'd really like to hug her, but he didn't dare go that far.

Instead he offered his hand. Would she take it? Or would she ignore it, pretend she didn't see it? Or even worse, show she did see it and still ignore it? There was something more than losing her dog wrong with this woman. She seemed almost afraid of him, not physically, but as if he had the power to hurt her some other way.

She looked at his hand, her forehead wrinkled in a frown; then she shifted her gaze to his face, almost as if she was searching for something there. And then, heaving a sigh of surrender, she shook his hand. Her fingers felt cold, small and lost inside his. He wanted to pull her against him and warm her up. Take that sad look out of her eyes. But she'd probably wallop him a good one if he tried something like that, to say nothing of the dog, who had a good set of teeth and was looking at him with distrustful eyes.

"Good-bye, Brad," she said. "Good luck finding your dog."

And then she was gone, swinging off down the street on those long jeans-clad legs. Not a word about how it'd been nice meeting him again, or talking with him. Or anything. But he knew where to find her. That was something. Not much, considering that she'd already turned down a date with him. But something.

Jenny hurried toward home. It was getting on to dark and she hadn't eaten yet. Too bad she didn't have something waiting in the oven, as he did. Or even in the fridge. For the first time in a long time she actually felt like eating. Well, a peanut butter and jelly sandwich and an apple would have to do. Maybe she'd go to the grocery store tomorrow, get a few more supplies.

She pulled her hood up. It was really getting cold. Too bad Brad hadn't found his dog yet. It was awful to keep worrying about an animal who was lost. The worry was always there in the back of your mind. And Brad seemed like the kind of person who really cared.

Funny, today he'd acted like a different man than the one who'd laughed at her the other night. She smiled. What a waste, a hunk like that spending his life photographing other people's little kids! With his looks he could have been a model himself. But when she asked him why he'd chosen such a career, he'd said that he liked it. He liked working with kids. Most kids. It was their mothers who sometimes drove him crazy.

And then he'd made her laugh with his stories of interfering mothers and kids who tried to eat the props, or fell asleep in the middle of the shoot, or seemed to know just when to move to wreck a shot. Strange that such a man should be living alone. Unless he was lying when he said he was. But why should he lie to her? He'd probably never see her again. Unless he found his dog. . . .

The time had really flown by. He was easy to listen to. Once she'd almost told him about Torrie. But she didn't want to cry. And the tears always came when she tried to talk about losing her.

Jenny sighed. She didn't like to cry in public; it was bad enough crying in private. She hadn't shed a tear when Hugh told her he loved someone else. Not then. Not even later. And she hadn't cried after she discovered that Morris had lied to her about the credit for the Smithers job. No tears for the likes of them. Her tears were saved for her best friend.

If only someone had found the other Fido, Brad's dog. If only someone was caring for her. There were probably hundreds of homeless dogs wandering around, a lot of them in Cleveland, even. And she didn't like to think of them, out there hungry and cold. But knowing Brad, knowing how much he missed his Fido, made her care even more what happened to his dog. Well, he said he was going to keep looking. And so was she. Maybe they'd find her.

And maybe Jenny would see him again.

She shook her head. None of that now. She'd broken the no-dogs rule; she wasn't going to break the no-men one.

She hurried up the back porch steps, Fido right beside her. She bent to take off the leash. You're really losing it, she told herself. What happened to no dogs? Well, this was an emergency. She couldn't leave him to freeze, could she? And besides, he was an exceptional dog. Not Torrie. But exceptional. He sat down, to the side of the door as before, and looked at her inquiringly, as if to say, "Do I come in tonight?"

She opened the door and still he sat there—waiting. "All right," she said, with a little laugh.

"You win. Come on in. And from now on you don't have to wait. You live here, too."

Fido barked once and stepped inside. Yep, he'd picked a smart human. She was a fast learner.

Chapter Five

The days went by—two, three, four. A week passed and Jenny hadn't heard a word from Brad Ferris. When she got home from work every afternoon she walked Fido, but she didn't see the other Fido. Or Brad. Maybe that was because she'd stayed away from the vicinity of Oak Street. Well, that made sense. After all, Brad was looking around there. So she'd look further out. Dogs could travel quite a long way. Still, she wished she knew whether he'd found the dog. Maybe his Fido had come home and he hadn't bothered to tell her. You couldn't really count on a man to do what he said.

"Well," she told Fido as she fastened the leash to his new collar on the next Monday afternoon, "I guess we could go toward Oak Street today. What do you think?"

He barked once, and she grinned. "Yeah, I think you're right. Oak Street it is. But first let me put my hood up. It's really getting cold out."

Fido waited patiently and then, when she started out, moved easily at her side. It was amazing how well he'd fitted himself into her life. She let him out first thing in the morning. Then she let him back in. When she came home at night he was waiting there for her, right inside the back door. No matter how quietly she came up the porch steps, he was sitting up, watching for her when she opened the door. And the house was spotless. You'd never know he'd been alone in it all day. Coming home was better now. Some nights she almost looked forward to it.

You understand, Torrie, she said silently. He can't take your place—nobody can. But he's company. And he needs a home. And somehow, some way, she felt Torrie heard her and approved. Whoever had said dogs didn't go to heaven had better think again. There wasn't anybody anywhere who deserved heaven more than a faithful dog. And there'd never been a more faithful dog than Torrie.

Jenny looked around. If she wanted to help Brad find his dog, she'd better start paying attention to what she was doing. "Fido!" she called. "Fido!" The Fido pacing beside her never twitched an ear. "Fido! Come on, girl!"

But no other dog appeared. A couple of

blocks from Oak Street, Jenny turned a corner and saw Brad Ferris coming toward her. She couldn't see his face at this distance, but she knew it was him. Though she'd only seen him twice, she'd know his walk anywhere; the easy way he moved, his long legs eating up the distance. And the breadth of his shoulders inside his jeans jacket. She swallowed hard. It was his dog she was interested in, not him. Better remember that.

When he got closer he grinned. How could that grin of his make her feel so warm inside, like something special was going to happen just because he was coming closer?

"Hi, there! I hoped I'd see you tonight."

Her heart jumped around in her chest. What was wrong with her? He was just talking about the dog. "Did you find her, then? Oh, I'm—"

"No," he said, raising a hand in denial. "She hasn't come home."

"Oh. Then why did you—That is, I'm sorry."

His eyes went dark, shutting her out. Whatever he'd meant by saying he'd hoped to see her, it didn't look as if he was going to tell her now. "I—ah—wanted to see how your Fido was doing." He gazed down at him. "I must say he looks great. Looks like he's filled out a little already."

It really had seemed as if Brad wanted to say something else, but she couldn't very well grill him about it. Besides, if it was personal, she didn't want to hear it. "He has. You know, he's the most amazing animal. So well trained. I can't understand why no one's claimed him."

Brad turned and walked alongside her. "Hard to say. Not everyone loves animals the way you do."

"I know. It makes me angry, how some people treat them. Abandoning them. Abusing them. As if animals don't have any feelings."

He nodded, his face grim. "I know what you mean. That really stinks."

"Have you been out looking for Fido every night?"

"Yeah. I've just about walked my legs down to stumps. My place is a real mess." He gave her a sheepish smile. "Not that I'm the best housekeeper in the world. But I do usually keep the dishes washed and stuff like that."

Funny to hear a man talk about housecleaning. Most men she knew could live in a mess and never even know it was there. "I wouldn't worry about it," she said. "Stuff like that isn't important."

He made a funny strangled sound, half laugh, half cough. "Better not let my mother hear you say that."

She glanced up at him. Why such a strange note in his voice? Usually men spoke of their mothers with respect. But she didn't hear that in his tone. She wasn't sure what she did hear, but it wasn't pleasant. "I take it your mother kept a clean house?"

"That's the understatement of the year. She kept a perfectly clean house. And woe to anyone who disturbed it." There was a smile on his face, but something else in his voice, something that gave her a strange, sick feeling inside. He was really hurting about this.

If only she could make a joke, something to chase the sadness from his eyes. But she didn't know what to say. "Well," she said finally, "you have your own place now."

"Yes," he said, his face brightening. "Growing up has its compensations. It's all mine." He chuckled. "Well, except for the bank's share."

She managed a laugh, too. "I know what you mean. The bank owns a big piece of mine. I suppose some people would think it silly, a single woman having a house of her own. But in our family, apartments are only temporary things. A person needs a house of her own. She's not a success till she has one." Now, why had she told him that? Well, it wasn't really that personal. Probably lots of people felt that way. "Tell me, though, why did you want a house instead of an apartment? I mean, you said you're not married."

He shrugged. "You can't guess? I wanted a place that was mine. A place that was a real home. Where I could keep a favorite chair, pound nails in the wall, have a dog."

She almost stopped in the middle of the sidewalk to stare at him. It was one thing not to have a dog because it kept a person from getting ahead, but for a kid not to have a dog, a kid she could tell had been unhappy, that was . . . "Are you telling me your folks wouldn't let you have a dog?"

"Afraid so." There was that strange laugh again. "My parents felt dogs were unnecessary. And far too much trouble."

She was silent for a few paces. Finally she said, "That's hard to imagine."

"Everything about my parents is hard to imagine. I was a mistake, you see."

How could he say such a thing and laugh about it? He had to be joking.

"They didn't want me."

That did stop her. Dead in her tracks. She turned to face him and swallowed a cry at the quickly shuttered pain in his eyes. "Surely they didn't tell you that!"

"They didn't have to say it in so many words. It was clear enough." He seemed to shake himself and then he smiled. "But it's all right. I learned to laugh at it. And I grew up okay." He grinned ruefully. "At least I think I did. Enough about me, though. Tell me about your folks. What are they like?"

And because she wanted to give him something else to think about, something happier, she told him. "My folks live in Iowa, on a farm.

My sister Sue lives with them. Sue and her girls, Fanny and Ellen. Sue's divorced. Her husband left her for a younger, prettier woman." Oh-oh. She hadn't meant to tell him that. Well, he couldn't know about Hugh unless she told him. And she wasn't about to do that.

"My folks," she hurried on. "My folks are the best. Mom makes the most wonderful homemade noodles this side of heaven. And her blackberry pie—it's beyond words. And Pop, Pop works hard and cusses hard, but inside, where it counts, he's a sucker for a lost pup or a stray kitten. Anything that's little or hurt. He buried my pony out back when he died. Dug the whole grave by hand himself." She had to stop and swallow. "Dad's that kind of man." Good grief, what was she doing, telling him all that? Brad didn't want her whole life history.

"Sounds like a wonderful family," he said, his voice heavy with longing. "I envy you belonging to people like that. It must have been great growing up in such a family."

"It was," she said. "It still is."

He looked at her curiously. "Then why'd you move to the city?"

"Well, they don't have much use for architects in the middle of Iowa farm country. And I had this crazy need to design buildings."

"*That's* what you do?" he asked. "You're an architect?"

"Yes."

His eyes showed admiration. "Wow! That's great. Where do you work?"

"Morris and Pleasant. Downtown." Try as she would, she couldn't keep the hint of anger out of her voice.

"And you don't like it there?"

She looked at him. "What makes you think that?"

He chuckled. "Well, for one thing, there's the expression on your face. And then there's the tone of your voice. They're both dead give-aways."

He was on to her. No sense denying the truth. Besides, it'd be a relief to talk about it to some-one she could trust not to run back to Morris and tell tales. "Well, you're right. I don't like it there."

"Then why do you stay?"

"It's not that easy to leave. For one thing, I have a house to pay for." She glanced down at Fido. "Two mouths to feed."

"I understand," Brad said.

And for some reason she felt he did. He didn't pursue the subject either, and she appreciated that. He just let her say as much as she wanted to, and didn't push.

They walked in silence for a few minutes. Then he sighed heavily. "Well," he said, "my Fido's been gone well over a week now. It doesn't look like I'm going to find her. So I guess I might as well give up."

Jenny stopped again. He couldn't mean that. She turned to face him. "Give up? You mean, not look anymore?"

He shrugged those magnificent shoulders. "Yeah, that's what I mean. What's the use? She's gone for good."

"How can you say that?"

"Because it's true. She ran off and she didn't come home. Guess that means she doesn't care as much for me as I thought. And anyway, I can't go on looking for her forever. I have a life to live, you know."

She couldn't believe it! "It hasn't been that long. You can't give up yet."

"Isn't that up to me?" He gave her a strange look. "She's my dog."

Just like a man, thinking only of himself. Anger washed over her. Anger that almost robbed her of the ability to speak. "You're right," she said finally. "She is your dog. And no one can *make* you keep looking for her. But I can tell you one thing—if she was mine, I'd never stop looking. Never!"

And before he could say anything more she left him standing there. The jerk!

For a little while there she'd even felt sorry for him, for the little boy whose parents hadn't loved him. But she wasn't going to feel that way anymore! He didn't deserve it.

* * *

Pacing along beside her, Fido considered the peculiar actions of human beings. They got angry so easily. But maybe that was because they didn't have a good pack leader. They had to manage by themselves. Not that he couldn't understand Jenny's anger; he'd felt like growling at the man himself when he talked about forgetting his dog. Jenny was loyal, his human; loyal to the bone. She'd never desert anyone she loved. Fido smiled to himself. He'd made a good choice. A real good choice.

Brad watched them go, cursing himself for a fool. Now he'd put his foot in it. And just when he and Jenny were getting along so well. He might have known she'd be like that about his looking for the dog. Jenny obviously had a real soft spot for animals. She just wasn't the sort to give up.

He sighed. Imagine growing up in a family like hers; imagine being loved like that. He wasn't sure he *could* imagine it, but he'd give just about anything if he could have been part of such a family. It sounded like the kind of family he'd always wanted to belong to, the kind he'd dreamed about as a kid.

He hadn't told Jenny, of course, but one of the reasons he'd gone into photographing kids was because he liked seeing mothers who loved their babies. Even the brattiest kids or the bossiest mamas had that bond of love between them. And seeing that reassured him.

That was what love looked like, the love he'd never had. He'd been right to move away from his parents. He gave them respect; they had raised him, after all. They hadn't put him up for adoption—though sometimes he'd wondered why not, and if it might not have been better for him if they had. At any rate, he gave them respect, but he kept his love for Fido, Fido who wanted it, who accepted it, and who'd loved him unconditionally in return.

Jenny was right. He couldn't stop looking for Fido. Not ever.

He swung off down the street. "Fido! Fido! Come on, girl. Come on home."

Still no answer. He'd just keep looking. Fido would do as much for him.

He went around one block and turned down another. "Fido! Come on, Fido! Here, girl."

"Woof! Woof!"

He stopped in his tracks. Could it be? "Fido? Fido, is that really you?"

"Woof!" She almost knocked him off his feet, launching herself into his arms like a missile.

He clutched her to him, hardly able to believe it was really her. "Fido! Where've you been?" He swallowed hard. Where'd that lump in his throat come from? She didn't seem thin—she must've been eating. And she smelled faintly of some flowery perfume.

"Lady? Lady?"

The soft voice came from his right, from the doorway of a yellow house that had seen better days. He turned toward it. Fido whined and tried to wriggle out of his arms.

But he held her tighter to him and made his way up the sidewalk. "Hello, ma'am. Has my dog been here with you?"

The woman inside the doorway smiled sadly. A tall, thin woman in an old-fashioned house-dress, she twisted a faded pink apron in nervous hands. "Yes, she has. I knew she had an owner somewhere. But she seemed so lost. And it was cold outside. So I let her in. I hope you didn't worry about her too much. I didn't know how to find you."

"I put a notice outside the grocery store," he said, wondering why he wasn't angry. "Maybe you didn't see it."

"I don't get to the grocery store much," she said apologetically. "I don't drive anymore. Can't see too well. A friend brings my groceries in." She gestured toward the interior of the house. "Would you like—Do you have time to come in? Maybe have a cup of coffee?"

Her voice held such a note of pleading that he didn't even hesitate. "Yeah, sure, I've got time for that."

She stepped aside and motioned him in. He looked around. A house out of the past. The kind of house he'd dreamed of as a kid, with big, overstuffed slate blue furniture, worn but still nice. Doilies on the backs and arms, and on all the tables. Old-fashioned globe lamps with flowers painted on them—and that soft, out-of-the-past glow that had filled his daydreams of what a home should be. "Wow," he breathed. "This is a great place. So homey. So cozy."

"Why, thank you, young man." The old woman looked at him in surprise. "I know it's old-fashioned, but it's mine. My Horace, he liked it. We had a good life here." Her voice trembled, but she managed a little smile. "I lost my Horace last year. My children, they don't live around here. They want me to go into a home. But I won't." She chuckled. "I'm a grown woman. I do what I want. And I want to stay here, where Horace and I were happy. It's a little lonely now, but I have my memories. And this house is my *home*."

"I understand," he said. He might not have ever had such a home, but he could sure understand its value.

She searched his face, wonderment in her eyes. "Yes, I think you do. Thank you, Mr. . . ."

"Ferris; Brad Ferris." He extended a hand.

Her fingers were warm, her skin dry as parchment. "Clara," she said. "Clara Kelly. I'm glad to meet you, Mr. Ferris." She turned. "The kitchen's down this way. The coffee won't take but a minute. I'm so glad for your company."

Chapter Six

An hour later Brad approached 515 Pine Street. He'd finally pried himself loose from Mrs. Kelly. He hated to leave her, the old woman seemed so pathetically grateful for his company. But finally he'd torn himself away, pleading the lateness of the hour and the fact that he had to tell a friend he'd found his dog.

There were lights on in the back of the house. Jenny must be home. "Well, Fido, she said she wanted to know when I found you. And maybe she'll get over being mad at me, now that you're back. I hope so."

He took a deep breath and marched up the steps to the door. Before he could knock, the dog inside started barking. Good dog, protecting Jenny.

Brad knocked once. The door opened. Jenny had on faded jeans and a big flannel shirt, and her bare feet were shoved into faded pink slippers. Looking just great silhouetted against the cozy kitchen behind her, she stared at him, wiping soapy hands on a dish towel. "What are you—" She glanced down, finally seeing the dog. "You found her! Look, Fido, Brad found his dog!"

The dog appeared beside her, his head cocked inquiringly, and leaned against her leg.

Brad pulled in another breath. Well, she hadn't slammed the door in his face; that was good. Maybe she'd gotten over being mad at him. "You said you wanted to know right away if I found her. So I took a chance on coming over. I didn't want you to be worrying about her for another night."

"I appreciate that," Jenny said, giving him a funny look.

He gazed with longing at the lighted kitchen behind her. He wanted to be in there—with her. He wanted it really bad, with the kind of yearning a kid feels and can't put into words. "Do you suppose I could have a cup of coffee?" he asked, forcing a shiver. "It's cold out here."

She hesitated, looking around uncomfortably, but finally she stepped back. "Of course. Come in."

He stepped through the door. Into heaven.

The dog eyed him once, then stepped up to his dog and started sniffing noses.

"You can let her off the leash," Jenny said, closing the door. "I imagine she's well trained."

"Yes," he said. "She is, but—"

"He won't hurt her. Honest."

Brad took her at her word and unleashed Fido. She sniffed the other dog's nose and headed for his food bowl. Brad took a step after her, but Jenny's dog just sat and watched while his dog helped herself to the food.

"I told you," Jenny said, laughing a little. "He's a perfect gentleman."

He'd never seen such a thing. Dogs were usually really territorial. "I guess *so.*"

"Sit down," she said, motioning him to the kitchen table on which sat a pot of pink African violets. "I'll make you that coffee. I'm afraid it'll have to be instant."

"That's fine." The last thing he needed was another cup of coffee, but he hadn't been able to think fast enough to come up with anything else. And he really wanted to get into that kitchen, to be in there with Jenny. "Thanks."

"Tell me how you found her," she said, filling the tea kettle at the tap and then putting it on the stove.

"Well, after you left me I realized you were right."

She swung around, lifting an eyebrow in surprise. "You did?"

"Yeah. What's so strange about that?"

She shrugged, and a strange, embarrassed look crossed her face. "Nothing. I guess I'm just not used to people admitting I'm right."

"I realized you were right," he repeated, "that I couldn't desert my friend. So I kept on looking for her. I went around one block, and on the next one, Denver Street, I was walking along, calling for her. And suddenly there she was, barking. Jumped right up into my arms."

"I can't believe it," Jenny said. "After being gone two weeks." She set out two coffee mugs.

"Well, I found out why. This old woman, Clara Kelly, saw Fido—she called her Lady—wandering around outside lost, felt sorry for her, and invited her in."

Jenny poured hot water into the mugs and passed him the jar of instant coffee. Then she settled into the chair across from him. "And that's where she's been all along?" she asked, stirring coffee into her mug. "With Mrs. Kelly?"

He reached for his. "Yeah. She asked me in, too. She has the most marvelous house. You wouldn't believe it. Like something out of the forties." He laughed. "Like the Beaver's house."

She smiled at him, a little-girl smile. "Like our house at home," she said.

"You're so lucky."

"I guess I am." She glanced at his mug. "Listen, I'm sorry I don't have any pie or cake to offer you with that. It's just that there's so much stress at work, I figure I'd better take care of my body. So I eat healthy." She laughed. "Besides, it takes less time to eat raw fruits and vegetables than to cook up elaborate dishes."

He took a sip of coffee. "I guess you're right about that. But I have a sweet tooth—doughnuts, cookies, ice cream. You know, all that bad-for-you stuff."

She shook her head. "Really, for an intelligent man you have some weird ideas."

He laughed. "Who says I'm intelligent?"

She looked down at her cup. "I do," she said softly.

Now why should that make him feel so good? Like he was Superman, or had just climbed Mount Everest. "Well, thanks. But sometimes I'm not sure. Those kids can be demons. And their mamas . . ." He shook his head. "You haven't known stress till you've come up against one of those mamas."

She straightened and shook her head. "I bet they couldn't hold a candle to Mr. Morris. He's such a pain. And the world's biggest crook." Her cheeks turned pink as the African violets in their pot. "Whoops! Forget I said that."

Crook? He didn't like the sound of that. Or the troubled something in her eyes. "Crook?"

"Please, just forget I said it."

"Come on, Jenny, I can't forget it! You shouldn't be working for a crook."

Her face turned pinker. "Don't you think I know that?"

"Then why do you do it?" For a second he couldn't breathe right. "He's not . . . You're not involved in anything shady, are you? I mean, really illegal? Good grief, I don't want to see you in jail!"

Her eyes grew bigger, and then she laughed nervously and spread her hands wide. "Oh, no. It's not like that."

He let out a big sigh. "Whew. That's a relief. What are you talking about then?"

"He steals from me," she said, looking over his shoulder, not at his face. "In a way, at least. He tells people that my designs are his. He takes all the credit for them."

"The devil you say!" No wonder she'd flown off the handle. She couldn't have much of an opinion of men after being treated like that. "Can't you do something about it? Report it to your professional organization or something?"

"I could," she said. "But then I'd be without a job."

"But if you're good, can't you get another one?"

She shrugged. "I'm not really sure. It's hard to fight the old-boy network, you know."

"I suppose so. But it still stinks." *Stinks* wasn't the word for it. It made him want to bust something, preferably Morris himself, for treating Jenny that way.

"Don't worry about it," she said. "Listen, this woman, this Clara Kelly, you say she's all alone?"

"Well, she said she has kids, but they live out of state. And she has a friend who brings in groceries. But she seemed awfully lonely. Sorry to see Fido leaving."

Jenny glanced down at her Fido. "Yes," she said, "a dog can be a lot of company. If Mrs. Kelly lives on Denver Street, maybe I could go see her."

"That's a great idea!" Why hadn't he thought of that? Another chance to get to see Jenny. "I'll go, too. We'll see to it that she has company."

"Well. . . ." Jenny looked away from him again. "I meant to go alone. But I guess we could go together sometime."

He finished off his coffee and hoped he could get home before he burst. "Sounds good. Guess I'd better go. I haven't had my dinner yet. And I suppose Lady Fido will gobble up whatever I give her, even though she ate your Fido's supper."

He looked at Jenny. She looked good enough to eat herself. "You know, at Mrs. Kelly's the dog answered to Lady. Maybe I should call her that. Avoid confusion, you know."

For a minute he thought she'd ask him what confusion he meant, hoped she'd ask him, but she just got to her feet and went to the door with him. They stood there together, looking down.

The dogs were curled up together, looking like they'd known each other forever.

"Smart dogs," he said. "They know when they've got something good."

She sighed. "Life's a lot easier for them, I guess."

She sounded so wistful, so lost. He wished he was a dog so he could curl up with her, give her the comfort she so obviously needed. But he wasn't a dog, and neither was she. Besides, sniffing noses wouldn't be enough for him. She was a beautiful woman and he wanted to kiss her.

He wanted to. And the next thing he knew, he was.

She was soft and warm in his arms, fitting perfectly. He had one glimpse of her startled face as he pulled her closer and then he went to work on kissing her, kissing her good. She kissed him back, too—for a few seconds. Then she stiffened and tried to pull away.

He let go of her, the coldness hitting him, the knowledge that he'd made a mistake. Better brace himself. Now she was going to clobber him.

But she didn't. She just stood there looking at him with those great soulful eyes, eyes that seemed to hold all the hurt in the world. "I don't date," she reminded him. "I told you that."

"Sorry," he said, feeling like the world's biggest heel. "I saw the dogs. I wanted to—You looked so—Well, it seemed like a good idea at the time."

"Forget it," she said, her voice flat. "You'd better go home and get your dinner."

"Yeah." If only he had some way to tell what she was thinking. If she'd slapped him, he'd have at least known that she was mad. This way he didn't know anything. He didn't want to leave her angry with him. There'd been too much of that already. Besides, he didn't want to leave her at all. But he had to. She was standing there waiting, expecting, him to go. "I'll call you about going to see Mrs. Kelly."

Jenny hesitated, her expression uncertain. If only she didn't shrug him off. He wouldn't, couldn't, let her do that. "I know she'd like to see us," he said. "She seemed really lonely."

Finally Jenny sighed. "All right. And I'm glad you found your dog. Really glad."

Standing beside Jenny, Fido watched them go—the male human and his dog. Now they were getting somewhere. That kiss had really heated up the room.

He twitched his tail. He was glad the man had found his dog, too. That Lady was a real looker. Not too smart, though, if she couldn't find her way home from a couple of blocks away. Still, with a good teacher she could learn. And he was one of the best.

* * *

Jenny sighed. She *was* glad Brad had found his dog. And it was a good idea to go visit Mrs. Kelly. The old woman certainly sounded as though she needed a friend.

Jenny turned back into the house and closed the door. But that kiss . . . She hadn't expected that he'd kiss her. Or that she'd like it so much. Or that even though she could hardly breathe she'd be able to feel his mustache tickling her upper lip and his hands warming her back and . . .

Cut it out! No dogs. No men. That's what she'd promised herself. Well, she might have changed her mind about dogs, a little anyway. Fido was a free spirit. He could take off any time.

But she wasn't changing her mind about men. She didn't mean to get emotionally involved with one again. They couldn't be trusted. Especially when they kissed like this one!

Chapter Seven

Around two the next afternoon someone knocked on Jenny's office door. She looked up from the computer screen and made a face. Why wouldn't they leave her alone so she could get some work done? "Come in."

Phil Burton stuck his bald head in. "Hi, Jen. The boss wants to see you. ASAP."

She swallowed a curse. The new project wasn't going as well as it should, but talking to Morris wasn't going to be any help. "I'll be right there."

Phil nodded sympathetically and scurried off. Poor Phil, like a mouse with a cat always after him. She didn't know how he'd taken working for Morris as long as he had.

She saved what she was working on and got

to her feet. Why did old man Morris have to bug her now? She was having enough trouble without him on her back. But when the big boss hollered, his staff had better answer. Quick.

She smoothed her hair, tried to settle a busy look on her face, and hurried down the hall. Giving her a harried look, Morris's secretary, Marian, motioned her into the inner sanctum. Something must be up. Marian looked even more haggard than usual.

Jenny stepped in and closed the door behind her. "Mr. Morris?" she said. "I understand you wanted to see me."

He didn't raise his head right away. Ensconced behind a gigantic ebony desk that he evidently didn't realize dwarfed him, he looked like a little boy playing big business. A small, pale man with mean, wizened features and a shock of black hair that looked as if he'd stolen it from someone younger, he studied a folder on his desk and ignored her.

But Jenny knew better. When she'd first come to work there Burton had warned her. When Morris looked like he was busy on something else he was really watching *you*. So she stood straight, breathed normally, and waited.

Finally the great man condescended to raise his bushy black head. His mean little eyes squinted at her over the huge desk. "The Viking job's behind," he said. No preamble. No "how are you," or even "good morning," or "hello." Just jump on you with both feet.

"Yes, sir," she said. Excuses were no good either, Burton had warned her. Just let Morris run down and wait till he dismissed you. That's what Burton had told her. And that's what she did.

"I'm disappointed in you," Morris said, twirling a pencil in his fingers. "That job should be nearer completion."

"There have been some problems, sir. I'm working on them." That was good, her voice was steady, the way she wanted it.

"I should hope so." He straightened to his full height, and she had to admit that if she hadn't known what a little runt he was, he'd look imposing. Word had it that his chair had been raised to give him as much height as possible. Still, though he might *look* imposing, nothing could make him a man to respect. At least, not to her.

He let her stand there a while longer in uncomfortable silence, but she knew better than to say anything. Burton had trained her well.

Morris cleared his throat. "I want this project done. I want it done by the twenty-fifth. Absolutely no excuses." He glared at her. "Do you understand me?"

"Yes, sir."

"Good. Then get out of here and get to work!"

Swallowing the scorching words she longed

to say, she went back to her cubicle and shut the door. Softly, because she knew that the people in the outer room, though they were pretending to be busy, were watching her, wondering exactly what Morris had said to her, wondering how she was reacting to being called on the carpet.

She threw herself down in her chair. Now she'd lost another half an hour and she was upset to boot. The irritating little S.O.B.! Who did he think he was? And how did he expect her to finish the stupid job by the twenty-fifth when he kept making changes in what was supposed to be in it? Well, she'd give him a finished job, but it wouldn't be good. It couldn't be good—not in that length of time. Her unconscious needed a certain amount of time to play with an idea—uninterrupted quiet time. Exactly what Morris wouldn't give her.

She leaned back in her chair and tried to breathe deeply. Think about something else, she told herself. Anything else. Think about Fido. What did he do all day when she was gone? What did he think about? Did he think? Why did he insist on staying with her? Maybe she'd take him with her to visit Mrs. Kelly.

Or think about Brad. Though thinking about him wasn't all that relaxing. Think about the way he'd kissed her last night. His mouth, the way his mustache tickled, his . . .

What would it be like going with him to see

the old woman? It was hard to imagine being all alone like that. Well, maybe not. Hadn't she felt that way after she lost Torrie? She'd had her folks, of course, but she'd still felt lost. They loved her, but they hadn't insisted she come home to live. They knew she had to be on her own.

She swung her feet down to the floor and turned to the computer. All right. Morris wanted his stupid project finished by the twenty-fifth. He'd have it. And if it wasn't as good as it could have been, it would be his fault, not hers.

It was almost dark when Jenny finally reached home. She felt worn to a nub. All she wanted to do was scrounge up something to eat. Anything at all. Then she'd take care of Fido. But he'd have to do without a walk tonight. And then she could fall into bed and stop thinking.

She was nibbling on a carrot and pouring a glass of milk when Fido looked at the back door and barked. "Someone coming? Okay. Good boy."

She opened the door. And wished she hadn't. Brad stood there. A couple of curls had worked their way out of his ponytail holder and clustered around his ears. His face wore a sheepish look. And the cutest beagle puppy squirmed in his arms. "Hi," Brad said. "Can we come in?"

She motioned him inside. Might as well. Otherwise he'd probably just stand there. What was he doing with a puppy, anyway? "Expanding your dog family?"

He looked surprised. "No, no. I got him for Clara Kelly."

Jenny stared at him. "A puppy for a tired old woman? Have you completely lost your mind?"

A wounded look crossed his face. "No. I just thought she'd like to have a dog. Company for her and all. So I went to the pet shop and bought her this pup. Isn't he cute?"

Men! Didn't they ever think before they did things? Jenny retreated to the table and sank into a chair. "Of course he's cute. But Clara Kelly's an old woman. At least, that's what you told me. How's she going to take care of a puppy?"

"It's not that hard," Brad said.

She shook her head. No wonder his dog ran away! "He has to be housebroken. Taught to heel. Taught to obey. Socialized."

"Good grief," Brad said. "You want a dog or a robot?"

She didn't have time for this. She just wanted to go to bed. Sleep and forget everything. "Look at Fido," she snapped. "Does he act like a robot?"

Brad snorted. "Of course not."

She pointed out the obvious. "And that's because someone trained him. He wasn't just born like that, you know."

Brad looked surprised. "No, I guess he wasn't. But I still think Mrs. Kelly's up to taking care of this pup. It'll give her something else to think about—something beside herself."

From his bed in the corner Fido watched the man put down the pup. He skittered across the floor, sniffing at everything on the way, and took a swipe at Fido's tail. Fido twitched it out of the way, raised his upper lip a smidgen, and growled softly, just enough to let him know who was boss here. The pup gave him a surprised look and backed off, retreating to press against the man's pant leg. Pups weren't so bad. Give him a couple of weeks with this youngster and he'd whip him into shape.

Fido put his head on his paws and considered these people into whose lives he'd invited himself. They were two of the densest humans he'd ever seen. First they liked each other, then they didn't. Then they did, then they didn't. And they hardly ever talked about what they were really feeling. What they were feeling was plain enough to *him.* He could smell wanting in the air, smell it on both of them. But they didn't let on to that. Oh no! They just talked about some other human, some old woman. And Jenny couldn't even make up her mind. He could smell that she wanted the man, but he could also smell that she was afraid.

Humans! Who could understand them? They

were so hard to train sometimes. This man human had shown up with a squirming nosy pup, when what Fido wanted to see was that classy Lady. The name fit her. Now there was a lady he could settle down with. He was getting tired of all this roaming around. What he needed was a nice place and a family.

Jenny put her elbows on the table and propped her chin in her hands. She was too tired to argue. "I don't know. Maybe you're right. Maybe a puppy is just what Mrs. Kelly needs. But a puppy's an awful lot of work."

"Hey," Brad said, staring at her with worried eyes, as though he was just really seeing her. "You don't look so good. Something wrong?"

She sighed. "Nothing that unusual. It's just that Morris wants the job done immediately. Like always. And I've had some problems."

Brad bristled. "Well, he doesn't have to work you into the ground! If I were you, I'd tell that dirty so-and-so where to put his job!"

"I'd like to," she said, managing a little smile. That was something she'd like to see—Brad tangling with Morris! "But not yet. I need another six months." She rubbed her temple where the headache that had nagged all day had grown into a full-blown raging pain.

Brad scooped up the puppy under one arm and got to his feet. "Listen, I'll talk to you tomorrow. I shouldn't have bothered you tonight.

You look beat. You'd better get to bed." He paused halfway to the door. "Anything I can do for you? Bring you some junk food, maybe?"

She chuckled weakly, appreciating his effort to make her laugh. "No thanks. What I need is sleep."

He grinned. "Want me to walk the dog?"

"No need. I'll let him out and he'll come back."

"Yeah." He shook his head. "I forgot. He's not like Lady."

He took a step toward her, as if he might try to kiss her again. It probably wasn't a good idea, but she didn't back away. And then Fido was there between them. Not snarling, not growling, not doing anything really, just standing there, keeping Brad from getting too close to her—as if he could anyway, with the puppy squirming in his arms. She didn't know whether to be relieved or disappointed, and she was too tired to decide. "Good night. And thanks."

"I'll call you," Brad said, with a funny look at Fido. "If you're still willing to go with me to see Clara Kelly."

"Yes, yes. I am."

Brad slammed the wagon door and plunked the pup down on the seat beside him. Damn that Morris! Jenny looked just awful. If only he could persuade her to get out of that place. Better to work for minimum wage than be beaten into the ground by a slave-driver.

Brad sighed. He'd like to wrap her in his arms and carry her home with him. Put her in his bed and treat her like a princess. Wait on her hand and foot till she was laughing and happy again. But he hadn't known her long enough to do that. He didn't have the right to take care of her. If she'd ever let any man do that.

She was so standoffish. Most women got soft and clingy after they were kissed—at least, that's what he'd heard—but Jenny seemed even more distant, as if his kiss had offended her in some way. But she hadn't said so, hadn't sent him packing. He had that much, at least, and he meant to build on it.

He'd wanted to kiss her again tonight. How he'd wanted to! He'd hoped, when he came barreling in with the pup, to hear her tell him what a good idea he'd had. To see her smile and laugh, and show him how much she liked seeing him there. And when he left, to kiss him back. His mouth tingled just thinking about it.

But instead of that he'd found a walking zombie, a woman who looked out on her feet. Who lit into him about what he'd thought had been a good deed.

Whoops! Something familiar here, Brad boy? Hadn't he lit into her a few days back? Laughed at her, when she thought *she* was doing a good deed. No wonder she'd gone stomping off in a huff that day.

If only he'd had more sense. It was so obvious now. Jenny was really on edge over this job business. And she didn't have anyone to comfort her, anyone but the dog Fido. Brad grinned. That Fido was one smart cookie, getting between them like that. It was uncanny. He seemed to know just what Jenny wanted him to do. Well, it was just as well. If Jenny didn't want him to kiss her, he wouldn't. He didn't want her to draw away from him. It raised too many old memories—bad memories. He'd been ignored and rejected as a kid. He didn't have to take it as an adult.

And he was a big boy now—he wasn't going to let this throw him. A dog could be a lot of comfort to a woman, true, but a man, the right man, could be even more. And he was going to prove it to Jenny.

She was the best thing that had come into his life in a long time. Probably ever. And he meant to hang on to her, no matter how much work it took.

He looked over at the little beagle, busy playing with his own tail. "I'm not so sure buying you was a good idea, young fellow. But now that I've got you, we might as well give it a try. Yeah. We'll give it a darn good try!" And he wasn't just talking about the dog.

Chapter Eight

The next evening, when Jenny unlocked the back door, the phone was ringing off the wall. She hurried to pick it up. "Hello."

"Jenny," Brad said. "Glad you're home."

"I just got in." Why had her heart started pounding like that at the sound of his voice? Why were her lips tingling? Good grief! The man wasn't even in the same room with her.

"Working late *again?*" he asked, exasperation tinging his voice.

She shrugged, though he couldn't see her. "It's my job. It has to be done."

There was silence on the other end of the line. She could almost hear him counting to ten. Finally he said, "I called to see if you're up to going to Clara Kelly's with me tonight. To take the pup. We don't have to stay long."

Jenny sighed. She just wanted to fall into a chair and not move. But it was better for the puppy to get to his new home right away. He had a lot of learning to do. She just hoped Clara was up to it. "Okay. What time?"

"Pick you up in half an hour?"

She swallowed her sigh. "All right. I guess I can make that."

Half an hour later she'd eaten a peanut butter and jelly sandwich, drunk a glass of milk, and changed from her business clothes into jeans and a flannel shirt. "I won't be gone long," she told Fido when she let him back into the house. "I'm sorry you have to spend so much time alone." She ruffled his ears. "You're a great dog. I was lucky the day you chose me."

He shoved his head into her hand. "Okay, okay. You deserve to be petted, I know. You deserve a lot. I don't know what I'd do if you hadn't come along when you did. I was so awful lonely."

And stubborn, too, Fido thought. Imagine cutting herself off from dogs. That was really dumb. People *needed* dogs. Well, he'd taken care of the dog part. And that man human was trying to connect her with people again. Basically he was trying to connect her with himself. But that was all right. People needed people. People needed love. So did dogs, he thought, wishing

Brad would bring Lady over again. There was something about her . . .

Jenny straightened. Brad should be there soon. She liked Brad well enough, but nothing was going to come of it. Nothing romantic. After what Hugh had done to her, she was through with that kind of thing.

Brad pulled into the driveway and honked. "See you later," she told Fido, giving him a last pat.

Brad held the puppy while she climbed into the station wagon. When he let him go the little beagle clambered into her lap. "Hello there," she said.

"Hello," Brad answered. "You look better tonight."

"I think I'm going to make Morris's deadline. It won't be a really good job. There isn't time for that. But it'll be done."

He reached over and patted her hand. "Good."

She stroked the beagle's soft head, rubbed his ears. Better not to think about touching Brad. Much better. "Does Mrs. Kelly know we're coming?"

He shook his head. "Not exactly. I mean, not tonight. I told her we'd be coming over sometime. And she said she never goes out."

"Okay." No sense arguing with him. Just get

the puppy delivered and hope that Mrs. Kelly could handle him. Though she still wasn't sure.

The little yellow house had seen better days. Its paint was beginning to chip and fade. But the flower beds showed the remnants of summer flowers. So Clara Kelly must come outdoors sometime.

Holding the little beagle to her, Jenny climbed out of the wagon and followed Brad up to the door. He knocked three times.

"Are you sure she's home?"

He looked a little worried. "She said she never goes out."

He knocked again. And the door opened. "Mr. Ferris! How good to see you."

Brad smiled. "Hello, Mrs. Kelly. This is my friend Jenny. The one I told you about."

Mrs. Kelly motioned them inside. "Do call me Clara. Please." She turned to Jenny. "How nice of you to come visit me, my dear. Come in. Come in. I'll put the tea kettle on."

"You don't—" Jenny began.

"Oh, it's no trouble." Clara smoothed her apron, a fancy patchwork yellow trimmed with green rickrack. "I made some doughnuts." She gave Brad a shy smile. "You said you'd come back to visit and I wanted to have something good for you to eat."

Clara had a grandmotherly smile. She was like Mom, Jenny thought. Had to feed people the minute they got in the door. Otherwise she didn't feel right.

The puppy squirmed in Jenny's arms and tried to climb up her front. She passed him to Brad. Let him hold the wiggle worm for a while.

In the kitchen Clara put the kettle on and motioned them to a table covered with an embroidered cloth. "Sit down. Please. Did you get a new puppy? How nice of you to bring him to visit."

Brad grinned. Jenny wasn't sure if it was a real grin or one caused by a late attack of nerves. "Well, we didn't exactly bring him to visit," he said. "We brought him to live here. With you."

Clara's mouth dropped open. It hung open for a moment while Jenny wondered if the woman would keel over from the shock. Finally Clara shut her mouth. "With me?" she squeaked, her eyes opening wide. "To live with me?"

Brad kept smiling, but he didn't look so happy. "Yes. We thought you'd enjoy some company."

Clara looked around the kitchen, as though trying to gather herself together. Or maybe find some help, Jenny thought.

"Why, that's—" She gulped. "How nice of you. It *is* lonely here by myself."

Brad gave Jenny an I-told-you-so look. What was wrong with the man? Did he really think that odd expression on Clara's face was joy?

Hadn't he seen the woman's hesitation? Couldn't he tell she wasn't all that happy about this?

Clara turned away to set out delicately painted china cups and saucers and heaps of doughnuts on a crystal plate. Jenny could see Brad eyeing the cups. "What lovely china," she said before he could spoil things by asking for a mug. "How kind of you to go to so much trouble for us."

Clara flushed and twisted her hands in her apron. "Well, I don't have much company anymore. My Horace passed on, and a lot of my friends are gone. So when Mr. Ferris here came to visit me it was a real treat. That's why I hope you'll come to visit me often. Both of you."

"We will," Jenny promised. It was easy to see that Brad was right about one thing—the woman was really lonely.

Brad put the puppy on the floor and he ran around the room sniffing at everything he could reach. Then he turned around a couple of times, squatted, and left a puddle in front of the fridge.

Brad turned scarlet and made an odd, strangled sound, while Clara tried valiantly not to notice. Jenny got to her feet. "I saw some paper towels over here. He'll behave better after he's trained, you know. Puppies are like children; they need to be brought up properly."

Before she could stoop to clean up the mess, Brad took the towels from her. "I'm sorry," he told Clara. "I guess he just got excited."

"It's quite all right," Clara said, though her smile was beginning to look really strained. "It was time to wash the floor anyway."

Since the floor was spotless, Jenny guessed Clara was trying to spare Brad's feelings. Well, they weren't off to a very good start, but puppies did get excited. Surely Clara would realize that.

They visited a while longer. Brad ate practically every doughnut on the plate and Clara beamed fondly. Yes, Jenny thought, food was Clara's way of showing hospitality.

Finally Jenny said, "I'm sorry, but I've got to go. I have a full day's work tomorrow and I'm trying to meet a deadline."

Clara got to her feet. "Of course, my dear. But do come see me again. And Harry, of course."

Brad looked startled. "Harry?"

"The puppy," Clara said. "I'm naming him Harry."

"I told you she'd like the pup," Brad said as they climbed into the wagon. But he made his voice sound more confident than he actually felt. "I think it was a good idea."

"Of course she *said* she liked him." Jenny wrinkled her nose, and a nice nose it was, too. As nice as the rest of her. "Clara didn't want to hurt our feelings." She sighed heavily. "But I don't know whether she'll be able to handle him."

Brad sighed, too. She was being really delicate about the puddle thing. "That puddle on the floor wasn't much of a beginning, I have to admit. But he's little. He'll learn."

"Maybe you're right," Jenny said. Her voice sounded really tired. What was that ass Morris doing to her now? Why didn't she get out of there?

"How's work?" Brad asked, trying to sound as if he was discussing the weather and not a subject that ate at his guts every time he thought about it. It really galled him to think of Jenny having to put up with Morris and his crooked ways.

"Work?" She made a face. "The same as always. I manage. I have to."

He wanted to ask her more, but the look on her face stopped him. Better leave it alone.

"How's Fido?"

Jenny brightened. "Fido's great. I can't believe I tried to run him off. I love having him there waiting for me when I get home." Her voice changed, trembled a little. She gulped. "Don't laugh, but I think my old dog knows and approves of him."

"Why should I laugh?" Brad said, swallowing over the lump in his throat. Didn't he remember Mrs. Vincent's dog Tuffy? The closest thing to a pet he'd ever had. The pain he'd felt when Tuffy died, the awful emptiness. And the sense of her approval, though it was years after her death when he got Lady. "We can get really close to dogs. I know."

Jenny turned to look at him, her gaze searching his face. He read understanding in her eyes. "I think you do," she said. "I think you do know."

It didn't take long to reach her house. Damn! Now what did he do? Should he or shouldn't he? Tonight there wasn't any Fido to get between them. But if he tried to kiss her and she got ticked off . . . He didn't want her to push him away again. It was too much like the painful memories of when he was little, when he'd tried to kiss his mother and been pushed away. When he'd felt that there must be something terribly wrong with him. He knew better now.

But being a man was touchy business. It was hard to know what to do next.

He pulled into her driveway and turned off the motor. "Thanks for going with me," he said. "I think Clara really enjoyed our visit."

"I think so, too," Jenny said with a big sigh. "Now I'm going in and get to bed."

Well, that settled that. No chance to go into her place tonight. He took a deep breath. "How about dinner Friday?"

She sighed. "I appreciate the offer. I really do. But like I said, I don't date. And I'm too tired anyway."

Too scared, he told himself silently, seeing the withdrawn look creep into her eyes. Some man had hurt her real bad. Hurt her in a romantic way, not by stealing her designs, bad as that was.

"I hope you understand," she went on.

He cleared his throat. "You will go with me again to see Clara, though, won't you?"

"Yes, of course. She needs some friends. And we'll want to see how Harry's doing."

Well, that was something. He'd better be content with it. Jenny reached for the door handle.

"I'll go to the door with you."

"There's no need."

"I know." He got out of the wagon and went around to her side, but by the time he got there she had the door open and was getting out.

She pulled up her hood and shivered. "I'm glad our dogs are safe inside."

"Me, too. Real glad."

He went with her up the steps to the back door. Would she open it and let Fido get between them again? She put her key in the lock and then she turned to him. "Thanks again. And that was a kind thing you did for Clara."

He smiled. "Even though you think it's a mistake."

She shrugged, her eyes turning dark. "Your intentions were good. That's what counts."

"My intentions are always good." He managed a shaky grin. "And I don't *always* make mistakes." He wanted to kiss her so bad he could taste it. "Do I?" he asked.

"No," she said, giving him a little smile. "Not always."

"Thanks for the kind words. Though I'd rather—"

"Good night," she said, leaning forward to give him a peck on the cheek.

He jammed his hands into his pockets to keep from grabbing her and pulling him into his arms. His body remembered her hands on his bare chest, wanted them there again, remembered the shape of her in his arms, her lips against his. He swallowed hard. Not now, he told himself. Not till she wants it. "Good night, Jenny. Sleep well."

Her eyes grew wide as saucers. Had she *expected* him to grab her, to kiss her? Had he lost some kind of chance by not doing it? Too late. She opened the door and went inside.

Holy Toledo! Would he ever understand women?

Chapter Nine

The work week finally came to a close. On Friday night Jenny could hardly wait to get home, change her clothes, and relax. Thank goodness Fido wasn't the sort to run away. She could let him out and let him in, and not worry. At first she'd watched him out the window, but he never left the yard. Just did his business and came back to the door to give the one little yip that signaled that he was finished.

She opened the back door and smiled at his hello bark. "Hello yourself," she said, bending down to ruffle his ears. "We're going to have a wonderful, relaxing weekend. Just the two of us. Well, maybe we'll go visit Clara. See how Harry's doing. Would you like that?"

Fido barked again and nosed her hand.

She laughed and scratched behind his ears. "You're really good company, you know."

An hour later she'd fed him, eaten her dinner, and was relaxing on the couch, just lying there doing nothing. The first time she'd relaxed all week. Fido lay on the floor beside her, his nose on his paws, the picture of contentment. She stretched and smiled. Wonderful! She'd left everything at the office. Morris might expect her to work over the weekend, but she wasn't going to do it. She could only preserve what sanity she had left by forgetting about Morris and his stupid ultimatums. For the weekend, anyway.

Fido's ears came up. He raised his head and looked toward the back door. Then he got to his feet and started toward it.

"Don't tell me someone's coming." She got up, too. So much for relaxing. Well, unless it was some late-working salesman, it must be Brad. What few friends she'd made since she got to Cleveland were as overworked as she was, and anyway, they called before they came by.

She went to open the door. Brad stood there, his hand raised to knock, a sheepish look on his face. "Hello," he said, smiling. He didn't move, just waited. But Lady had no such scruples. She marched right in without an invitation, dragging Brad behind her.

"Sorry," he said, glancing down at the dog.

"She hasn't got any manners. Doesn't know she ought to wait to be invited in."

Jenny had to laugh at the rueful expression on his face. And, truth to tell, she was glad to see him. Here was a friendly person, one who wasn't always watching her, one she could trust not to go running to Morris. "Well, since you're already in . . ." She shut the door. "But it's still instant coffee, and I still don't have any pie or cake. In case you haven't figured it out yet, I'm not much for cooking."

Brad grinned. "That's okay." He patted the t-shirt over his lean stomach, and her mind gave her a picture of his bare chest the way she'd seen it that first day, covered with those little golden wisps of furry hair. Her fingers itched to . . . Enough! This wasn't the time to think about that.

"Gotta watch my girlish figure," he went on.

A lot of people watched his figure, she bet. A lot of women, anyway. But she kept her thoughts to herself.

"Watcha doing tonight?" Brad asked, while Fido and Lady moved around each other, exchanging sniffs.

"Just relaxing. For a change."

"Sounds good," he said, his voice wistful. "Can I relax, too?"

What was he getting at? "I guess that's up to you. Can you?"

He grinned. "You know what I mean. Can I

relax with you? Maybe watch some TV?"

He glanced toward the living room, toward the couch. Her heart did a little skip and jump. Sitting beside him, just snuggling into his side, her arm across his chest, and feeling his arm around her; that would be good. Better than good. Just thinking about it made her feel all warm inside, made her breath catch in her throat and her heart start to pound. But it wasn't a good idea. No men, she reminded herself. She wasn't going to be hurt like that again. She'd sworn off men. For her own protection.

"Maybe we should go see Clara," she suggested. "See how Harry's doing."

Brad didn't look too happy about it, but he said, "If you want to. What about the dogs?"

"Fido can stay home. But maybe Clara would like to see Lady again."

Fido moved over and shoved his head into her hand. What did she mean he could stay home? He wasn't going to stay here if Lady was going.

He put on his mournful look. That always got her. Funny, Jenny was good at picking up on his feelings. Why couldn't she pick up on Brad's? Well, humans were difficult to understand sometimes. He nosed her hand again to make sure she got the message. He wanted to be wherever Lady was.

* * *

Jenny patted Fido's head. Poor dog. He looked so sad.

Brad laughed. "Doesn't look like Fido *wants* to stay home."

"I guess not. Well, he can come along. I was going to take him over there later this weekend anyway." She turned toward the back door. "Shall we walk or drive?"

"Let's drive," Brad said. "It's cold out there. Gonna be Thanksgiving before too long."

She sighed. "Don't I know it. The fifteenth is just around the corner. My stupid deadline." No! She wasn't going to think about work. She went to get her coat.

A yellow globe lamp sent its soft glow from between the lace curtains of Clara Kelly's front window. Brad pulled into the driveway and sat there. Feelings of longing welled up in him, making it hard for him to speak. Finally he conquered the lump in his throat enough to say, "It looks just like I always imagined a home should."

Jenny gave him a questioning look, but all she said was, "I wonder how Harry's been doing."

Trust Jenny to get down to the nitty-gritty. He sighed. "You still think he's too much trouble for her, don't you?"

She hesitated. "Well, we'll see. I could be wrong."

But she didn't really think so. He could see

that in her face. He grabbed Lady's leash before he opened the door. He didn't feel like chasing after her tonight.

Clara had the door open before they got to it. She looked down to where Harry frisked about, biting at the toes of her sturdy shoes. "Come in," she called. "Oh, do come in. I'm so glad to see you."

Brad followed Jenny into the house, into the dream home of his imagination. Into—! Good grief, what had happened here? The place was a shambles. The cozy living room was barricaded with straight chairs turned on their sides. The lace tablecloth on the dining room table sported ragged edges turned up onto its top. One corner of the carpet was covered with some kind of white powder and the unmistakable pine odor of cleaning solution hung in the air.

"Come on into the kitchen," Clara said, with a worried glance at the pup. "I'll put the kettle on."

"Thanks."

He followed Jenny and her dog into the kitchen.

"Sit down," Clara said.

He sat and took the leash off Lady. She went to investigate Harry's bowl, but he was too busy giving Fido the once-over to notice.

"I'm glad you brought the dogs to visit," Clara said, turning away from the stove. "I think Harry needs some company."

Brad swallowed. No use waiting. He might as well take the bull by the horns. "So, Clara, how's Harry doing?"

Jenny made a strangled sound, but he didn't look at her. He was too busy watching Clara's face. Her mouth came open and twitched once or twice, but nothing came out. She swallowed and twisted her hands in her apron, pale green today to match her housedress. Finally she said, "Well, he—he's a little difficult to train. He—he wants to chew on everything. Just everything. He ruined the corner of my living room rug. Chewed a hole right through it. That's why I've got the room shut off. And my lace tablecloth. And—" She ground to a halt, her face turning pink. "Oh, dear, I am sorry. It was so kind of you to bring him to me. But I'm afraid—well, I have to tell you—I'm so sorry, but I just can't handle him."

Brad still didn't look at Jenny. She could say I-told-you-so later. "I'll take him back, of course," he said. "I'm sorry for the damage he's done to your beautiful home." Finally he risked a glance at Jenny, but she wasn't smiling. In fact, she looked at him with sympathy. "I just thought you'd like to have a dog," he went on. "For company. I didn't mean to make you any trouble."

"I know," Clara said, smiling at him. "It was a real kind thought. Lady was a lot of company. But if you could just take Harry back—" She glanced at the corner where the pup had started worrying Lady's tail. "If you could just get me an older dog." She smiled apologetically. "Maybe from the animal shelter. I don't care what breed she is." She gave a funny little laugh. "Just so she's housebroken." She chuckled. "And she can't run faster than I can." She hesitated. "Maybe, maybe take one no one else wants."

"What a wonderful idea," Jenny said, such enthusiasm in her voice and on her face that his heart beat faster. Why, if she ever looked at him like that he'd probably keel over! He had to hand it to her, though. Jenny knew how to make Clara happy. The old woman was really grinning. "You'll give an old dog a home," Jenny said, "and you'll have company, too."

Tears filled Clara's eyes. "Oh, my dear, I can't tell you. I'm so relieved. I didn't want to seem ungrateful. You were so kind to bring me the puppy. But Harry—" She shuddered delicately. "Harry never stops. Never. And I'm just an old lady. I can't keep up with him."

"We understand," Jenny said gently. "Don't worry about it." And she looked at him and raised an eyebrow.

"Sure." He picked up his cue. "No problem. We'll take Harry with us tonight. And tomorrow morning we'll go to the animal shelter and find you an older dog. Say, maybe you'd like to come along."

Two tears slipped down Clara's wrinkled cheeks. She wiped at them hastily with the edge of her apron. "Oh, I couldn't do that. I know it sounds silly, but they'd haunt me forever—the ones I didn't choose. You go for me, please. You know what I want."

He'd never thought about that happening at the shelter, but from the look on her face it seemed likely Jenny had. That didn't surprise him. She had a tender heart.

"We'll go for you," Jenny said. "Don't you worry now. You get a good night's rest and tomorrow you'll have a new friend." She laughed. "One that won't literally eat you out of house and home!"

"Oh, thank you." The kettle whistled and Clara went to pour the tea. "I made some more doughnuts," she told him. "And some sugar cookies. With butter frosting."

"Great. I can't wait." He'd already had his quota of goodies for the day, but he wasn't going to pass up Clara's doughnuts, flat stomach or not.

About an hour later Jenny emptied her tea cup for the third time and sighed. The homemade doughnuts were delicious, and the cookies, too, but one of each was her absolute limit. At first she'd worried about hurting Clara's feelings by not eating more of them, but when she saw how Brad was shoveling them in she knew he could take care of the eating. She concentrated on conversation instead, drawing Clara out.

But finally Jenny ran out of things to talk about, and fatigue crept over her, numbing her mind. She hated to say anything about going home. Clara was beaming so, obviously having a really good time, and even Harry was behaving. Jenny rested her chin on her hand. She was so tired. Her head felt as if it was going to fall, crash on the table if she didn't prop it up, and she'd be asleep just like that. She stifled another yawn.

Brad put his cup back on the delicate saucer. "I think we'd better get going," he said to Clara. "Jenny's had a rough week and she needs to get to bed."

Jenny felt an unfamiliar warmth spreading through her. It had been a long time since anyone paid enough attention to her to notice how she felt. Hugh had seldom noticed such things. Many times she'd sat through the most boring meetings with him, and he'd never even thanked her. And now Brad had seen and . . .

"Of course," Clara said. "Thank you so much for coming. And I *am* sorry about Harry." She started twisting her apron again. "I'm really—"

"It's all right," Brad said. And he said it as if he meant it. "He's a cute little guy. He'll find a home in a hurry."

Brad pulled on his jacket, put Lady on the

leash, and gathered up the puppy. Jenny reached for her coat and followed him to the door, Fido right behind her. Clara trailed after them, her face wreathed in a huge smile. "Do come back," she said. "Anytime. I do love having company."

"We will," Jenny said. "We will."

Fido scrambled into the back of the wagon and Lady followed him. Jenny settled into the front passenger seat with a sigh and took the puppy from Brad. Harry was tired and snuggled into her arms. "What are you going to do with him?" she asked.

Brad raised an eyebrow and backed the wagon out onto the street. "No 'I told you so'?"

"Nope," she said. "I don't believe in that kind of thing."

Brad shook his head. "Are you for real?"

"Of course." She made a face at him. "Now, what are you going to do with Harry?"

"Guess I'll take him back to the store. I don't think Lady'd be happy to have a companion, especially one so young. She wasn't at all pleased that night I had him at the house." He grinned ruefully and ran a hand through his hair, making it go even curlier. "I don't have a nice place like Clara's, but what I do have I want to keep. And I'm gone a lot."

"Yes," Jenny said. "Harry needs kids to play with. Too bad we aren't closer to the farm. I'd buy him from you for Sue's kids."

"Yeah. I bet they'd like him. Well, at least Clara liked the part about having a dog for companionship. Are you going with me to the shelter in the morning?" He searched her face.

"I—" She didn't want to go with him, but she didn't want to tell him why. "I've got a lot to do and—"

He snorted. "Come on, Jenny. Be honest. You feel the way Clara does, don't you? Like the dogs you left there would haunt you."

He was too perceptive. Hugh would never have guessed that. Or if he had, he'd have laughed at her. But Brad wasn't laughing. "Yes," she admitted, wondering why Brad's being like this made her feel so good. "I do feel that way."

He smiled gently. "I understand. Think you can trust me not to pick a bad one?"

She had to laugh at the anxious expression on his face. "Let me put it this way—I think you've learned your lesson."

He laughed, too. "Have I ever! Okay, I'll return Harry in the morning and then I'll go get a dog for Clara, a housebroken old-lady dog. One she can keep up with."

He pulled into her drive and left the engine running. "Shall I hit your place around noon tomorrow?" he asked, turning to take the puppy from her. "That way you can sleep late."

"Sounds great," she said. "And thank you for understanding."

"What's to understand?" he asked, surprise in

his voice and on his face. "You've got a tender heart for dogs. Nothing wrong with that. I've got one myself."

And that was when she did it, did it without thinking about it. She leaned across the seat, across the squirming Harry pinned between them, and kissed Brad. She meant it to be a peck, like the other night, but somehow the kiss fell full on his mouth. Surprise hit her—that without any contact but their lips a kiss could be that good. She pulled away reluctantly.

"Wow!" he said, his eyes shining. "What was that for?"

"Just for being you," she said, opening the door and motioning to Fido to get out. "But don't get a swelled head. See you tomorrow. Noon."

Chapter Ten

Jenny woke the next morning around nine. Fido raised his head from her slippers and looked at her. It was about time! Even the best of dogs could only wait so long.

"Thanks for being patient," she told him. "You're a good dog." Slipping on her robe, she went to open the back door for him.

The sun was shining. The sky was blue. The air was crisp and cold. He pulled in a big lung-ful of it. A beautiful day. Too beautiful to go back to bed.

Jenny spent the morning doing little chores she'd been neglecting. And then, finally, she got around to paying attention to him. "You've been such a good dog," she crooned, ruffling his ears just the way he liked her to. "I wish you could talk to me," she said. "I wish you could tell me what you think of Brad."

Fido looked at her. *He* wished he could talk to her, too. But she probably wouldn't like what he had to say. For example, he'd want to know why she was dillydallying the way she was. It was plain to him that Brad was attracted to her. And it was pretty clear that she felt the same way about him. Couldn't she understand that humans were made to love each other? All living creatures knew that. Even the smallest runt knew it, knew he was supposed to have love, and went searching for it, even before his eyes opened.

Well, give her time. He hadn't been around her very long, and training a human was a complicated, time-consuming project.

He tried to tell her with his looks that he understood what she was talking about, that Brad was a man she could love. She seemed to pick up a little of it, but not enough.

"I guess you like him," she went on. "I mean, if you didn't you'd probably snarl at him or something. Wouldn't you?"

He raised his lip obediently and gave her a halfhearted snarl, then changed it to his most appealing grin.

She chuckled. "I bet you'd have bitten Hugh!"

From what she'd said about this Hugh, she was right. But biting didn't sound like enough.

This Hugh deserved a good chewing out. At the very least.

"Yeah," Jenny went on, "I guess you like Brad, all right. But liking him and—" She shook her head. "This is stupid. You're a great dog, but you can hardly give advice to the lovelorn." A funny expression crossed her face. "Not that *I'm* lovelorn." She patted his head. "I've sworn off men, you know. I just wish I had someone to talk to about Brad. Someone who could talk back to me."

Fido thumped the floor with his tail. If only he could tell her. It was so simple. Love the man. Just love him.

He raised his head and sniffed the air. Speaking of Brad . . . That was his smell in the air. Fido glanced toward the back door.

Jenny grinned. "Well, that nose of yours is working all right, anyway. I guess he's here. You'd better stay home this time, fellow. He's got the new dog with him. I'll see you later." Smiling, Jenny grabbed her coat and went out.

Fido settled in his bed and put his head down on his paws. This time he didn't mind staying home. Didn't mind at all. If Brad had picked out another juvenile delinquent like that Harry, this dog would be just as happy not to be there. But probably Brad had learned his lesson. For Clara Kelly's sake, Fido hoped so.

* * *

"Thanks," Brad said when Jenny opened the passenger door. "I was hoping you'd be watching for me."

"Fido heard you pull in. He has great hearing." She climbed in hurriedly and slammed the door.

"No need for that," Brad said with a little chuckle. "I have a feeling Duchess isn't going anywhere. I don't think she's the running-away type."

"Duchess," Jenny said, turning to look over into the backseat, "that's a nice—" Her heart came up in her throat and threatened to choke her. "Oh, Brad!"

He slammed on the brakes, his eyebrows going up in alarm. "Don't tell me I goofed again!"

"No, no!" The lump in her throat was so big, she could hardly get the words past it. "It's just—She's—beautiful."

Brad made a funny strangled noise. "Come on, you're pulling my leg." He finished backing out of her driveway. "She's no great shakes to look at, just a short-haired, medium-sized black mongrel, running to fat, actually. But she's housebroken and she's old—about ten, they said—and she seemed to be what Clara ordered."

"Oh, she is. She is." Jenny swallowed hard. Clara would love Duchess—Duchess who looked enough like Torrie to be her twin.

Brad cleared his throat. "Well, that's good. I

was worried there for awhile. 'Cause we—that is, I—have another problem."

She turned back to him, not liking the sound of his voice. "Problem? What's wrong?"

He made a face. "Plenty. The pet shop won't take Harry back. I was there this morning. I did my darnedest, used every argument I could think of. But no go. Seems they've got a twenty-four-hour return policy. It's printed right on the receipt—which, of course, I didn't bother to read."

She hadn't thought about anything like that. "Oh, my."

He smiled ruefully. "Oh, my, is right. Now I've got two dogs. One that runs off every chance she gets. And one that tries to eat everything in sight. Some deal! What am I going to do?"

"You didn't take him to the shelter." She said the first thing that came to her mind.

He stared at her, his mouth falling open. He shut it with a snap. "Come on; I couldn't do that. But I've got to find a home for him. Wouldn't like another dog, would you?"

"Not me!" She shuddered. "I doubt if even Fido could keep Harry in line. Besides, I didn't want any dogs at all."

He shrugged. "Well, it was worth a try. Here we are at Clara's. Reach back for Duchess, will you?" He grinned. "She's on a leash, but I think we'll make better time if we carry her in."

Jenny grinned, too. "Come on. She's not that fat, or that old."

"Sure."

Clara opened the door as they came up the walk. "Ohhhh!" She stood there, clasping her hands, a bemused expression on her face. "Look at her. She's beautiful. So beautiful." She shook herself and stepped aside. "Come in. Do come in."

Inside the door, Jenny unsnapped the leash. Clara bent to fondle the dog's ears. "Her name is Duchess," Brad said. "I suppose you could change it if—"

"No, no. It fits her. It's perfect." Clara turned. "Come. Come into the kitchen. I've washed Harry's bowls and bed and made everything ready for her." She smoothed the dog's hair. "Jenny, Brad, I can't tell you how much this means to me. How really much."

Jenny felt the tears stinging behind her eyes. She blinked and swallowed. "We're just glad you like her."

"Oh, I do. I do." Clara's voice trembled and she wiped at her eyes with a corner of her apron. "Enough silliness, now. This is a happy time."

Duchess crossed the spotless kitchen floor, sniffed the bowls, took one lap of water, and came back to stand by Clara's side. Clara moved to the tap to wash her hands and fill the tea kettle. Duchess followed her. Clara put the kettle on the stove. Duchess went with her.

Clara giggled. "I think she likes me."

"Of course she likes you," Jenny said, trying to control the break in her voice. "She knows you belong to her."

Clara's smile was watery, but it was a smile. "My, what a lovely day this has turned out to be!"

Jenny looked at Brad just in time to see his Adam's apple convulse. This was getting to him, too. He had a soft heart. Pop always said a man with a soft heart was a real man, that a real man wasn't afraid to have feelings.

Jenny sighed. She sure missed Mom and Pop. And Sue and the girls. She hadn't been home since Labor Day weekend, and it seemed like years instead of just a few months. If Morris hadn't been such a jerk, if he'd given her enough time to do this job right . . . But Morris was Morris, and he wasn't going to change. Forget about Morris.

"I think she's perfect," Clara breathed, setting out a plate of cookies that would feed an army. "Just exactly what I had in mind." She giggled again. "Why, I believe I can run faster than she can!"

Brad laughed, that deep hearty laugh that made Jenny feel good inside. "That's why I chose her. Something told me she'd be just right for you."

"You were right," Clara said. "I know we're

going to get along real well." She took the delicate cups and saucers out of the cupboard and set them on the embroidered tablecloth. Then she set down a dainty teapot.

"How beautiful," Jenny said, leaning forward to admire the tiny painted violets and gold gilt that decorated it.

Clara smiled. "It's very old, dear, my grandmother's. I decided to get it out again now that I'm having company."

"It's beautiful," Jenny breathed. "So delicate."

"Thank you," Clara said. "It was Horace's favorite, too." She smiled. "Horace was a tea man, you see. After he retired we had tea together every afternoon." Her smile turned wistful. "It was a good time for us."

Jenny swallowed. Would she ever have anyone to love like that? To love her? She stole a quick glance at Brad. What if he . . . No! She'd sworn off men—she had to remember that. She wasn't going to lay herself open for that kind of pain again. Being alone wasn't so bad. She'd get used to it.

Several hours later Jenny followed Brad out to the station wagon. A beaming Clara stood in the open doorway, Duchess leaning against her leg. Clara lifted a hand to wave.

"You did it this time," Jenny said, waving back as Brad turned the wagon toward home.

"You picked the absolutely perfect dog for Clara."

"Thanks." He expelled a deep breath. "I was worried, scared I'd goofed again."

She leaned over to pat his hand. "You did just great."

Brad sighed. "I'm glad about that, but I've still got the problem of Harry."

She couldn't help giggling. She hadn't felt so good in a long time. "I'm sorry," she said after a minute, managing to compose herself. "Harry must be a real trial to you."

"Trial?" Brad exclaimed, his voice spiraling upward. "Nightmare's more like it. You know what the little demon did last night?"

"No, tell me. What did he do?" She wouldn't laugh. She wouldn't. But she couldn't help grinning.

"I thought I had him closed off in the kitchen, but somehow or other he weaseled his way out. He got into the bedroom and decided to snack on my hundred-dollar loafers."

"Oh, no!"

"Oh, yes," Brad said, his face a study in disgust. "And that's not all he's been chewing on. Sometimes I think his father must have been part goat."

She laughed, but hundred-dollar shoes . . . This wasn't funny any more. "What are you going to do?"

Brad pulled into her driveway and turned off

the engine. "Well, I've got a kind of idea. It came to me while we were at Clara's. Do you suppose I could come in and discuss it with you?"

She hesitated. If she let him come in . . . She shouldn't have kissed him last night. It might have given him ideas. For sure it had given her some. She didn't want to hurt him. He'd been a good friend. And if he came in tonight . . .

"Please," he begged. "It won't take that long." He shivered dramatically. "It's so cold out here. You wouldn't leave a stray dog out in this weather, now would you?"

She had to laugh at the exaggerated expression of woe on his face. "That's a low blow, Brad Ferris, and you know it."

"Yeah, I know it." He grinned. "But did it work?"

She laughed aloud. "Oh, all right, come on. But I still don't have any goodies."

He groaned and clutched his stomach. "Oh, please. Don't mention goodies. I don't want to *see* another cookie, let alone eat one. I must have eaten two dozen today."

"At least." She opened the wagon door. "Come on, you poor thing. I'll make you some coffee."

Brad went in and sat down at the kitchen table as if he lived there. But for some reason she didn't mind. There wasn't any reason she should. Surely she could have a friend. She turned to ruffle Fido's ears and put fresh water in his bowl. "You're a good dog," she said, going to wash her hands.

Brad chuckled. "Too bad it isn't catching."

She put the kettle on the stove and got out the mugs. Then she settled in the chair across from him. "Okay, now give. Tell me about this idea."

He looked into her eyes. He had great eyes, sort of a cross between green and gray. And so warm. Somehow they invited her to trust him.

"It's just an idea," he said. "I don't have it all worked out yet. But let me tell you the whole thing before you decide, before you say anything."

She raised an eyebrow. "I don't know about this. It doesn't sound so good."

"Please?" he begged. "Give me a chance. Just listen."

"All right. Tell me. I won't interrupt."

He heaved a great sigh. "Good. Now, these are the facts, ma'am. The store won't take Harry back. I can't have him chewing up everything I own. And you can't take him."

She nodded.

"Well, the other day you said you have a sister with two kids. So, I thought, why don't we take Harry and go to Iowa and—"

"What!"

He gave her a stern look. "You promised not to interrupt. We could take Harry to the farm and you could give him to your sister's kids. They'll have time to chase him around."

She stared at him. Go to Iowa? With Brad?

"You can talk now," he said. "What do you think?"

She said the first thing that came to her mind. "Iowa is over six hundred miles away."

He shrugged. "I know that. I have a road atlas."

The kettle whistled and, grateful for the interruption, she got up to make the instant coffee. To go home, even for a little while, would be so good. But she had to be sensible. "It takes time to drive six hundred plus miles," she said, putting a full mug down in front of him.

He nodded. "I thought about that. We can do it over Thanksgiving. We could leave at noon the day before. Drive six or seven hours. Stop to sleep. Get up early the next morning and be there in time for Thanksgiving dinner—if my being there isn't a problem. From what you said about your family, they'd probably be glad to see you."

He was right about that. They'd be excited to have her visit. They were always asking her when she was coming home again. And there was always room for more at their table. Oh, it sounded good. Real good. But it was crazy to drive all that way for just a couple of days. Besides . . . "What about Lady and Fido?"

He wrapped his fingers around his mug and looked thoughtful. "We could leave Lady with Clara. But I'm not sure that's such a good idea.

Not the way she likes to run off. And Clara has Duchess now anyway. Besides, I knew you wouldn't want to leave Fido at home. So we'll just take them along."

Jenny stared at him. The man must have had too many cookies—the sugar had affected his brain. "Take them along? Three dogs shut up in a car with us for six hundred some miles? Have you lost your mind?"

"Not yet," Brad said, making a face. "But if I have to keep Harry much longer, I will. When I was out this morning I bought him a cage. I hate putting him in it, but I can't let him wreck the place."

He took a sip of coffee. "We'll put the cage in the back of the wagon for him. Lady and Fido will behave . . . I hope. They get along with each other. So they shouldn't be any problem."

She sipped her own coffee. "What if Lady runs away again?"

"I can keep her on a leash. Fasten it to the cage." He gazed at her with pleading eyes. "Come on, Jenny. I don't know what else to do. You'll have your project finished by then. You must have some time off coming."

She hesitated. It'd be great to see the folks again. And Sue. To be home just for a little while. Home, where she knew she was loved. Home, where she didn't have to think about Morris or his projects. And she *would* be through with this latest project by then. She could be off from the Tuesday afternoon before Thanksgiving till the Tuesday morning after. Once she'd finished his precious project Morris could afford to give a little.

"How are you going to find a motel that'll take three dogs?" she asked.

"I'll call the Auto Club," he said. "They have lists of places that allow pets. Can we do it?" He stared at her, his eyes full of anxiety. "Say yes, please say yes."

"Yes," she said finally, matching the grin that spread across his face. "I think I need my head examined, but yes."

Brad jumped to his feet. "Thank you! Thank you so much. I'll go home now. Start making calls. Get everything together."

"We've got ten days," she said, infected by his enthusiasm in spite of herself. She got up, too. She should call Mom and tell her company was coming. What would she say about Brad? Just a—

"I know," he said, moving toward the door. "But I don't like to leave Harry in the cage too long. I need to take him and Lady for a walk." He looked at her with hope in his eyes. "You want to come, too?"

She should call Mom, but . . . when he looked at her that way what could she do? "Well, I guess Fido could use a walk. I've been neglecting him this week. When I get home I'll call the folks and tell them we're coming."

"Great." Brad took a step toward her and stopped, a funny expression crossing his face. He stood there for a minute, swallowing. "It'll work," he said finally. "You'll see. Your sister's kids'll love Harry."

Now why did she think he was talking about something else that would work? And why did her heart start to pound when he moved toward her? She'd sworn off men, that was the one thing she was sure about.

In the corner Fido gave a sigh of relief. At last! A nice long weekend with Lady. And if Jenny and Brad couldn't get it together in that length of time—Well, he'd have to do something drastic, that was all.

Chapter Eleven

The days passed quickly. Determined to finish the project on time, Jenny pushed herself unmercifully. She thought sometimes that if it hadn't been for Fido and Brad, she'd have just stayed all night at the office and never stopped working at all.

But Fido was at home waiting for her. And Brad came around every evening, insisting that after she ate she and Fido go with him to walk Lady and Harry. Sometimes she thought she went along because it was easier than getting him to leave her alone. But in her heart she knew she owed him a lot. Her health for one thing. Fido's too.

Brad made her walk, but he also made her laugh. Every night he regaled her with hilarious stories of the kids he'd been photographing, or, sometimes even funnier, of their doting mamas. "I wish you'd come watch me work," he said more than once.

"Maybe later," she said. "After I finish this Viking thing."

"I'll hold you to that." His eyes gleamed. "After we come back from Iowa. Before that jerk can give you another project that takes over your whole life you can come in on a Saturday and watch me coax the kids into smiling."

"All right," she'd agreed. She'd like to see him with kids. See how he handled them.

Every night they walked the dogs and on the weekend they visited with Clara and Duchess. In her spare moments Jenny packed her suitcase, putting in her rose-colored suit for church. Mom and Pop would insist on their going to church, she told Brad, and he said okay, he'd pack some church-going clothes. She didn't tell him about the questions Mom had asked about this *guest* she was bringing home with her, the first one ever. Or how vaguely she'd answered them.

And then it was Tuesday afternoon. The Viking project was actually, really, finished. It wasn't as good as she'd like it to be, but it was as good as anyone could make it in the time Morris had given her. She'd called Marian that morning and told her she'd be bringing the finished Viking project at three o'clock.

At two-thirty she finished the last line and gathered all the material, putting it in the proper order. Then there was nothing to do but wait till it was time to beard the lion in his den. Morris wasn't much of a lion as looks went, but he had a loud roar. She had a pretty good idea, though, that in spite of the roar he was really a coward. A man with real power didn't need to roar like that, or barricade himself behind a huge desk to make people think he was someone important.

At five till three she straightened the skirt of her blue suit, smoothed her hair into place, and set off for Morris's office. Marian gave her a weak smile and waved her on in. Poor Marian, how could she stand it, being that close to Morris all the time, taking the brunt of his bad temper? As usual he was ensconced behind his huge desk. Come to think of it, Jenny couldn't remember ever seeing him anyplace else.

She stood there, clutching her finished work, and waited, feeling like a schoolgirl called to the principal's office. But she wasn't going to let Morris rattle her. She was going to turn in the project and tell him she was taking some time off—through Monday. And then she was going to leave. Freedom! She was going to have six wonderful days of freedom. She wasn't sure she could imagine freedom anymore. In the year she'd been in Cleveland, Morris & Pleasant had more or less taken over her whole life.

Finally Morris raised his bushy black head and stared at her with his beady little eyes. "You've finished the Viking project?" he snapped.

"Yes, sir."

"Put it there." He pointed to the corner of the desk.

She deposited the material and stood erect again. "I'm taking some time off, sir," she said, proud that her voice was firm and strong, that she looked him right in the eye. "I'll be back in on Tuesday morning."

He glared at her, but she wasn't backing down. Not for anything. She needed this rest. Needed it bad. Let him fire her if he wanted to—that'd give her unemployment, at least. And she wanted to leave here anyway.

Morris cleared his throat. "I have a new project for you. It has to be finished in January."

So much for saying thank you. But then, why did she expect the man to behave like a decent human being? He never had before. He wasn't likely to start now.

"I'll start it on Tuesday," she said. "I need to clear my mind of Viking."

He continued to glare at her, but she didn't look away. Finally he grunted. "I expect this new project to be finished by mid-January."

"I'll start as soon as I get back."

He picked up a folder from his desk and slid it across to her. "Take this with you."

She swallowed hard. One of these days . . . But it was too soon to give him a piece of her mind, much as she'd like to do it. She picked up the folder. She'd take it back to her office, but he couldn't make her take it to Iowa with her. Even Morris couldn't go that far.

"You're dismissed," he said. "But don't forget, the workday isn't over yet."

"Yes, sir." The words stuck in her throat, but she got them out. She wouldn't be taking this kind of thing forever. By spring she'd have enough money saved up. Then she'd be able to tell Morris where to go and she'd get another job. Anything would be better than working for him.

She made it through the big room without meeting anyone's gaze and shut the door to her office carefully behind her. She didn't feel like answering questions. Making a face, she dropped the folder on her desk. The nerve of the man! All the extra hours she'd put in on the Viking job, working herself to exhaustion, almost, and he didn't even thank her. What a jerk.

He had to be crazy, thinking she was going to start a new job this soon, before she even had a holiday. Not even giving her a breather. Well, it didn't matter what he wanted. *She* wasn't going to do it. She wasn't going to open the stupid folder. She didn't even want to see what the job was about. Not till next week, when she got back. Morris couldn't make her look at it. He wasn't going to come in here to get on her case. He wasn't going to come out from behind his desk.

A knock sounded on the door. She pulled the folder toward her, just in case. "Come in."

Phil Burton opened the door a crack and eased in, the mouse still trying to be invisible. "Finished the Viking job?"

"Yes." The word came out of her mouth like a sigh. "At last."

Phil rubbed his bald head. "Satisfied with it?"

She looked at him carefully. What was he getting at? "As much as I could be with the time he gave me. Why?"

Phil shrugged. "No particular reason. I just wondered how you're adapting to the pressure. It's hard on people who aren't used to it." He sighed. "It's hard on those who are."

"You can say that again."

He glanced at the folder on her desk. "I see he gave you another project."

"Yes." She wasn't going to say any more about it.

"Does it look bad?"

"I only just got back from his office," she said. "I haven't had time to look at it yet."

"Lucky he gave it to you today."

"Lucky?" What made him say a thing like that?

"Yeah, you can start tomorrow. And you'll have the weekend, too."

"I'm going away."

Phil's eyebrows went up. "He gave you time off? Morris gave you time off?"

She shrugged. "I guess you could say he gave it to me. I told him I was going away and wouldn't be back till Tuesday."

Phil's eyes almost popped out of his head. "You *told* him?"

"Yes."

"Wow!" He shook his head and rolled his eyes heavenward. "You *told* him and you're still here. You must be good."

Jenny shrugged. This conversation was making her uneasy. She'd depended on Phil to learn the ropes here and so far he'd been a good friend, but she was beginning to feel that he needed more backbone. If everyone in the firm didn't kowtow to Morris, maybe he wouldn't be such a martinet. Of course, Phil had five kids to think about; he probably felt he had to do whatever Morris wanted.

Phil turned toward the door. "Guess I'd better let you get back to work. You'll want to get a good idea of the new job before you leave tonight."

She didn't correct him. Phil would be shocked if he found out she had no intention of opening the folder till after she got back. "Have a nice Thanksgiving,"

Phil nodded. "See you Tuesday."

As he closed the door behind him, Jenny

leaned back in the chair and pulled in a deep breath. Relax. Take it easy. An hour and half till she could go home. After all the hours she'd worked late, she deserved to leave this very minute. But there wasn't any sense pushing her luck.

She looked around. Well, this place could use a good cleaning. But whatever else she did, she was *not* going to open that folder.

At six Brad was at Jenny's back door, Lady and Harry straining on their leashes beside him. He hated to keep badgering Jenny about these walks, but if he didn't she'd probably just fall into bed every night without even eating. The walks helped her unwind and gave her an appetite. At least he hoped they did.

He searched her face. He hadn't been happy with the long hours she'd been working lately. She really needed this trip back to Iowa. Thank goodness he'd thought of making it.

"Thought maybe we'd walk over to Clara's tonight," he said. "Say good-bye before we leave tomorrow."

Jenny smiled and shrugged into her coat. When she reached for Fido's leash, on its hook by the door, the dog was already standing at the ready. "Sounds like a good idea," she said, straightening.

"So," Brad said, as they went out the door, "did you get the Viking job turned in?"

"Yes." She made a face. "And the jerk didn't even thank me."

Brad snorted. "I think you ought to get away from that dictator."

"Me, too. May, that's when. By May I'll be able to swing it. Till then I don't dare rock the boat."

He turned to look at her. The suspense was driving him crazy. He couldn't wait any longer to find out. "You did get the time off, didn't you? To go to Iowa. How did it go? What did he say?"

"I got the time off." She grinned. "Told him I wouldn't be back till Tuesday."

"Told him?" His own face broke into a grin. "Good for you!"

"Not so good," she said, looking a little worried. "He didn't much like it." The worried look turned to indignation. "And get this—he had another job for me to start right now. Wanted me to take it with me to Iowa."

"No way!" Man, he'd like to give that little pipsqueak a piece of his mind. A piece of his fist, too, though he wouldn't hit a smaller man. What was wrong with the guy, anyway? Jenny was a person, not some kind of machine. She'd been working so hard these last weeks that she had dark circles under her eyes. Looked like she'd lost weight, too. "Somebody ought to do something about that guy," he snapped.

"Somebody will." She grinned. "In May."

* * *

Pacing along beside them, Fido listened happily. Yep, Brad had it bad. Now, if Jenny would just get on the ball, this trip ought to bring them together.

Chapter Twelve

Late the next morning, pulling out of his drive with both dogs yapping in the backseat, Brad had a moment when he wondered about his sanity. Three dogs in a car for six hundred miles? But it was only a moment. Harry had to have a home. Jenny's nieces would love him. And that little devil Harry'd have the whole farm on which to sharpen his teeth.

Brad grinned to himself. And besides finding a home for Harry, *he* would have six wonderful days with Jenny. If he couldn't get closer to her in six days . . . well, he'd just have to keep trying. She was softening toward him; he could see it in her eyes. And she talked to him now, really talked, like that stuff about her job. Jenny treated him like a friend.

Of course, what he wanted was to be more than a friend to her—much more. That's why he'd seen this long weekend as a golden opportunity. Thrown together all the time, they'd get to know each other better. They'd have to.

Jenny had her suitcase sitting on the back porch. Leaning against it was a bag of dog food and another bag holding Fido's bowls and bedding. As he turned off the motor, the back door opened and Jenny came out, Fido right behind her.

The dogs behind him kept up their insane yapping. Muzzles—maybe he should have thought to bring muzzles. He'd go nuts if they kept up that noise for long.

He got out and went for Jenny's stuff. "Good morning," she said.

"It is now." She gave him a funny look, but didn't ask him what he meant. A good thing, he supposed. It was too soon to talk about his feelings for her. Heck, he'd only kissed her a couple of times. But he knew. He knew this was the woman he wanted to spend the rest of his life with. He just had to convince *her*.

He opened the tailgate, hefted her suitcase in beside his, took the dog food and Fido's bag from her, and put them in. And all the while Lady and Harry kept up that infernal yapping. "I hope you brought your earplugs," he said, making a face. "They're kind of noisy this morning."

"Up, Fido." She motioned with her hand.

Fido jumped in and sniffed noses with Lady and Harry. They shut up like someone had pulled a switch. Fido turned around three times and sank down next to Lady. Brad looked from him to Jenny. "How'd he do that?"

She giggled. "Don't ask me. Fido's a prince."

"I guess so," Brad said. "Those two have been barking constantly since I put them in the car."

"They'll be all right now," she said. "Everything'll be all right."

He couldn't believe the difference in her face. Just overnight she looked younger, happier, full of spunk and ginger. If he could just get her away from that Morris for good, have her look like this all the time. But Jenny wasn't the kind a man could push. As much time as they'd spent together, there was still something distancing in her glance, something that kept him away from her. A line she wouldn't let him step over.

"Got everything?" he asked.

She grinned. "I hope so. Oh, Brad, this was a great idea! I can't wait to get home. Thank you." And right there in the driveway she gave him a quick hug. Too quick. But he didn't try to prolong it. Let her move at her own speed. At least it was a hug. She wasn't so afraid of him now.

"I owe you the thanks for finding Harry a home," he said. "I'm getting absolutely nowhere trying to train him."

Jenny laughed, a good strong belly laugh, the

first he'd ever heard from her. "Don't worry about it. The girls can handle him."

I won't worry, he thought happily. *I won't worry about a thing.*

Jenny settled back and fastened her seat belt. They were on their way, really on their way. Tomorrow she'd be home in Iowa. She felt so light, almost giddy, as if a great weight had been lifted from her. And it had—the weight of the Viking project.

She sighed. Of course, there was the new project waiting for her when she got back. But she didn't have any idea what it was about. A couple of times yesterday afternoon she'd been tempted to sneak a peek in that folder, but she'd resisted. If she didn't know what the project was, she *couldn't* think about it. And that was the way she wanted it to be. She wanted her mind to be free to enjoy this trip.

What would Mom and Pop think of Brad? Would they like him as much as she did? And Sue—would Sue feel bad seeing her sister with a man when hers was gone? But not Sue. Sue was too loyal and loving for that. And maybe by now some decent man had found out what a gem Sue was. Besides, Brad wasn't *with* her; not in that sense.

"Tired?" Brad asked.

"Not really." She swiveled in the seat to look at him. He looked so happy and relaxed. Maybe he needed to get away, too. He'd left his jacket open and his red plaid shirt was unbuttoned at the throat. A few wisps of golden hair peeked out above a red t-shirt. Her fingers itched to touch his chest, to feel the warm flesh move beneath—What was it with her! The man had a nice chest—so what?

They were friends. Just friends. Thinking of anything more would get her in trouble. In fact, she shouldn't have hugged him there in the driveway. But she'd just felt so good, like she wanted to hug the whole world if she could.

"You look happy," she said, looking for something to talk about. "Are you glad to get away?"

"Yes." He grinned and rolled his eyes. "I love my work, but yesterday I must have had the three most demanding mothers in the city of Cleveland. You wouldn't believe . . ."

She giggled. She actually giggled. "Tell me about them. Tell me every horrendous detail."

And while the dogs slept in the backseat he told her.

The miles sped by. About an hour out, they went through a drive-in, a place with salads, and got lunch. A little later they stopped at a roadside rest area and walked the dogs.

"Do you want me to drive for a while?" Jenny asked.

Brad shook his head as Fido bounded out of the wagon. "No, I'm fine. I'm enjoying it." He grinned. "Besides, I want you to relax."

"I am," she said. "I really am."

Brad looked at Fido, taking a leisurely smell of the rest area. "I can't believe that dog. No leash."

"He doesn't need it," she said. "He won't leave me." She didn't know how she knew that, but she did.

Lady and Harry weren't as lucky as Fido; they had to stay on leashes. Brad handed her Harry's. "Here. Would you mind walking him? I'm getting tired of having him tangled around my legs."

"I don't see why," she said, grinning. "You wanted a dog."

"So I did," he said. "So I did."

Soon they were back in the car. They stopped again in midafternoon, and again a couple of hours later. The sky was starting to darken when Brad said, "We're coming into Gary, Indiana. Shall we stay here or go on a little farther?"

She looked out the side window. In this old steel town everything was gray. Gray buildings. Gray railroad yards. Gray parking lots. Even gray sky. She shivered. "I don't like the way it looks here. If you're not too tired, let's go on a little farther. I don't want to get up to a gray sky."

"I'm with you," he said. "We deserve blue skies. The bluest."

The sky grew darker and the grayness of Gary dropped behind them as night fell. "Thanks," Jenny said. "By the way, you did bring the list of dog motels, didn't you?"

"Of course," he said, patting his pocket. "In a little while we'll stop for supper. We can take a look then. Joliet might be a good place."

At the second Joliet motel Brad came back to the wagon, a sheepish look on his face. Jenny rolled down the window and shivered. A cold wind was blowing up. "What's the matter? Isn't this the right motel?"

"Oh, yeah," Brad said, pulling his coat tighter around him. "It's the right place."

"Then it takes dogs?"

"Yeah. It takes dogs."

Well, something was wrong; she could see that. "Brad! For mercy sakes! Will you please tell me what it is?"

"There's a dog show in town. And they only have one room left."

She couldn't believe it. "Only one room?"

"Right," he said, looking sheepish. "Listen, I asked about other places. They even called around for me. But all the motels that take dogs are full. So I paid for the room before someone else could snap it up. You can take the dogs in there. I'll sleep in the wagon."

"You'll do no such thing," she said, not even

bothering to think about it. "Why, you'd freeze to death. We'll manage."

He hesitated. "Well, if you're sure . . ."

She wasn't sure at all, but she couldn't leave the man outside in this kind of weather, not after he'd been kind enough to drive Harry all the way to Iowa for the girls.

"Let's walk the dogs," she said. "Then we can settle in. We'll leave a wake-up call and get an early start in the morning."

He went around to open the tailgate and she joined him. "Guess we'd better take Harry's cage inside," she said.

He made a face. "Yeah. I don't want to pay for chewed-up motel furniture."

"Why not give me the leashes?" she said. "I'll feed the dogs and walk them while you set up inside. Division of labor. You know."

"Okay. Listen, Jenny, I'm really sorry. I never thought about—"

"Brad." She put a hand on his arm. "It's all right. It's really all right. Now give me the dogs and get the stuff inside."

"Yes, ma'am," he said, giving her a quick hug. "And thanks."

It was such a quick hug she didn't have time to protest or wiggle out of it before it was already over. And anyway, hadn't she hugged him this morning? Friends could hug each other. That didn't need to mean anything. It didn't need to—but it could. And was she wishing it did? No, no, and no.

"Jenny?" He looked at her oddly. "You okay?"

"Sure. Give me the dogs."

He passed over the leashes. "They said to walk them over there on the left."

"Okay."

What on earth was wrong with her? Just because Brad was a nice guy, just because she could talk to him, that didn't mean anything special could come of their friendship. And anyway, she didn't want it to. She'd sworn off men, and she meant it.

By the time she got the dogs fed and walked and got back to the room, he had Harry's cage set up in a corner and the rugs spread for Fido and Lady. He'd carried in both suitcases and put them side-by-side on the lowboy. And he was putting two chairs together, seat-to-seat.

She put Harry in his cage and took the leash off Lady. "What are you doing?"

He motioned toward the bed—the one king-sized bed. "You take the bed. I'll sleep in these chairs."

"Brad! Be sensible. You can't sleep in that and then drive tomorrow. I'll sleep in the chair."

"No." He stuck his hands on his hips. "I'll sleep on the floor, then. Do you want the bathroom first?"

"Sure. Just let me get my things." She smiled. "I won't take long."

Chapter Thirteen

Fido settled on his blankets with a big sigh. These humans were really beginning to annoy him. They were so slow at picking up on things. He closed his eyes for a moment and tried to concentrate. What they needed was a good pack leader, someone to take charge of things. Well, he was a smart dog, with a lot of experience. He ought to be able to come up with *something* that would bring these two together.

Lady dropped down beside him, a little rift of scent from her fur skittering over his nose. Rain coming in soon. He opened his eyes. Hmmmmmm. Rain. That could work. He nuzzled Lady. Now all he had to do was get that Brad to open the door.

* * *

Standing by his open suitcase, Brad surveyed the motel room. It wasn't the greatest, to say the least. But it was clean. It was done in a sort of a dull monotone—the same earth tones, browns and dirty yellows and rusts that most motel rooms seemed to be decorated in. Maybe those colors didn't show wear-and-tear as much. A nondescript picture hung over the bed. Good thing he wasn't aiming for a romantic evening here. This was definitely not the place for it.

But then, he'd never taken a woman to a motel for romance, and he wasn't about to start now. Actually, he hadn't had much romance in his life. He wasn't one for casual relationships. They reminded him, in some strange way, of his parents. Maybe because such relationships didn't mean anything—and neither did theirs.

What he wanted was a relationship that *did* matter, a woman he could really love. And until Jenny there hadn't been one. No one had ever affected him the way she did.

Crazy, he told himself. He was crazy to even be thinking about romance. But then, she was driving him crazy. So far all he'd had from her were a few kisses, a couple of hugs. No dates as such, just lots of dog walking. And visits to Clara Kelly's. Lots of talk, too. He'd learned a lot about Jenny from their talking. Maybe that was why he loved her.

He did love her—there was no sense denying

it. He shook out his pajamas and robe and hung them over a chair. Good thing he'd brought the robe. He'd figured he might need it at the farm.

But not here! He'd expected them to have adjoining rooms, never dreamt of something like this. Jenny was really being a good sport about it. He'd meant what he said—he'd been prepared to sleep in the station wagon, though he sure hadn't been looking forward to it. It was cold out there! Did her insisting that he come inside mean she had more feelings for him than she let on? Or was it just because of that tender heart of hers, the way she felt about strays?

He wished he knew. He was getting in deeper and deeper with her. Well, he already loved her past the point of pulling away. There was nothing to do now but go forward—see what happened. He sure hoped—

What was that noise? He looked up. Fido was whining, standing by the outside door. Good grief, Jenny had just walked the dogs. Why did Fido need to go out now? The dog scratched at the door and looked reproachful. Well, it was obvious he did need to go out. Being in the car all day could have messed up his schedule. The dog whined again. He wasn't going to be denied.

"Okay! Okay!" Brad said. "I'm coming." He looked around. Lady lay curled up, her eyes closed, her nose tucked into her tail. Already asleep. He'd just open the door and let Fido out for a minute. She'd never know the difference.

He opened the door—and all hell broke loose. Instead of going out, Fido stood there in the doorway while Lady streaked past him like the proverbial bat. Brad made a grab for her, but she slipped through his hands. She was gone, disappearing into the darkness, with Fido right after her.

"Jenny!" Brad yelled, racing to pound on the bathroom door with his fists. "Jenny, Lady got out! I gotta go after her."

The door opened. Jenny stood there in pink silk pajamas that took his breath away. For a minute he couldn't move, couldn't do anything but stare. "Go! Go!" she cried, pushing him toward the door. "I'll be right there."

He grabbed his jacket and lit out, yelling, "Lady! Lady!" What the hell was going on here? If he didn't know better, he'd swear the dogs had planned the whole thing. Man, he was really losing it. These were dogs, not super spies. And Lady had always been keen to slip out. He fastened his jacket and turned up his collar, heading toward the woods.

"Lady! Lady!" He was never going to find her in this darkness. He shivered. A roll of thunder sounded, not too far away. Just what he needed—rain.

He stumbled over a tree root and mumbled a couple of curses. This whole trip was rapidly going from bad to worse. Jenny would think he was a real dork. And maybe he was.

"Brad? Brad? Where are you?"

"Over here."

A thin wobble of light came toward him. Good for Jenny; she had some sense, anyway. She'd thought to bring the flashlight out of the wagon.

"Did you see which way they went?" she asked, handing him the light and pulling up her hood to tie it.

"No."

She took back the light and started off through the darkness, shining it in sweeps across the surrounding brush. "Well, I guess this is as good a way as any. What happened?"

"Fido whined and scratched at the door. I thought he had to go out. I looked at Lady. She was asleep. At least I thought she was. I opened the door. And bam—out she flew."

"Funny Fido having to go out again so soon," Jenny mused.

"Yeah." He didn't say anything about her dog being in the way so that he couldn't slam the door. And he certainly wasn't going to tell her that he thought the dogs had *planned* the whole thing. She'd think he was losing it for certain. Besides, everything had happened so fast that he couldn't be sure of anything. Except that the stupid dog was gone, and he was left feeling like a first-class idiot. "Maybe you ought to go back to the room," he said. "They might come back there."

"No," she said. "I don't think so. Anyway, I'm out here now. I might as well help you look."

He didn't argue with her. Truth was, he wasn't even sure which direction the motel was from here. "Are you any good at directions?" he asked, avoiding a low-hanging branch. "I wouldn't want to get lost out here."

Jenny actually giggled, bless her heart. "I've got a pretty good sense of direction," she said. "Iowa farm country looks a lot alike, you know. I learned early how to find my way home."

"That's good, because being a city boy, I never learned how to get around in the country." He managed a weak chuckle. "We have signs in the city, you know. Out here I haven't the least idea where I am." He was feeling more and more stupid. He was supposed to be the one who knew what he was doing. Wasn't he? "Lady! Fido! Come on, now. Quit messing around."

They worked their way deeper into the woods. The beam of the flashlight played over branches and thickets and grass. A few late bugs flickered in its light, but no dogs. He called, Jenny called, but it was useless. The dogs were long gone.

The thunder sounded again, almost overhead now. "Oh oh," Jenny said. "We'd better—" And the rain came down. Came down hard, in great spattering drops that pelted through the leafless trees.

In less than a minute they were soaking wet, their jackets and jeans stuck to them, mud squelching under their shoes. This was ridiculous. He grabbed Jenny's hand. "Come on! Let's get out of here!"

They slipped and scrambled through the mud and pouring rain, over roots, around fallen logs, through dead leaves. Suddenly he hit a slippery patch and his feet went out from under him. He went down on his behind, smack dab into a puddle. A cold, wet, muddy puddle. Seconds later Jenny came down on top of him with a force that knocked him backward and drove all the air from his lungs. And there he was, on his back in the mud with Jenny's body pressed against his, her mouth only inches away from his.

And then it wasn't the force of the fall that left him breathless. Her whole weight was on him. He could feel her body against his. It was wet and muddy, but it was still her body. So he kissed her. He was a man, after all. He kissed her hard. And she kissed him back, a long, deep kiss so hot it was a wonder the puddle didn't turn to steam.

He was still lying there in a state of shock when she scrambled to her feet. Pulling at him, she yelled, "Come on. We've gotta go."

He was tempted to yank her back down and

lie there in the mud forever, but she kept pulling at him, so he got up.

Slipping and sliding, they hurried back toward the motel room. They reached it finally. Half-drowned and covered in mud, they slid to a stop. He could hardly believe his eyes. To one side of the door, under the little overhang that protected it, Fido and Lady waited, both of them perfectly dry.

Jenny took one look at them and burst into laughter. The next thing he knew, he was laughing, too. Laughing fit to be tied. Dripping like crazy, they unlocked the door and stumbled into the room, the dogs ambling after them.

He shut the door. Jenny was still laughing. She stood in the middle of the floor laughing. Her beautiful hair was plastered to her head and straggled down her soaked jacket to drip onto the floor. A streak of mud crossed from one temple to her chin. She swiped at her face with a mud-covered hand, leaving more mud there. Her jeans were muddy and her sneakers were big blobs of mud. She kicked them into the corner. "W-we've got to get out of these wet clothes." Her hands shook as she tried to undo her jacket. She looked like a drowned rat. And he'd never seen a woman he wanted more.

"Here. Let me help."

His own hands felt like blocks of ice, but his lips still tingled from her kiss. And inside he was on fire, the fire of wanting her.

"Th-thank you," she stammered, looking up at him, her eyes great brown pools of . . . Was that longing he saw there? Desire as heavy as his own?

Whatever it was, it pulled at him, drawing his lips to hers. He gathered her sopping-wet muddy body into his arms and kissed her long and hard. "Oh, Jenny," he breathed finally, his lips near her ear. "I want you. I want you so much."

Her arms were around his neck, her face nestled in the curve of his shoulder. "Me, too," she whispered.

"You mean—"

"Yes." The word was so soft, he could hardly hear it.

"Help me." She giggled. "Help me get out of these things or I'll be frozen solid. You won't want an icicle."

"Yes, yes, I will." Finally he got her jacket unzipped and stripped it off her. Under it the pink silk pajama top was molded to her chest, her nipples standing out against the soft fabric. His heart came up in his throat. He wanted to rip the shirt right off her. He didn't, of course.

"It's so c-c-cold," she said. "Where did I put my robe?"

He kicked off his shoes and dropped his jacket beside them. "You don't need it," he said. "I'll warm you up." He searched her face. "If you really meant it."

Jenny stood there watching him. His shirt was soaked. And under that shirt was his furry chest, those little wisps of golden hair. She felt like a cat yearning to rub against forbidden furniture. Only this furniture could rub back.

Her heart jumped around like a kitten chasing its tail. She'd told him she'd go to bed with him! Just like that! Out there in the stormy darkness, lying in his arms, she hadn't wanted to get up. She'd wanted to do it right there, in the mud and the rain. She wanted to have a man again. She wanted to have this man.

She didn't love him, of course. How could she, when she wasn't going to love anyone again? But she had needs, just as a man might. Couldn't friends help each other that way, too? If she had something else a friend needed, food or clothes or money, she would give it to him. Why couldn't she give him this?

People did go to bed together, people who hardly knew each other at all. Sometimes people did it on their first meeting. Just because they wanted to. She'd never done that, of course. It wasn't the sort of thing she'd ever do. Or Hugh, either. At least he wouldn't have approved of *her* doing it. She wasn't sure anymore what Hugh had approved of, or what he'd done when he was away from her.

But she didn't want to think about Hugh. That was over. This was Brad. Brad wanted her. She wanted him. And he was a kind, gentle man. Out there in the darkness he hadn't snapped at her, hadn't complained about getting soaked, or her falling on him like that. Instead, he'd been concerned about her. She could depend on him to be careful. So what harm could it do?

"You did mean it, didn't you?" he asked when she remained silent for so long, his eyes questioning, his face anxious.

"I—Yes, I meant it." There, she'd said it again. "But I think we'd better have some ground rules. Like, this is a one-time thing. No strings."

He stared at her, his eyes gone dark. "A one-time thing?" he repeated slowly, as if he wasn't sure he understood. "No—strings?"

"Yes." She forced herself to be calm, logical. "I don't date, remember?"

A strange look crossed his face. "I remember."

"But we're friends, and friends can do things for each other. Can't they?"

"Of course." His face lightened. "Like that song, 'Help Me Make It Through the Night'?"

She breathed a sigh of relief. He did understand. "Yes."

He moved closer. "Let's get you out of these wet things then."

His fingers brushed her chest as he unbuttoned the silk pajama tops. A shiver went down her back, but it wasn't from being cold. Not this time. She watched his face while he undid the buttons. His forehead was furrowed in a frown and he drew his bottom lip between his teeth as he concentrated on making his fingers work. A blob of mud had streaked his forehead and darkened one corner of his mustache. She could still feel that mustache against her mouth as he had kissed her. It had felt different wet than it had dry. From what she could see, the back of his head was mostly all mud. They were muddy messes, both of them.

Finally he got the shirt unbuttoned, but he didn't open it. She managed to undo her jeans and let them fall to the floor. "I'm all muddy."

"Me, too." He grinned ruefully and dropped his jeans beside hers. "Not very romantic, is it?"

She didn't look down, kept her gaze on his face.

"No. I'm afraid I need a hot shower."

He shivered. "Me, too. But you go first."

"We could—" What on earth had come over her? She'd never behaved like this before! But she didn't want to be away from him, not for a second, not now. She could feel the blood flooding her face, but she said it anyway. "We could take it together."

His face lit up like a Christmas tree. "Oh, yes!" He pulled her closer, warming her with his body, except that his shirt and her top were both soaked. "A nice hot shower and we'll both be good as new." He chuckled. "Maybe even better."

For some reason her hands were on his chest,

on his wet shirt. His heart was pounding under her fingers, pounding as hard as hers. His arm was still around her, his hand warm at her waist. And his voice had dropped an octave, stirring something deep inside her. "I—" she began.

"I promise you won't regret it." And he kissed her again.

In the bathroom she stood awkwardly by the shower stall while he took off his shirt and dropped it in the sink. What did she do now? "You might as well know," she said. "I don't do this. That is, I've never done this before."

He turned, shock on his face. "You're a virgin?"

She giggled again. "Well, no. Not exactly."

"Me neither," he said, grinning. "Not exactly. But that was a long time ago. Let's see if we can forget then and only think about now."

"Yes, let's." She stepped out of her panties and put her pajama top in the sink with his shirt. When she turned the look on his face made her forget all about being cold. And then she saw that his shorts were gone. He stood there, and his body was everything she'd dreamed it would be. She *had* been dreaming about it, she admitted to herself.

"Last one in has to scrub the other's back," she cried, wondering if she could have been

Chapter Fourteen

The water was good and hot. Jenny let it stream down over her head, rinsing away the mud and the chill. She started to move to one side to make room for Brad, but he hooked an arm around her waist and kept her where she was. "Let's share," he said, that mischievous glint back in his eyes. "They taught me in kindergarten that sharing is good."

"Me, too. Sharing is good." As his hand found the curve of her hip, she caught her breath. "Real good." She looked up at his face. Not that she didn't want to look at his body again. She did. But it seemed sort of childish. After all, she'd seen a man naked before. It was no big deal. She was just trembling like this because she was cold. And because she'd never, ever done anything so outrageous before.

He reached for the soap. But he didn't ask her to turn around so he could wash her back. Instead he came closer and put both arms around her, moving so their heads were out of the stream of water. "Best way to warm up I've ever heard of," he whispered, his lips brushing her ear. "Maybe we ought to patent it."

"Ummmmmmm." How could one body against another feel so good? Each little hair on his chest seemed to give its own caress to her sensitive breasts. They felt as if they'd been waiting forever for his touch.

And the rest of her, the rest of her got warm in a hurry. She stood there, more conscious of her body than she could ever remember being. How could anything feel so good?

"Want me to wash your hair?" he asked, pulling it aside to kiss her shoulder.

She moved back a step so she could see his face. "Y-you? But men don't—"

"This man does," he said, his eyes dark. "If you want me to."

He pulled her back into his arms. The most wonderful sensations went running through her body. "All right. My shampoo—"

"I see it."

She stood there under the water while he soaped her hair. She let him move her here and there, positioning her for the best flow. Finally he stood in front of her. "Tilt your head back. That's it."

She didn't want to tilt her head back. She wanted to tilt it forward, to look down. She wanted to lean against his chest, to feel the rest of him against her again. But she did as he asked.

"All finished," he said finally. "Now for the rest of you."

"The rest?" she squeaked.

"Yeah." He grinned and started soaping a washcloth. "I think I've discovered a new career. I'll hire myself out as a people washer."

A lump of jealousy rose in her throat. Where on earth had that come from? She had no strings on him. He could bathe anyone he wanted to.

"On second thought, though," he murmured, sliding the cloth from her shoulder down across her breast in a movement that left her quivering, "I think I'll stick to just one customer. I believe I could make this my life's work."

Laughter bubbled out of her. "Now you're being silly," she said.

He grinned. "Nothing wrong with that. I guess I'm due some silliness. I spent most of my childhood alone. Ever try to be silly by yourself?"

"No," she breathed, steadying herself with a hand on his shoulder as his cloth moved down across her stomach and lower, lower.

She wasn't sure how much longer she could wait. She wanted him so much, so— "Ummmmmmm."

Finally he straightened. "All finished. Clean as a whistle."

She managed a smile. "It's a good thing. Much more of this and I won't be able to stand up."

His gaze met hers, questioning. "I guess that means you liked it."

She giggled. "I guess it does."

"Good. Give me a minute to do my hair and I'll—"

"Let me."

His mouth actually fell open and he stared at her.

"What's wrong?"

"Wrong? Nothing. I just—"

"You'll have to bend down a little," she said, reaching for the shampoo bottle.

She stood at his side as he bent so she could shampoo his hair. Her breasts brushed his arm, an exquisite sensation. With one of his hands he fondled her leg, tracing delicious little lines on it. She'd never imagined lovemaking could be like this. And they hadn't even done anything yet.

With a deep sigh he straightened and took her in his arms. "This is great, but if I wait much longer, I'm going to explode."

"Me, too," she whispered against his wet neck.

"Then let's get out of here and get this show on the road." His laugh was deep and warm. "I'd like to carry you just like that, all wet and slippery, right to the bed. But it's the only bed we've got, and we'll need to sleep in it afterwards. So I guess we'd better be practical and dry off first."

"I guess so." But how was she going to dry off? All her nerve endings were on fire with longing for him. Touching a towel to her skin seemed like too much.

He turned off the water and stepped out. "I'd like to dry every inch of you," he said. "But—" He looked down at the evidence of his desire.

"Me, too," she said. "Let's hurry."

Brad went into the bedroom ahead of her and got the bed ready. He still wasn't sure how this had happened. But he was glad it had. Glad! What a insufficient word for the joy exploding through him. He'd thought he loved her before—now he knew it. He loved her, loved her madly. And in a minute he was going to show her how much.

She paused in the doorway from the bathroom, toweling her hair, her beautiful body highlighted by the light behind her.

"All ready," he said, swallowing over the desire that clogged his throat. "My lady's bed awaits her."

She threw the towel back in the bathroom and crossed the carpet toward him. She was so beautiful, yet no more beautiful to him now than she'd been a while ago, covered in rain and mud. "Thank you," she whispered.

He couldn't wait any longer. He pulled her to him and kissed her again. "Oh, Jenny, I've been wanting to do this for a long time." Oh, no! Why had he said that? She might think that he'd planned the whole thing. Now he was getting stupid again. How could he plan for the dogs to run away? Well, he might, but he hadn't. "I mean—"

"I know what you mean," she said, kissing the corner of his mustache. A little shiver rippled through her and she pressed closer to him.

"Let's get in the bed," he said. "I don't want you to get cold."

She laughed, the laughter of a young, carefree girl. "Cold?" she said. "We'll be lucky if we don't scorch the sheets!"

He laughed, too. "I can at least pick you up and put you into the bed."

"What's this thing you have about carrying me?" she asked, her head against his shoulder.

He chuckled. "It's a man thing, you know, like in *Gone with the Wind*, when Rhett swept Scarlett into his arms and carried her up that great staircase to the bedroom." He kissed her neck, left a trail of kisses down to her nipple. "Where he had his way with her."

"Oh." Her eyes were dark with desire. She touched his shoulder with her tongue. "Is that what he did?"

Laughing, he lifted her into his arms and turned to the bed. "Yes, that's what he did." He put her down carefully. "And now—"

But her arms were around his neck and she didn't let go. Instead she jerked him down on top of her. "And now that's what *you're* going to do. Have your way with me."

Her body was warm and soft; her breasts crushed against his chest were driving him crazy. He didn't know what to do first. He wanted to kiss her mouth, her eyes, her breasts, her belly. He wanted to kiss every part of her—and all at the same time. But more than anything else he wanted to be inside her, to feel that she was really truly his, even if it was only for that brief moment, even though she'd said "no strings."

He kissed her forehead, her nose, her eyelids.

"Brad," she whispered, her voice gone husky. "Please. I want you. I want you—now."

"Anything to please," he said. "Just give me a second." He reached for the foil packet he'd left on the nightstand and made sure he was protected. Then, tenderly, he turned back to Jenny.

She was ready for him, open and eager, and he slid in as though he'd always belonged there.

"Ummmmm," she murmured, her lips against his shoulder. "Ummmmmn."

He wanted to take it easy, to go slow and make it last. But all that stuff in the shower had him so primed, he was almost afraid to move.

Then she kissed him, kissed him so hard that his body moved on its own. And they were going at it, her body arching up against his, moving in rhythm with his. "Yes," she whispered. "Oh, yes."

Then there was no sound but their labored breathing, the wonderful, urgent breathing of their passion. He was afraid he wasn't going to hold out. He didn't want to leave her unsatisfied. But while he was trying to think of some way to tell her she convulsed under him and gave a muffled scream against his throat. He felt the quivers of delight that went through her, felt them on his skin, and felt them deep inside her, where they triggered his response. Then he went over the top, heart and soul off on some wild flight into eternity, and he collapsed on her with a groan of exultation.

Across the room Fido drew closer to the sleeping Lady. Strange creatures, humans. They did the thing in such a peculiar way, face-to-face. But they'd obviously enjoyed it. And that was what counted. Now maybe they'd see what had been right under their noses. These two were meant to love each other. Any fool could see it.

Chapter Fifteen

Jenny came to awareness with a smile. What a nice, nice dream. She'd been snuggled in Brad's arms, all safe and cozy, the warmth of his chest under her fingers and . . .

There *was* something warm under her fingers, something that rose and fell, rose and fell. Cautiously she opened her eyes. Daylight was peeking through the drapes and she could see Brad's chest. Her hand was lying on top of it and her head was nestled in the hollow between his neck and his shoulder.

And then she remembered—and her body went hot. Last night! Last night they had made love. They'd showered together, washed each other. Made wonderful, glorious love together. They must have fallen asleep like this, their arms still around each other.

Now what did she do? From the looks of the daylight it was only just dawn. Did she try to draw away and wake him? Or stay here till he woke? She swallowed a giggle. Why did she feel so young and silly?

"Good morning," Brad said.

She twisted till she could look up into his face. Not a good idea, because it brought her mouth perilously close to his and made her even more conscious of the warm flesh beneath her fingers—and the rest of his body, pressing against hers. "Good morning," she said, trying to ignore the feelings going through her. "Thank you for your help last night."

Brad grinned. "Nothing to it. I specialize in helping maidens in distress."

She didn't know how to answer that. She hardly knew how to say anything with him so close to her and nothing, nothing at all, between them. "I—Do you think we ought to get up? Get an early start? Maybe?"

"I suppose so," he said. "But it's awfully comfortable here." And his fingers curled around her breast.

She tried to ignore it. It wasn't easy. "They'll have a comfortable bed for you at the farm," she stammered, trying to think of something to say that didn't sound stupid.

"But I'll have to sleep in it alone." He grinned. "Won't I?"

"Of course."

If only he'd kiss her the way he had last night. If she looked at him much longer, she'd be the one doing the kissing. "I do think we'd better get up." She didn't really, but she couldn't believe her behavior last night. It wasn't like her at all.

He heaved a sigh that she felt through her whole body. "All right, slave driver. But could you, maybe, give me a little jump start?" His eyes twinkled at her, the warmest gray-green eyes. "Help me get going again?"

"And how can I do that?" she asked. Why did his chest have to feel so warm under her fingers? Why couldn't she just stay there in his arms forever?

"Just a little kiss," he said. "A quickie. Just to give me an incentive for getting out of here."

She couldn't help it—she laughed. "You're impossible, Brad Ferris. Absolutely impossible."

"I know. But will you give me a kiss?" he wheedled. "Just a little one?" His fingers were moving on her breast, making her want—

"Oh, I suppose I could spare one. Just one, though."

"I'll take what I can get," he said. "And be grateful for it." And for some reason she didn't think he was teasing anymore.

She wiggled a little to get closer to his mouth. Another mistake, raising feelings so fast that they swamped her. She'd never felt like this before. Then he was kissing her, or she was kissing him, she couldn't be sure which. And all the things they said in books really happened—time stood still. She forgot to breathe. She forgot to think. She forgot everything but the touch of his mouth on hers. They were going to do it again, and she was glad, glad that—

And then the mattress sagged and two wet noses sniffed their cheeks and two warm dog bodies wriggled over and around them. Brad released her mouth and sucked in a deep breath. "Well, I guess the decision's out of our hands. The dogs say it's time to get up. You want the bathroom first?"

"Okay." She pulled in a breath, too, trying to get back to reality. "Fido, get down. I don't know what's wrong with him. He's never gotten up on the bed before."

Brad chuckled. "It's all right. At least this time he didn't get between us till *after* I got my kiss. And last night he was a real doll."

He took his arm from around her shoulders. "Same detail as last night? You do the feeding and walking, and I do the loading and clean up in here?"

"Okay." She pushed herself off his chest, though if the dogs weren't there she'd probably have burrowed back against him and—Well, maybe not. But it sure was tempting. She rolled out of bed.

She shrugged into her robe, laughing as she collected her clothes.

He sat up, and her breath caught in her throat. The sheet fell away, revealing the chest that her fingers longed to touch. She gripped her clothes as though they might run away, just like her feelings. She wasn't going to touch him again. She wasn't.

She hurried into the bathroom.

When she came out Brad had the blankets put away and Harry out of the cage on a leash. "See you in a bit," he said, giving her a little kiss, handing her the leashes and opening the door.

Fido and Harry ate heartily, but Lady kept pulling on her leash, refusing the food. Finally the others were done. "Come on," she said, pulling Lady after her. "You'll have to eat later. I don't know why you don't have better manners." She glanced down at the puppy. "Harry I can understand, he's only a baby. But you're a full-grown dog. You should have more sense than to run off from your master, especially from one as nice as Brad."

But Lady didn't seem to care. She just kept pulling on the leash, trying to drag Jenny away from the motel. Finally Jenny turned back. "Don't you dare go to the bathroom in the station wagon," she warned. "You've had plenty of time now."

When she got back to the wagon Brad had Harry's cage and the suitcases loaded. "All set," he said.

She glanced toward the door of the room. She wanted another look at it. Well, she'd really like to go back inside and—If only they hadn't promised to be at the farm in time for dinner. But they had.

He grinned. "Go check," he said. "Make sure we didn't leave anything behind."

"I—"

"Go on," he said, almost as if he knew she wanted one last look at the place.

Was the man psychic? How did he know what she wanted to do? And almost before she knew it herself.

"Okay. I will."

She stepped in, looked around, and smiled. She'd never forget this place. Maybe someday she and Brad would—

"Confound it, Lady! Get back here!" Brad's yell made her jump. Then Harry started yapping.

Jenny hurried out. "What happened?"

Brad's face was turning red. "The stupid dog jerked the leash out of my hand and lit out," he explained over Harry's yapping. "I've had enough! I swear, I'll leave her here."

"Now, now, take it easy." Jenny stared at the puppy and growled deep in her throat. "Harry! Hush!" Harry shut up. She looked around. "Where's Fido?"

Brad looked sheepish. "He lit out, too. Guess he's not the prince you thought he was."

"I can't believe—" And then she looked over his shoulder and burst into laughter.

He scowled at her. "What the hell are you—"

"Look."

He swung around to where she pointed. There was a moment of stunned silence, and then he started to laugh, too. Here came Fido and behind him, not too willingly it seemed since the leash in his mouth was taut, trotted Lady.

"Good job, boy!" Jenny bent to take the leash from Fido's mouth. "Good job!"

And Brad echoed her. "You're a dog hero, Fido. That's what you are."

She passed the leash to Brad. "Now, can we get this show on the road?"

He saluted with his free hand. "Yes, ma'am. Right away, ma'am."

They reached the farm a little after eleven, after another drive-through breakfast and several stops for dog walking. Jenny'd been smiling for the last half hour, soaking in the familiar sights and sounds, breathing in the clean air. Oh, it was good to be home again. So good.

"Does it always look like this?" Brad asked.

She turned to him. "Like what?"

"Like some kind of painting or picture postcard."

"Yes," she said. "It does. Except in the spring, when it's a lot greener. And it always smells this way, too." She laughed. "Well, except when the farmers spread fertilizer. Then it's not so nice."

Brad laughed with her. "I can believe that."

"Look! There it is. The old house."

She turned to Brad. He was smiling. "I like it," he said. "It's almost the way I pictured it."

"Almost?"

He chuckled. "Remember, I'm a city boy. Lady's the only animal I've ever had close contact with. Except for Mrs. Vincent's dog Tuffy, when I was a little kid. And in case you haven't noticed, I haven't done so well with Lady."

"So, what did you imagine the farm would look like?" she asked, curiosity getting the better of her.

"Oh, fields of cows and horses. Goats, maybe. And some pigs. A big old white house with a veranda around it. A big red barn bursting with hay. Chickens and a henhouse. Maybe a pond with a few ducks swimming on it."

She stared at him for a minute. "Well, that's a real, complete farm, all right. We've got the house. Just a front porch, though; no veranda. Got the barn. Cows, yes. But they're probably sticking close to the barn in this kind of weather. A couple of horses. No goats. No pigs. But we do have chickens, and ducks on the farm pond. And a big old willow tree beside it."

"Great. Sounds perfect." He looked to where the farmhouse sat nestled in some trees. "Were you born in that house?"

"In the hospital in town," she said. "But I came home here, lived here all my life, till a year ago, when I moved to Cleveland."

"Why'd you go so far?" he asked. "Can't they use architects in Des Moines?"

She hesitated. "Yes. But I wanted to get farther away." That didn't sound right. "I wanted to see the world."

After last night it didn't seem right not to tell him the truth. "Actually," she said, staring hard out the window, "I wanted to get away from my fiancé, my ex-fiancé, who by then was someone else's husband."

"Hugh," Brad muttered.

She turned in surprise. "How did you know that?"

He looked straight ahead. "You were dreaming about him in the night. You called his name."

"Yes, Hugh. He broke our engagement and married Melodie Marin. Her father owns half of Des Moines."

"I see."

"Not quite," she said, wondering why she felt that she *had* to tell him all this. "Melodie's not satisfied to have a wealthy father. She's also a gorgeous blonde."

"I like brunettes," Brad said, giving her a warm smile. "With hints of red in their hair. Always have."

Now why should that make her feel like laughing?

"Look," she said as they drew nearer to the house. "They must have heard the car. Here come the girls. And Sue."

Chapter Sixteen

Brad pulled the station wagon to a halt by the porch and climbed out. He grinned. A real front porch with wooden rockers on it. They were upside down and leaning against the wall, but he could see them in the summer with . . .

Two little girls with hair as dark as Jenny's threw themselves at his legs, threatening to pull him down onto the porch floor. "Where is he?" one demanded.

"Where's our puppy?" the other asked.

"Girls! Where are your manners? And your coats?"

The woman in the doorway was older than Jenny, but she had the same dark hair and eyes.

He bent down to the girls. "Go inside. Aunt Jenny and I will bring the puppy. I promise."

They sent one longing look at the wagon and obeyed. The woman clutched her sweater tighter around her and shook her head. "You must have kids. You know how to handle them. Is there anything I can help carry?"

"No, no," Jenny said, giving her sister a quick hug. "It's cold out here. Go on in. We'll bring the stuff."

"Okay."

Jenny joined him at the tailgate. "I forgot to warn you about the girls. They tend to get excited."

He grinned. "So do I. What say we take the puppy in first? That'll keep them busy while we unload the rest."

Jenny laughed. "Good idea!"

He let down the tailgate and unlatched Harry's cage. Pulling out the wriggling pup, he passed him to Jenny. "You take him. And I'll bring the cage. I figure they'll need it."

Jenny laughed again. Lord, how he loved that laugh. If only he could keep her laughing like that. Well, at least she had the weekend. The long weekend.

He pulled the cage over the cage and lifted it. "Lead on."

Inside the front door the little girls were waiting. They grabbed Harry from Jenny with giggled thank-yous and ran off squealing. A motherly woman stepped toward him. Her dark hair had a few streaks of gray and her figure had spread a little, but she looked the way a mother should. She wiped her hands on her apron and held them out to him. "Hello, Brad. It's good to meet you."

He set the cage to one side and let her take his hands. For a minute he thought she was going to hug him, wished she would, but then she released his hands and stepped back. "Dinner'll be ready in about an hour. I'll leave Jenny and Sue to help you settle in. Afraid I've got things to attend to in the kitchen." She started off, calling back over her shoulder, "Hope you brought a big appetite."

"Come on," Jenny said. "Let's get the dogs and the suitcases. Mom said the dogs can stay in the house. I don't know about Lady being loose, though. I mean, it's hard to make the girls remember about not leaving doors open."

"Maybe I can tie her somewhere." He wasn't too happy with that idea, though. Tied at home, Lady made a mess of anything within reach.

"Maybe we ought to keep her in the barn or something," he said as they went back outside. "I don't want her to wreck anything in the house."

"I don't know," Jenny said. "Let's walk them down that way and see what Pop says."

"Okay." He untied Lady's leash from the door handle and stood aside so she could jump down. Fido followed her. "Why can't Lady be like Fido?" he asked.

Jenny shrugged. "I don't know. But then, Fido's a dog in a million."

Brad grinned. "You can say that again."

But she didn't. Instead she took a look toward the barn and lit off at a run, calling back over her shoulder, "There's Pop. Pop! Pop! We're here."

Brad followed more slowly. Give her time to say hello to her dad. He tried to understand what it was like for her, coming home to a family that loved her. Wanting to see them, to hug them the way she'd hugged her sister and her mother, the way she was hugging her father. But that was hard to imagine. His own homecomings were always painful, times of cold hellos and wishing that he was somewhere else, anywhere else. And never any physical contact. If he got within a couple of feet of Mother, she pulled back as if he was contagious. And Father was even worse.

Brad shook his head. There was so much love around here he could almost feel it spilling over on him. He came up to the barn, where a man not much taller than Jenny was bent over, ruffling Fido's ears. "Looks like you got a keeper here," he said. "A real good dog."

"Yeah, Pop." Jenny turned. "And this is Brad. And his dog Lady. I met him when he lost her. I found Fido and thought he was Brad's dog, so I took him to his house and—That's how we met."

The man turned. His face was weathered and wrinkled from years in the outdoors, and the hand he extended to Brad was hard with calluses. But his eyes were bright and warm—dark eyes like Jenny's. "Good to meet you, Brad," he said. And somehow Brad felt he meant it.

"Good to meet you, sir. Jenny's lucky to have such a great family."

Jenny smiled. "I was telling Pop about your problem with Lady. And he has a suggestion."

"Anything," Brad said. "I'm really tired of her running off."

"Dad thinks if we leave them both loose, her and Fido, that Fido will go with her if she runs off. And bring her back. Sort of the way he did at the motel, only without the leash." She looked at him with concerned eyes. "But it's up to you. If you don't want to do that, we can keep them in the tack room."

He looked down at Lady, straining at the leash. She was raring to go, all right. And over beside Jenny and her father, Fido sat, as though he'd spent his whole life here and was determined not to leave Jenny's side.

Brad heaved a sigh. He didn't want to lose Lady, but if the idea worked . . . It'd be great. And such a relief. "Let's try it," he said. "Maybe he *can* teach her." He bent toward Lady.

"Wait." A little flush stained Jenny's cheeks. "I've got to talk to Fido first. Explain it to him."

He saw in her eyes that she was waiting, waiting for him to say something smart. Or maybe laugh. He looked at her father. He was waiting, too. Brad nodded, as if the people he knew always explained things to their dogs. "Of course. I'll walk her down that way and back."

Jenny's father gave a nod of approval and her eyes brightened. Well, if that had been some kind of test, he'd obviously passed it. He clucked to Lady. "Come on, girl. Let's stretch our legs."

Jenny watched Brad walk off. He hadn't laughed. He hadn't stared at her as if she'd lost her mind. He'd really understood. Pop cleared his throat. "Well, I got work to do afore we eat."

"Sure, Pop. See you later."

"Yeah." He looked after Brad, his forehead wrinkled in a little frown. "Think maybe you've got *two* keepers." Then he gave her a grin and hurried off.

Jenny swallowed over the lump in her throat. Trust Pop to have his say. Take one look at a man and decide on his character. But she'd never known Pop to be wrong about a man. Never. He'd tried to warn her about Hugh more than once, but she'd been too stubborn to listen.

Fido pushed his cold nose into her hand. "Okay, okay. I get the message. Come on over here where we can talk." She settled down on a bale of straw. "Listen, Fido, you know what a pain Lady's running away is. And you brought her back this morning. So we're going to leave it up to you. You keep track of her, okay?" She stared into his soulful eyes. "Can you do that?"

Fido barked once. Of course he could. What? Did she think he was stupid or something? Besides, Lady wasn't going to leave *him*. Not now that they had an understanding.

He shoved his nose into her hand again. It looked as if she needed reassurance. Well, he was the dog for the job.

Jenny smiled at Fido. He looked so eager, sitting there. Almost as if he wanted to say something back to her. What was he thinking? Did he really understand her? She believed he did. Pop believed it, too. And Brad.

She'd never known a man like Brad. Well, she hadn't really known any men but Hugh. Hugh had never been much for animals, but she'd accepted that about him. Just as she'd accepted his need to be noticed, his wanting to always have the spotlight. She'd accepted him the way he was, though there were some things about him she hadn't cared for that much.

But it turned out he hadn't accepted her. She hadn't realized it then, that he was waiting to see if someone better came along. She could see it now, though, with hindsight. Why else had he been so insistent that they should wait till she finished college before they married? Because *he* wasn't sure, that's why—because he was looking for something better.

She saw that, finally, when he told her about Melodie and the wonderful life he was going to have with her. Jenny sighed. Hugh had never accepted her as she was. He'd always wanted her to be something more: smarter, prettier, richer.

Fido licked her hand, barked again, then got up and trotted after Brad and Lady. Jenny stood, too, tears in her eyes. Fido understood her, all right. Now would Lady understand him?

Brad grinned as Fido came trotting up. "Guess you gave Jenny the go-ahead," he said. "I sure hope this works."

He squatted down on his haunches and looked into Lady's eyes. Talking to a dog wasn't so weird, but expecting her to understand this kind of thing was. To him at least. Still, he was going to do his part. "Now, listen, Lady," he said. "We've only got a few days here. I don't want to keep you chained up, so I'm going to let you loose. I'm counting on our pal Fido here to keep you in line. Okay?"

Damn, he'd swear the dog nodded her head! He unhooked the leash. "Go on now; run!"

The two of them took off into the adjoining woods. He swallowed a sigh. Give it a chance.

Heck, even if she ran away, she had a few days to find her way back.

"Don't worry," Jenny said, coming up behind him. "Have faith in Fido."

He turned to face her. She looked so beautiful, her face all glowing that way. "I do," he said. "But most of all I have faith in you. In your judgment."

She giggled. "Don't say that! Now if she doesn't come back, it'll be my fault."

"No," he said. "It won't. And anyway, she'll be back. No one in their right mind would run away from you."

Chapter Seventeen

"This is where you'll sleep," Jenny said, standing aside so Brad could carry his suitcase into the room. "I'll be bunking in with Sue. They brought up the rollaway. That's her room. Across the hall, catty-cornered." She pointed. "The bathroom's down that way."

Brad put his suitcase on the chair and looked around, taking in the pale lavender curtains and bedspread, the furniture painted white. "This was your room."

She nodded. "Yes. When Sue came home again she went back to her old room and fixed a place in the attic for the girls. They think it's just great to be off by themselves."

"I bet. But you don't have to give me your room. I can sleep on the couch or—"

"Oh, no," she said, shaking her head. "Mom would never hear of such a thing. She'd be insulted."

He looked at the narrow white bed and grinned. "Not very big, is it?"

"No," she said. "I'm afraid not."

He heaved a great sigh. "I knew I should have stayed in bed this morning."

The thought of being there, in the bed with his arms around her, made her catch her breath. "Behave yourself," she said, glancing at the door, but she couldn't help smiling.

"Yes, ma'am."

She looked at her watch. "Mom said dinner'll be ready in fifteen minutes. I'm going down to see if I can help. Come down when you're ready."

He took a step toward her, and her heart came up in her throat. But he didn't kiss her. Instead he took her in his arms and hugged her, really hugged her. Then he stepped back, his face serious. "Jenny, I can't tell you what it means to me, being here, with a real family. It's—it's—" He swallowed.

"It's all right," she said, taking pity on him. "I'm glad to share them. See you in a little bit."

Brad looked around the room—her room. He left the suitcase where it sat and went to the bay window, to the window seat upholstered in deep forest green. He kicked off his sneakers and sat down on it, pulling up his knees and wrapping his arms around them. Off in the distance, beyond the barn, he could see the pond, the big willow bending low over it. And to the right, on the other side of the barn, he could see the pine tree that she'd told him marked her pony's grave and, closer to the house, a smaller tree, the dog's grave. Her father had put them where she could see them from her room. What a man her father was. A real man. A man with a heart.

And her mother and sister, real women, women with feelings. She was so lucky to have them. She knew she was lucky, of course, but she couldn't know *how* lucky. No one could know that unless they'd grown up without love, without a family that cared.

When he thought how his family had treated him, drawing back whenever he came near them, as if he was carrying some kind of terrible disease . . . When he remembered the hurt of that little boy who hadn't been able to understand why his mother didn't kiss him, didn't hug him, didn't love him . . .

Well, his parents were what they were; that wasn't his fault. Finally he'd come to see that, though it had taken some years of therapy. Finally he'd come to know that there was no use feeling sorry for himself, that his life would be what *he* made of it.

Those days were over, anyhow. He was going

to spend Thanksgiving in this house, with people who cared about each other. And with Jenny, the woman he loved. Now *there* was something to be grateful for!

He smiled and leaned closer to the window as two streaks of fur raced from the barn and out toward the pond. So, Lady hadn't run away yet. Maybe this place was big enough that she wouldn't.

He glanced at his watch. Better freshen up and get down to dinner. Jenny'd be happy to get some decent food for a change, instead of drive-through stuff.

Brad paused in the dining room doorway. The table looked gorgeous. The whole nine yards—white linen tablecloth, fancy china, shining silverware, and, in the middle, flanked by tall candles, a big ceramic cornucopia spilling out gourds and Indian corn. A Thanksgiving table to be remembered. He knew he'd never forget it.

Mrs. Carruthers bustled in, carrying a covered dish of something. She put it on the table and smiled at him. "There you are. George'll be along in a minute. Had something to do in the barn." She frowned toward the living room. "Maybe *you* can get the girls to put that puppy away long enough to eat. I'm not getting anywhere with them."

"Of course," he said, wanting to be polite.

How had he gotten to be the child expert? Oh, well. He followed the sound of squeals and found the girls tickling the pup. From the looks of him, Harry was eating up all the attention.

"Hi, there," he said.

Two pairs of bright eyes peered up at him. "Hi," the older girl said.

He bent closer. "Listen, Fanny, will you girls do me a favor?"

Fanny looked at Ellen. Ellen looked back at her, but neither one said a word.

"I did bring you that puppy," he went on.

They exchanged another glance and nodded solemnly.

"Well," he said, hunkering down to eye level with them, "if you don't put him back in the cage and come to dinner, I'm going to get in trouble with your grandma. Your momma, too." He tried a grin. "You wouldn't want that to happen, would you?"

They looked at each other and burst into girlish giggles.

Well, he was making some progress at least. "Your grandma made a scrumptious dinner. Turkey and—"

"And dressing."

"And mashed 'tatoes," the littler one added, licking her lips. "Grandma makes great mashed 'tatoes."

"Let's go," they said together. Ellen picked up Harry, gave him a noisy, sloppy kiss, and passed him to Fanny. Fanny gave him a matching kiss and put him in the cage. Ellen shut the door.

Brad checked the latch as they ran off, but Harry didn't look as if he was planning on doing anything but sleeping. He'd already curled up in a ball and closed his eyes. One tired pup. Brad grinned. Looked like Harry had met his match in those two.

By the time Brad reached the dining room again the girls were coming from the kitchen, passing a towel back and forth between them as they dried their hands. "You sit here," Jenny told him. "Beside me."

He looked at the table, at the dishes covering it, and for the first time he understood what was meant by a table groaning under the weight of food. He'd never seen so much food in one place before, at least not in a private home.

The others took their seats. "Girls," Sue said. "Quiet now while Grandpa says grace."

Brad bowed his head, too. His thanks were silent, but he was convinced they were every bit as genuine as those of Jenny's father.

"We give you thanks, Father," Mr. Carruthers said, "for this good food. And for our family being here together. Especially for Jenny and her friend getting back to be with us. Please bless us all. And help those who aren't as fortunate as we are. Amen."

"Eat hearty now," Mrs. Carruthers said, passing Brad the heaping platter of turkey. "There's plenty more in the kitchen."

"More?" he said in surprise. "More than this?"

Jenny laughed, and her father said, "Sarah's always afraid there won't be enough. Cooks enough for an army, that woman does."

Mrs. Carruthers took the teasing with a smile. "Tomorrow you'll be wishing we still had all this food. You wait and see." And she passed him a huge bowl of mashed potatoes.

Brad sampled everything: turkey, stuffing, mashed potatoes—real ones, not out of a box—gravy, cranberry sauce, creamed corn, green Jell-O salad, homemade rolls, real butter. He had seconds of everything and then thirds, and finally he had to stop eating. He was so full, he was almost afraid to lean back in his chair. He heaved a great sigh of contentment.

"Some more turkey?" Mrs. Carruthers asked, reaching for the platter.

"Oh, no, not me," he said. "It was the most delicious meal I've ever eaten. But I'm so full I couldn't eat another bite. Honest."

Jenny chuckled. "You mean you don't want any of Mom's homemade pumpkin pie?"

He looked at Mrs. Carruthers and smiled. "Pumpkin pie? Hmmmm. Well, maybe I could squeeze in a small piece."

"Better," Jenny's father said, a grin wreathing his face. "Best pie in the county, Sarah's is. She wins all the prizes at the fair."

Mrs. Carruthers beamed. "Oh, it's nothing. I just love to cook. That's all."

"What're your plans for the weekend?" Sue asked, looking to Jenny.

"Nothing special," Jenny said. "I thought I'd show Brad around the farm." She gave a big sigh. "I'll need to walk off this meal!"

"You needed a good meal," her mother said with a frown. "You're looking kind of peaked. Have you been eating right?"

Jenny grinned. "Yes, Mom. Real healthy."

"I can vouch for that," Brad said with a smile. "She eats plenty of fresh fruit and vegetables."

"How's the job?" her father asked.

Jenny's smile faded. "Not so good, Pop. Mr. Morris is a real stinker."

Mr. Carruthers raised an eyebrow. "What's the matter with the man?"

Jenny flushed. It looked as if she hadn't meant to say so much. But with her father looking at her like that, he knew she'd have to go on.

"Well, he's mean, Pop. To everyone. I just finished a real hard job, one he didn't really give me enough time to do. He didn't even say thank you." She shook her head. "And when I turned it in, he gave me another one right off. Wanted me to bring it along with me!"

"That's terrible. I hope you told him what's what!" Mrs. Carruthers said, her eyes flashing.

Jenny looked a little embarrassed. "Not yet,

Mom. But I'm going to. I'm saving my money. Come May I'm fixing to quit."

Mr. Carruthers cleared his throat. "You've got no call to work for a man like that, girl. You know you can come on home any time you want. There's always a place for you here."

Jenny's gaze met Brad's, and he knew she didn't mean to tell her father about Morris's dishonesty. "I know, Pop. I know. And thank you."

Across the table Sue coughed. "Pop, Jenny doesn't want to live back here. You know that. And you know why."

Brad straightened up and tried not to look interested, but he was all ears. They must be talking about Hugh.

"Is he in town?" Jenny asked, a stricken look crossing her face before she could hide it.

Yeah, Brad thought, feeling his stomach sinking, this *he* was definitely Hugh. So it looked like Jenny wasn't over him.

"I heard they were coming home for the holiday," Sue said, eyeing Jenny with concern. "I thought you ought to know."

Jenny shrugged. "It doesn't matter to me."

That wasn't true, Brad knew. He could see the pain in her eyes. He could hear it in her voice.

"We won't be going into town anyway," she said.

"We'll be going to church Sunday morning," Mr. Carruthers said quietly. "This family always goes to church."

Jenny nodded, her face serene now. "I know, Pop. I told Brad."

Her father gave her a funny look. "I guess you told him about Hugh, too."

She looked away. "Yes, Pop. I did."

Her father nodded, his face solemn. "Good. You made a mistake loving that one, but you found out in time. No need to be ashamed of that."

So, Brad thought, Mr. Carruthers hadn't liked Hugh. Well, that made two of them. Though he'd never laid eyes on this Hugh, he could truthfully say he despised the man. Anyone who would hurt Jenny like that . . . Would Hugh be in church on Sunday? Probably not. He didn't sound like the church-going type.

"Enough about that," Jenny said, her voice firm. "I'll go get the pumpkin pie."

Since his offer to help with the dishes was refused, the women saying no men were allowed in the kitchen, Brad went into the living room to watch the football game with Mr. Carruthers. His mind wasn't on the game, though. And neither was Mr. Carruthers's. Their conversation started out small talk, but it wasn't long before Brad found himself talking about the studio, and even telling the older man why he'd decided to photograph babies, and a little about his childhood and his parents lack of love. He wondered about that—he didn't make it a habit to talk about his parents. Now he'd told Jenny *and* her father.

"Life's hard on a man sometimes," Mr. Carruthers observed, sympathy on his weathered face.

"Yes, sir, it is. But I mean to find a good woman." Brad managed a grin, though he'd swear his knees were knocking. "Actually, I think I've found her. I want to settle down and raise a family. A family like yours, sir."

"That's good to hear, young man. Real good." Mr. Carruthers gave him a hard look. "Jenny's been hurt bad. Don't want to see her hurt anymore."

"I don't want to hurt her, sir. Not ever."

Mr. Carruthers grinned. "I believe you, boy. Listen, I'd rather you didn't call me 'sir.' Makes me feel like some kind of stuffed-shirt banker or something. Just call me Pop. And call the missus Mom. Everyone does."

Heat raced to Brad's cheeks and a lump formed in his throat. "You're sure, sir? I mean, Pop?"

"Course I'm sure. Knew the minute I saw you you were gonna fit in with this family."

Brad had to swallow twice before he could say, "Thanks." And still his voice broke in the middle of the word.

Mr. Carruthers—Pop—blinked and turned back to the football game. Brad barely had time to clear his own eyes before the women came in.

"All done," Jenny said. "Ready for a walk?"

He looked down at his bulging belly. "Looks like I need it!"

She patted hers. "Me, too. Let's get our coats. I'll give you a tour of the farm. We'll walk off some of that food."

"It was delicious," Brad said, with a glance to Mom. "The absolutely best meal I've ever eaten."

"Go along now," she said, beaming at him. "You'll be giving me a swelled head. Just go get your tour."

Chapter Eighteen

"So," Jenny said, shutting the door behind them and knotting her scarf under her chin. "How do you like farm cooking?"

"I love it." Brad grinned, turning up his coat collar. He looked at her in wonderment. "I don't understand how anyone can make such good-tasting food. I could eat it every day of the year."

She chuckled. "And you'd get fat."

He shook his head. "Pop's not fat."

"Of course not. He works—" She stopped halfway down the front steps to stare up at him. "Pop?"

Brad flushed a little, as if he was embarrassed, maybe. "Well, he told me to call him Pop. And your mother Mom. Told me while we were watching the game. I hope you don't mind."

"Of course not," she said. "I'm just surprised, that's all."

He grinned sheepishly. "You think *you* were surprised. You should have seen *me*. I couldn't believe your father liked me that much." He raised an eyebrow. "Or does he invite everyone to call him Pop?"

"No way," she said. "In fact, I've never known him to do it before."

"Well . . ." Brad was really grinning now. "That makes me feel real good."

"It should." It was good to see him happy. It made her feel happy, too. She tucked an arm through his. "Now, let's see. Where'll we go first?"

"Doesn't matter," he said, his eyes warm. Her heart started pounding, her body remembering last night, being in his arms, feeling his body against hers. "I'd go anywhere with you," he said, his voice gone husky. And she almost believed he meant it. But he was probably thinking about last night, too. And she had to stop doing that.

It had been a one-time thing—they'd both agreed on that. One time, no strings.

"We'll start with the barn. But first . . ." She whistled for Fido. "We might as well take the dogs along."

Brad looked around. His mouth was set in a smile, but his eyes were anxious. He was worried, and she knew it. She whistled again. *Come on, Fido. I'm counting on you.* But the dogs didn't come. Maybe Fido hadn't understood. Maybe he'd run off, too. Now she was getting stupid, imagining the worst thing that could happen. And when there was no need.

"It's all right," Brad said, trying to maintain his smile. "They're probably taking a walk, too."

He was trying so hard to look nonchalant, but she could tell he was really worried. Where was Fido? She steered Brad out toward the barn. "Come on, let's go. They'll be back later."

They walked for a long time, through the farmyard, through the barn, past the henhouse, through the woods, out to the willow tree by the pond. "It's a beautiful place," Brad said. "I'm surprised you could bring yourself to leave it."

She sighed and leaned against his shoulder. "So am I. I miss it a lot. But . . ."

She let that trail off, and Brad said, "But Hugh was here."

"Yes." Why was Brad so easy to talk to? She'd never talked to anyone about Hugh, not even Sue or Mom.

"Do you think you'll ever get over him?" he asked, worry in his voice.

She turned to look at him, grasping his arm tighter. Was that what he thought, that she was still hung up on Hugh? But that wasn't true. She didn't want Brad to think it was. "Oh, I'm over him already. It didn't take long, once I discovered he wasn't the man I thought he was."

He put an arm around her. "Would you—would you tell me about him?" he asked, his eyes going dark.

"There's not much to tell," she said, and realized how true it was. Not much at all, considering that she and Hugh had gone together for years. "I thought he was one kind of a person and it turned out he was a another. I thought he was a good person, like Dad. But it turned out he was a—snob, I guess you'd call it. He always liked the idea of my becoming an architect. But I didn't realize that that was because then he could forget I was a farmer's daughter." She sighed. "Hugh likes the fast track, you see: big money, big names, lots of power. He was always like that. I just didn't see it."

"You were young," Brad said, tightening his arm around her. "And growing up here, with such a great family, how could you know about people like that?"

She leaned against him. "It's nice of you to say that. The truth is, I was carried away by his good looks. And his popularity. He was class president three years in a row. Star of the basketball team. You know, the whole thing."

Brad nodded. "What's he look like? I mean, you said he was good-looking, and he was popular."

Was that anxiety in his voice? She didn't look to see, instead staring out at the calm water of the pond. "The usual—tall, dark, and handsome. As I said, he was a basketball star, class president, and his folks were rich and important in town. But it wasn't enough for him. It just wasn't a big enough town to satisfy him. He wasn't content to be a big frog in a small pond. He wanted to rule the big pond."

"He hurt you really bad," Brad said, genuine sympathy in his voice. "I'm so sorry."

She looked up at him in surprise. "Oh, I'm not. I mean, I was upset at the time, but I was lucky that he dumped me. Real lucky. We'd never have made it together. I know that now."

Brad's face changed as she watched it, went from sadness for her to joy for himself. "Not as lucky as me," he said. And then he swung her into his arms and kissed her. Kissed her as she'd been longing all day for him to do. Kissed her till she had to hang on to him to stay standing up, until she wished they were back in the motel in Joliet, back in the king-sized bed together.

"Sorry about that." He finally released her mouth, but he kept his arms around her, and he didn't look the least bit sorry. In fact, he was grinning. "You see, I've got this addiction."

She leaned back to look up into his face. "Addiction?"

"Yeah." He kissed her again. "See?"

"Addiction to kisses?" she asked, sudden giggles bubbling out of her.

He shook his head. "Not exactly. I mean, not just kisses. *Your* kisses."

Waves of heat swept over her, but she managed a laugh. "Flatterer!"

"No." His face turned sober and he hugged her to him again. "It's the truth," he said into her hair. "Jenny, you've got to know how I feel about you. Can't you at least give me some hope?"

Her heart rose up in her throat. "I—" She wanted to tell him how she felt about him, but the words wouldn't come. "It's too soon," she managed finally, the words muffled against his coat. "Give me some time." She raised her head to look up into his eyes. "Please. Give me some time."

"All the time in the world," he said. And kissed her again. Thoroughly.

She didn't want to leave his arms, his safe, warm arms. But they couldn't stand out here all night. "It's getting dark," she said. "We'd better head back to the house."

"Do you want to stop by the pony's grave?" he asked. "I saw the big tree from your bedroom window. The little one, too. That's the dog's, I guess. The dog who meant so much to you."

"I—" Tears filled her eyes. She hadn't been there since Labor Day, since she'd brought Torrie home for the last time.

Brad hugged her close again. "Would you rather go there alone? If you want to, I'll understand."

"No." She swallowed and gripped his arm

with both hands. "Come with me. Please. I want you to come with me."

They stood side-by-side near the big tree, silent. "Loving is so hard," she said finally. "It hurts so much."

"I know," he said, his voice husky. "When I was little I hurt a lot."

She kept silent. Maybe it would help if he could tell her about it.

"My mother—my mother didn't want to have children."

She bit her lip to keep from saying the harsh words that came to her. Let him do the talking.

"My mother didn't want me," he said, in that flat voice he always used when he spoke about his parents. He didn't look at her either, just stared straight ahead, as if he was seeing that little boy. That little boy who no one wanted, no one loved. "She didn't like the dirt of raising a child. I guess she's a very fastidious woman."

He was silent so long that she asked softly, "And your father? What sort of person is he?"

"He had no use for children either. Felt they made too much noise. He liked it quiet when he read. He liked it quiet all the time."

She slid an arm around Brad's waist and leaned against him. He needed comfort. She just wished there was more she could give him.

"But you're a very loving man," she whispered finally. "Someone must have loved you."

He put his arm around her waist. "Someone

did," he said. "That neighbor I told you about—Mrs. Vincent, and her dog Tuffy. They loved me. I always knew it."

Bless her, Jenny thought. Bless that wonderful, loving Mrs. Vincent.

"Thank you," Brad said, his voice breaking.

Why was he thanking her? "What for?"

"For saying that I'm a loving person." He still didn't look at her.

"Of course you are!"

"I've—I've wondered if maybe my upbringing left me—well, sort of deficient in that department. That's why I went into therapy."

She could hardly believe she was hearing this. "You mean—"

"I mean—I thought maybe I didn't know how to love. You know, because—"

She could hear the effort it took him to get the words out, the raw pain.

"That's not true," she said. "That's not true at all."

He turned to face her then, his eyes questioning. "How do you know?"

She thought fast. She couldn't let him go on worrying about such a ridiculous thing. "Well, look: You came after me when I stormed away that first day. And you stayed to visit with Clara instead of yelling at her. And you bought her Harry."

He started to smile and she swallowed her sigh of relief and hurried on. "You took Harry back—you didn't dump him in the shelter. You brought us all the way here so the girls could have him. You went to the shelter to get Duchess. Look how often you came over to make me walk and eat." She laughed. "Goodness, I could go on all night listing your wonderful qualities."

"You don't need to," he said, grabbing her in a big hug. "Because I want to believe you. You're a great girl, Jenny. A wonderful girl."

"I just told you the truth," she said. "Just the truth." It was awful what his parents had done to him. She'd never understand how he could have come through it so well, such a good person.

They went to the little tree next and stood there, their arms around each other, while tears rolled down her cheeks. "I'm—sorry," she said. "This is the first time I've been home since—since—" She wasn't sure whether she was crying for herself because she'd lost Torrie or for the little boy who'd been so lonely, who'd wanted love so much and been denied it.

"There's nothing to be sorry for," Brad said, pulling her closer. "They were your friends. You miss them." He took a handkerchief from his pocket and passed it to her. "As you said, sometimes love hurts."

He understood. He really understood how she felt. "Thanks," she began, wiping away her tears.

"Love hurts," he said. "But we can't stop loving because of that. It's a risk, loving is. Like my loving Lady. The hours I've spent worrying about that dog . . . Why, right now she might be gone for good. But I'm not sorry I loved her. Not sorry at all."

She managed a chuckle. "It's better to have loved and lost than never to have loved at all?"

"Yes," he said, and there was no laughter in his voice. "Take it from someone who knows."

He turned then and put his arms around her, holding her close. And she leaned into him, wanting to comfort him.

Then he drew in a deep breath and stiffened.

"What is it?" she asked, leaning back to look into his face, his beaming face.

"Look! Look who's coming!"

She turned. And there, coming toward them from the woods, trotted Fido and Lady. They passed them and went on toward the barn.

"He did it!" Brad cried, exultation in his voice. "He really did it! What a dog!"

And what a man, Jenny thought. What a wonderful, caring man.

She swallowed again. It was too soon to be thinking such things. Brad might be a wonderful man, but she wasn't sure she could risk loving him yet. And if she told him she could, and then she couldn't, that would hurt him even more. "Guess we'd better go inside. There'll be more pie and coffee. And cold turkey for sandwiches if you want."

He groaned. "More food? I couldn't possibly eat more food."

"Sure you can," she said. "We always say that, but we eat anyway." She took his hand. "The dogs'll be hungry, too. Let's go."

Later that night, after they'd bedded down the dogs in the kitchen near Harry's cage, Brad told all the Carruthers good night and followed Jenny up the stairs to the room that had once been hers. He couldn't remember ever feeling so happy, so contented. She believed he knew how to love. Only one thing could make him happier—if she'd tell him she loved him. And maybe in time she could do that. After all, she'd asked him to give her time.

She stopped with him outside the open door. "Good night," she said.

Her face was beautiful in the dim light of the hall, glowing with that inner beauty that was as much a part of her as her dark hair and eyes.

"Good night, Jenny. And thank you for inviting me here. It's been great."

She chuckled. "You won't thank me when you get home and step on the scales. Then you'll see those extra pounds."

He shook his head. "They don't matter." He looked up and down the hall. No one in sight. He reached out and took her by the shoulders, drawing her closer. "Listen, Jenny, I mean it.

Being here has been so good. It's been a nearly perfect day."

She smiled up at him, mischief in her eyes. "Nearly?"

"Only one thing could make it better."

She didn't say anything to that, but her eyes darkened.

He forged ahead. He'd started this—he'd better finish it. "One thing—if you were going to share that bed with me again."

She shook her head. "I can't."

"I know," he said. "But I had to say it. I wanted you to know. Good night, Jenny." He looked up and down again, but the hall was still deserted. He bent and gave her a quick kiss.

"Good nigh—" she began when he released her mouth. But he didn't hear the rest because from around the corner came a chorus of giggles.

"Jenny and Brad, sitting in a tree, k-i-s-s-i-n-g."

Jenny whirled from his arms. "Fanny! Ellen! You girls get to bed! Right now!"

Jenny turned, gave him a dazzling smile, and went off down the hall.

Smiling, he closed the door and turned to the narrow white bed. He'd better get to sleep. Tomorrow was going to be a busy day. A glorious, busy day.

* * *

In the kitchen Fido curled up around Lady and sighed in contentment. This was a great place, Jenny's home. Jenny's family was great, too. Good thing his gut had told him to go to Jenny that day she'd called to him in the yard. She was the human he'd been looking for. The one who was supposed to belong to him.

It looked as though this place was working its magic on her. She looked so much happier. The lines were gone from her face. She was eating better, too. Maybe in this good place she'd be able to come to her senses and see that love was what she needed, that it was worth the risk.

Lady's legs twitched and he nuzzled her ear. Chasing a rabbit in her dreams, he guessed. He closed his eyes. Rabbits could be fun sometimes, but he'd rather chase her.

Chapter Nineteen

When Jenny opened her eyes the next morning the sun was streaming through the window. It looked like a beautiful day. It seemed a little strange not to have Fido there beside her, his head on her slippers, but having him sleep downstairs had kept Lady and Harry quiet.

She grinned to herself. Fanny and Ellen had certainly taken to Harry. And Harry to them. The little demon would be kept good and busy, that was for sure.

She turned over, trying to do it quietly. The rollaway had a tendency to squeak. But Sue's bed was already empty, the covers carefully pulled up. Sue had always been an early riser. The girls, too.

Jenny stretched. How had Brad slept last

night? He seemed to be enjoying this break from work as much as she was. A flush spread up her body. *Enjoy* was a pale word for what had happened in the motel room in Joliet. In fact, there were no words to describe that experience. She'd never felt so loved, so wanted, before. In all the years she'd spent with Hugh, making love had never been so glorious. *And maybe,* she told herself, *that was because you were the only one making love. Hugh was just having sex.*

Still, what she'd felt then didn't mean she'd changed her mind about the no-men rule. There was more to a relationship than great sex. She'd meant what she told Brad—that night in Joliet had been a one-time, no-strings deal. Well, no strings, anyway. She wouldn't mind feeling that good again. And this was a vacation. Anything could happen on vacation.

She threw back the covers and looked at her watch. It was early, but maybe Brad was up. She didn't want to miss a minute of this wonderful day.

When Brad came back inside with Harry, Jenny was just coming down the stairs. In scruffy jeans and an old T-shirt, she looked good enough to eat. "Good morning, beautiful," he said, putting Harry back in his cage.

"You've been watching too many old Perry Mason shows," she told him, flushing a little.

"And *you* haven't looked in the mirror this morning. Your face is positively glowing."

She touched her cheek. "You're exaggerating," she said. "Though I have to admit I do feel pretty good."

"Have it your own way," Brad said. Why couldn't he stop grinning? But why should he? He felt like grinning. Actually, he felt like jumping up and down and singing. He was the luckiest man alive. "But I see what I see. And I see a beautiful woman."

"Enough flattery," she said. "Come on, eat some breakfast."

"Food?" he said, raising an eyebrow. "How could I possibly be hungry after what I put away yesterday?"

She grinned. "But you are. I know you are. Come on, you can eat a bowl of cereal."

A little later they pushed back their chairs. "What do you want to do now?" she asked.

Brad's devilish grin made her blush, especially as Sue had come into the kitchen and was getting breakfast for the girls.

"I need some exercise," he said, patting his stomach. "Lots of exercise. Let's take a walk."

"As soon as I help with—"

Sue shook her head and grinned at them. "Go on; I'll take care of your dishes. This is your vacation. Besides, now I won't have to entertain the girls. Harry's taken over that duty. For a long time, looks like."

"Thanks," Jenny said, giving Sue a quick hug. "You're a peach."

The air outside was crisp and clean. Brad pulled in a big lungful, tasting its freshness. As they came down the steps, Fido and Lady fell in behind them. "Looks like Pop's strategy worked," he said. "Lady's still here."

Jenny chuckled. "I don't think she'd leave Fido now. The two of them are really close."

"Yeah," he said, moving nearer. "Close is nice."

She made a face at him. "Let's walk."

By midafternoon Brad felt he'd walked ten miles. But he wasn't tired. He was full of energy; full of something else, too, he thought, as Jenny pushed open the barn door. He wanted Jenny. He wanted her so bad, he thought he'd explode. But he was a man of his word—he'd agreed to no strings. And he'd stick to it no matter how much he wanted something else. And he did. He wanted everything a man in love wanted. He wanted to marry the woman, have a family, and grow old with her.

She stopped inside the barn door and took in a great gulp of air. "Isn't it wonderful?"

He looked around. "What?"

"The smell. I love the barn smell—horses and straw."

He chuckled. "And manure."

"And manure," she agreed. "It's a good smell. A homey smell."

He'd never thought of anything like that. Smells to him were mostly to be avoided, like the exhaust that was sometimes so thick downtown that you could taste it on your tongue. He sniffed. She was right. It was a good smell, the smell of horses and straw and even manure; a natural smell. How lucky she'd been to be raised here. It had taken him many years in therapy to learn what had come to her so naturally: to appreciate the little things in life.

"You're right," he said. "It does smell good."

"Of course." Her grin was pure mischief. "Would I steer you wrong?"

He grinned back. "Never."

She pulled him farther into the barn. "Do you ride?" she asked.

Now she was going to see the worst of him. He was a real dork where any animal but a dog was concerned. And come to think of it, he hadn't done so well with Lady. Still he managed a grin. "Ride what?"

She poked him in the arm. "Horses, silly."

He shook his head. " 'Fraid not. The closest I've ever been to a horse is seeing one on TV."

She looked at him in surprise. "Really?"

"Really," he said.

"Too bad. I thought maybe we could go for a ride."

"I'm game if you are."

Her eyebrows went up. "You are?"

"I'm game for anything with you," he said. "Anything at all."

She blushed again and pulled him after her. "Come meet the horses."

He approached them carefully. They looked bigger in person. "What do you say when you meet a horse?" he asked, only half joking. Jenny probably did talk to horses.

And she did, because she took his question seriously. "You blow softly into their nostrils," she said. "That's how horses say hello."

He shrugged. "If you say so." He stepped up to a black horse that was eyeing him curiously over the stall door. "Hi there, boy. How are you today?" He blew softly into the horse's nostrils. The horse whuffled and tossed his head.

"He says he's fine." Jenny grinned. "His name's Midnight. Not terribly original, I'm afraid."

Brad reached out to smooth the glossy muscled neck. "He seems friendly enough."

"The friendliest horse around," Jenny said. "He's Sue's. And in the next stall is Cinnamon. She's my mare. Sue rides her for me sometimes."

The horse *was* the color of cinnamon. Brad blew into another pair of pink nostrils. "Hi, girl. How're you?"

"She's fine, too," Jenny said.

He stroked the horse's mane before he turned away. Jenny was staring at him.

"What?" he asked. "I've got something on my face? I didn't blow at her right?"

"No, no. It's just—well, usually guys don't want to admit to not knowing how to do things. Physical things, anyway."

He shrugged. "I might as well admit it. You'd know it anyway the minute I tried to get up on a horse's back."

She took a step closer and looked up into his eyes. "You know, Brad, that's one thing I really like about you."

His heart started pounding. He wanted to kiss her so bad, and she was only inches away. All he had to do was reach out and—He'd better behave himself. "What do you like?"

"That you're honest. That you tell me what you're really thinking."

There was his opening. He'd be a fool not to take it. "To tell you the truth, right now I'm not thinking about horses at all."

Her eyes sparkled. "You're not?"

"No."

"What *are* you thinking about?"

"About kissing you."

"Oh."

The word was an invitation. At least, he took it that way. He gathered her into his arms and kissed her. And kissed her again. She didn't object. She felt just right in his arms, as if she'd been designed to fit there and nowhere else. No strings, he reminded himself. She wanted no strings. But he wanted *her.*

"Wish it would rain," he murmured against her hair.

She leaned back in his arms and looked up at him in puzzlement. "Rain? Why do you want rain?"

The lump in his throat threatened to choke him. "Well, maybe we'd get caught in it, and fall in the mud, and have to take our clothes off, and—"

The look in her eyes made his tongue stick to the roof of his mouth.

"Rain does do strange things to me," she admitted, her eyes dancing. "But so do barns. You know, I've always wondered what it would be like—in the barn."

"You mean . . ." he stammered.

She grinned and put a little kiss on the corner of his mustache. "Yes. You *were* talking about what we did *after* we took our clothes off, weren't you?"

"Yes, yes, I was." He could hardly believe she was offering him what he wanted so much.

"I thought so. Well, are you really game for anything?"

"To—to do it here? Now?"

"Right. Here. Now." Her eyes sparkled with mischief. And something else. "A roll in the hay, I think they call it."

"But your father . . ."

"Pop's gone to town. Left half an hour ago. Won't be back till suppertime."

"Your mother and Sue—"

"Won't come to the barn for anything. They're busy in the house."

"The girls—"

"Will be taking their naps. But we can put the bolt on the door. Just to be sure." She tossed her head. "Of course, if you're chicken to—"

"Not me." He grabbed her hand. "Let's bolt that door."

Outside the door Fido heard the snick of the bolt sliding home. The smell of wanting was heavy in the air. And it looked as if Jenny and Brad were going to do something about it. The two of them were finally beginning to communicate—and without any help from him. Fido nuzzled Lady and headed for the woods. He had some communicating to do himself.

Chapter Twenty

Jenny watched the bolt slide home. They were safe from intruders now, the girls or anyone else, though she could hardly think of anyone who'd come to the barn looking for them. She could hardly believe what she'd just done. What had happened to her that she could talk so freely to Brad? That she could kid with him and practically tell him she wanted to have sex with him?

It had never, ever been like that with Hugh. In all their years together Hugh had always done the deciding. She could see it now, now that there was some distance between them. Hugh was a control freak; he had to be in charge of everything. But why was she thinking about him? Forget Hugh. He was nothing now.

"So," Brad said, leaning over to kiss the tip of her nose. "The door's bolted. What's next?"

She eased out of her jacket and dropped it to one side. He tossed his on top of it. She wanted to throw herself into his arms, but maybe a little restraint was called for. Well, just a little.

A giggle bubbled out of her, a giggle of pure joy. "Well, I suppose a blanket *would* help. Straw can be pretty prickly. And I don't think I want to keep half my clothes on."

His mouth fell open. Then he grinned. "Me neither. I like to look at you. And feel all of you. Against me." He took her hand. "So, where's that blanket?"

"You did say you like the smell of horses?"

He raised an eyebrow in puzzlement. "Yeah, I did. Why?"

"Well, I guess you're going to get a lot of it, because the only blankets out here are horse blankets."

He laughed then, a deep hearty laugh, and grabbed her by the waist to swing her around and around in dizzying circles till she could hardly breathe. "I—" He stopped and gulped. "You're crazy, Jenny Carruthers. But you're an awful lot of fun. Now, where's the horse blanket?"

Still a little dizzy, she wobbled over to the tack chest and pulled a blanket out of it. "Maybe in that corner would be the best place," she said, gesturing to a place out of sight of the window.

She still could hardly believe she was doing this. But she knew what she wanted. She wanted the touch of Brad's body, his hands on her, his mouth on hers, the tickle of his mustache as he kissed her, the sound of his breath in her ear, ragged and harsh with desire, then smoothing out after he—*Enough thinking,* she told herself, *just do it.*

She helped him spread out the blanket on the straw. "Now," she said, straightening, "I guess we're all set."

He took an anxious look at the door. "You're sure your father won't be back till suppertime?"

"Positive. He made a point of telling me so."

He stared at her as if he'd heard wrong. "He made a point?"

"Right."

He shook his head as though he was dazed. "I can't believe I'm standing here blithering like an idiot when the most beautiful woman in all Iowa—in all the world—is waiting for me to undress her."

"I wasn't waiting," she said, "but be my guest."

He stepped forward. "First, a little kiss." He grinned. "Or maybe a big one. I love your kisses."

He kissed her then, and it was even better than she remembered from the last time. "Oh, Brad. I love your kisses, too." She slid her fingers around the back of his neck and pulled off his ponytail holder, letting his hair fall loose against his collar.

"Hey."

"I like your curls." She wrapped one around her finger. "A lot of women would love to have curls like yours."

"Maybe," he said, "but I'm not a lot of women."

"No." She giggled again. "But you're a lot of man."

"Thank you, ma'am." He kissed the top of her head and dropped to his knees before her. "Shoes first. Okay?"

"Okay," she whispered. Anything he wanted to do was okay. Anything. But she couldn't tell *him* that.

He set her tennis shoes to one side, then kicked his own off. His fingers went to the waist of her jeans and flicked them open. Carefully he slid them down over her hips till they puddled around her ankles.

"They're not wet and muddy this time," he said, as he straightened up and she stepped out of them.

"No." She reached for the snap on his jeans. They joined hers on the floor. He was wearing navy blue jockey shorts that stretched taut over the evidence of his need for her. Her breath caught in her throat.

She moved her hands up, up, to the buttons on his flannel shirt. Under that shirt was his furry chest. She could remember it under her fingers, that first day, when touching it had been an accident, and that night in Joliet when it hadn't been. She didn't think she'd ever forget the feel of his chest. Or that she'd ever want to. "Flannel is nice," she said. "It feels soft."

"Not as soft as your skin," he whispered. "Nothing is that soft."

She felt the heat spreading up her throat. "A horse's nose is softer."

He stared at her. "I don't think so." In his stocking feet he crossed over to the stall and stroked Midnight's nose. Then he came back and stroked her bare thigh. "Nope. Your skin's softer."

She had to laugh. She'd laughed so much lately. It was good to feel like laughing again, to feel alive and happy. "Nobody's ever given me such a nice compliment." She reached out to stroke his chest. How she loved the feel of it. She eased off his shirt and bent to rub her cheek against the hair there, then dropped a kiss on each nipple and straightened.

He stood for a minute, a look of pure pleasure on his face; then he took hold of the bottom of her T-shirt. "One," he said. "Two. Three." And he pulled it up over her head.

There she stood, in only her bra and panties, her pink satin bra and panties. She blushed again. Would she never stop blushing?

His gaze traveled over her. "Pink satin?" he asked, a grin on his lips.

"I like pink. It's my favorite color."

"Mine, too, now." He ran a fingertip across the satin that covered her breast. He shook his head. "Nope."

"Nope what?"

"Satin's not as soft as your skin either."

"Flatterer."

"It's the truth."

Then she couldn't wait any longer. She walked into his arms, felt them wrap around her, hold her tight. He kissed her once more, long and lingeringly. Then he reached behind her to unhook her bra. It fell to the floor between them. She could feel his chest, his wonderful furry chest, brush against her breasts. She sighed in pure contentment. It was time for that blanket.

Half an hour later Brad turned on his side and kissed the tip of Jenny's nose. "So, Miss Curiosity," he said, "was your roll in the hay as great as you thought it would be?"

"Better," she murmured. "Absolutely perfect."

She turned a little, till her breasts were resting against his chest. The whole length of her lay against him. There were no words for how good he felt. He hardly knew what part of lovemaking he liked best—whether it was the foreplay or the act itself, or lying there like this afterwards, naked in each other's arms, while she played with the hair on his chest. Good thing he didn't have to choose. He wouldn't want to give up any of it.

It was all so wonderful. All except—A little quiver of doubt nagged at the back of his mind. No strings, she'd said. No strings. He didn't want to stick to that. He wasn't sure he could. If he had to give her up now, after he'd learned how much he really loved her . . . well, he wasn't sure he could do it.

He held her closer, kissing the top of her head. No sense in borrowing trouble. He'd just have to hang in there. She seemed really happy now. Surely she'd come to see that love *was* worth the risk, that without love, life just wasn't as good.

He could see that clearly enough now. He could hardly believe that he'd lived for so long without loving. If you could call that living. He wouldn't, not any more. Not since he'd been with Jenny. Not since he knew what love was really like.

"Penny," she breathed against his ear. "A penny for your thoughts."

"They aren't worth it," he said.

"Tell me anyway."

He swallowed hard. Did he dare risk it? "Well, I was just thinking that—" He gulped. He'd come this far, if he didn't risk—He couldn't expect her to read his mind. "That it'd be nice to do this often. To—be together."

She stiffened a little. He could feel her body tense against his.

For a long time she didn't say anything. He just lay there, holding her. Finally he couldn't stand the silence any longer. "Sorry. I know you asked for more time. I just—I just wanted you to know how I feel."

"Thanks," she said, burrowing against him again, her body softening. "I appreciate that. But it's still no strings."

"I hear you," he said, dropping a kiss behind her ear. "But you didn't say no hope."

"No, I didn't" She raised her mouth to his. "Kiss me again," she said. "It's a long time till supper."

When they unlocked the barn door it was almost time for supper. Jenny grinned. "We'd better pick the straw off our clothes." She'd loved watching him dress, loved every second of the time they'd spent together. This was vacation, and vacation was different, special.

"Yeah. We wouldn't want them to know what we've been up to." He pulled his hair back and fastened it with the ponytail holder. She might like his curls, but he never let them hang loose. "Of course, one look at your face and anyone with sense will know."

She nodded. "I suppose it glows like yours."

He made a fake frown. "You're sure your father won't take a shotgun after me?"

"I'm sure," she said, tucking her arm through his. "Now let's go wash up for supper."

But they only got halfway up the front steps before they met the girls coming out. Fanny looked at Ellen and giggled. "Where you been?" Ellen asked. "We been looking for you."

"We were busy," Jenny said. "I was showing Brad the farm."

The girls nodded. "Aunt Jenny," Fanny said, "can we ask you something?"

She heard the quick intake of Brad's breath. But he didn't need to worry. The girls couldn't have seen anything. "Sure. Go ahead."

Both girls giggled. "When you kiss him," Fanny said, "does his mustache tickle?"

She swallowed her laughter. "Fanny! What a question!"

Fanny shrugged. "We just want to know. Daddy didn't have a mustache. And Grampa doesn't. So we never kissed anyone with a mustache. And if we don't ask, how will we ever learn?"

"So," Ellen repeated, "does it tickle?"

Jenny managed a grin. "Yes," she said. "It tickles a little bit."

"I told you so," Fanny said to her sister with a smug smile. "Now where's that puppy gone and hid?"

And they ran off to look for Harry.

Jenny turned to look at Brad, and saw that he was trying hard not to laugh. "All right," she said. "They're healthy girls. With normal curiosity."

"I could shave it off," he offered.

"Shave it—"

"My mustache. I could shave it off because it tickles."

"No, no. Don't be silly." She smiled, wondering why she felt suddenly shy. "I like it the way it is."

Chapter Twenty-one

Jenny woke on Saturday still wearing a smile. She felt so good, it was incredible. Maybe she'd been wrong about men, maybe she *could* trust them. Well, one, anyway. Brad was so special. He wasn't like other men at all. Except maybe Pop. She'd always trusted Pop. Always would.

After breakfast she led Brad out to the barn. "You're sure you want to do this?"

He reached for her hand and she let him take it. Somehow it seemed natural to be walking hand-in-hand, their fingers intertwined.

"I told you," he said, squeezing her fingers, "I'm game for anything. As long as it's with you."

"Okay." He was such a nice man, a good man. "Which horse do you want, Midnight or Cinnamon?"

He made a funny face. "Which one's the slowest?"

She laughed. "Slow isn't always so good. A trot is slower than a canter, for example, but a trot can jar you right out of the saddle while a good canter is just like sitting in a rocking chair."

He chuckled. "If you say so. You're the expert on horses, after all. I'm just a city boy."

She pushed open the barn door. "So I've noticed."

A flush started up his cheeks. She'd never seen him blush before. Had she embarrassed him by calling him a city boy? "I'm sorry. I didn't mean—"

"Sorry?" he asked, raising an eyebrow. "Sorry for what?"

"I didn't mean to kid you."

His forehead wrinkled in puzzlement. "Kid me?"

"You blushed and I thought I'd hurt your feelings, calling you a city boy."

He shook his head. "Oh, that. I wasn't embarrassed. Though maybe I should be. I was remembering a few nights ago when a certain city boy fell into the mud. And then I was really remembering what happened afterward. And what happened here yesterday." He grinned and pulled her into his arms, where he held her close and kissed the end of her nose. "The memory sort of heated my blood. My skin, too, I guess."

She burst into laughter, but she didn't move out of his arms. It was good to stand there, good to feel him against her. "You're incorrigible."

He looked down at her, mischief in his eyes. "Really? I just thought I'd found a good thing and wanted to hang on to it."

"Well," she pretended to be thinking hard, "I guess it *was* pretty good."

He made another face. "Now my feelings *are* hurt. I thought it was stupendous, outstanding, out of this world. But if you think otherwise, maybe we should give it another—"

"Enough," she cried, easing out of his arms and reaching for Midnight's bridle. "You'll get me all heated up and I won't be able to do anything about it. Pop's not going into town today."

Brad heaved a big sigh. "That's a crying shame. Are you sure you can't think of somewhere to send him?"

She shook her head. "Behave yourself now, or I'll sic Fido on you." She looked over to where Fido and Lady were sniffing in the straw.

"You did that before," he said. "At least, you used him to prevent me from kissing you."

"We all make mistakes." She turned away before he could see her face. Was she making a mistake now, encouraging him this way? But Brad was a good man. She knew that. And, anyway, she'd told him no-strings attached; she didn't have to decide anything now. They had all of today and tomorrow. Two more days to be together. Two more wonderful days.

She slipped the bridle over Midnight's head and led him out of the stall. "Just hold him," she said, turning back for the blanket and saddle. "I'll saddle him up."

Brad took the bridle. "Should I learn how to do that?"

"Not necessary," she said, throwing on the blanket and then the saddle. She shoved a knee in Midnight's gut and pulled hard on the cinch.

"Doesn't that hurt him?" Brad asked, stroking the horse's neck.

"Nope. Horses learn early to puff out their bellies when you're saddling them. If you don't make them let the air out, the cinch won't be tight enough. And when you go to mount, the saddle will swing around and you'll end up hanging under the horse's belly. Or hitting the ground below him."

"Wow," Brad breathed. "You know so much about animals."

She shrugged. "Nothing to it." She'd never thought her ability with animals was unusual. It was just something she knew how to do. But she supposed it might seem strange to him, considering his upbringing. "I was raised on a farm. Just hold him while I get Cinnamon saddled."

It took her only a few minutes to saddle Cinnamon. Then they led out both horses. "Now," she told Brad, "you put your left foot in the stirrup and—"

"I've watched enough cowboy movies to know that," he said laughing, and promptly swung up.

"Good job," she said.

He shrugged. "I used to wish I could be a cowboy. I always wanted to do that running mount from behind—you know, where the cowboy sort of leapfrogs up onto the horse's back. But since I didn't have a horse I couldn't practice."

She grinned and swung up herself. "I tried that mount a couple of times, when I was around ten."

He raised an eyebrow. "How did it work out?"

She turned Cinnamon out of the barn yard, and Midnight followed. "Not so well, actually. I kept smashing my face into the horse's rump. Finally I gave up and went back to doing it the old way. I figured it was safer."

Brad laughed. "I'm glad. I wouldn't want to see that pretty nose all mashed flat."

"Let's go," she said. So, he thought her nose was pretty. "And remember, you can ease the wear and tear on your behind by standing in the stirrups a little."

"I'll try to remember that," Brad said. "Already I can feel bones I didn't know were there."

She chuckled and turned Cinnamon down the lane.

* * *

Coming out of the barn behind the humans, Fido woofed to Lady. They might as well follow along. A run would be good for them. The humans had been doing really well at communicating lately, but it wouldn't hurt to keep an eye on them.

There was no understanding some humans. Dogs didn't hurt each other unless they had to, to defend themselves or their pack, or were rabid or something. But humans—humans were just plain strange. They had a tendency to put themselves before the pack. No wonder they were always getting in such trouble.

An hour later Brad shifted painfully in the saddle. It didn't help. There wasn't a centimeter of his backside that didn't feel as though his bones were grinding his flesh to a bloody pulp. He sighed. "I'm afraid I'm not going to make much of a rider. I think my bones are coming right through my skin."

Jenny half turned in the saddle and gave him an encouraging look. "I'm surprised you've held out this long. The first time on a horse teaches you a lot about anatomy."

He groaned. "A lot I didn't want to know."

"You're doing all right." She looked out to the meadow, where Fido and Lady were running circles around each other and barking like pups.

Brad made a face. "I don't see how you can

say I did all right. When we trotted I must have looked like a sack of potatoes."

"Well," she admitted with a small smile, "maybe a little. But you make a nice, muscular sack of potatoes."

He grinned. He'd felt idiotic, bouncing up and down on the horse's back. And he did bounce, no matter how he tried to ride the stirrups as she'd suggested. Well, he hadn't hidden anything about himself from her. She might as well know this, too. He wasn't athletic—and he probably never would be. But maybe that wouldn't matter to her.

He wasn't good with animals . . . well, he was all right with Lady, but he wasn't anything like Jenny. He *was* good with kids, though. Real good. And he loved Jenny. That ought to count for something. It ought to count for a lot.

"Well, I've tried the trot," he said. "Are we going to canter today?"

"Let's go to the other end of the meadow," she said. "Then we can run back. The meadow's better for a run than the trail that follows the fence row." She gave him a sympathetic grin. "If you're sure your behind is up to it."

He loved that grin of hers. He hadn't seen it till he got her here to Iowa, away from the pressures of her job, but he loved it more every time he saw it. A little girl would grin like that, a little girl with Jenny's dark eyes and hair, a little girl who'd call him daddy. And a little boy—

"Oh," Jenny said.

He looked up, startled out of his daydream by the strange tone of her voice. A rider was coming, a rider on a gorgeous trotting palomino. The guy could ride—no potato-sack bouncing for him.

"Who—" he began. But then he got a glimpse of her face and the words died in his throat. She didn't need to tell him. The guy on the palomino had to be Hugh. Nobody else could wipe the smile off Jenny's face so fast and put that look of pain in her eyes.

"Guess that's Hugh," he said.

She gave him a startled look. "Yes." She started to turn the horse away, back the way they'd come. "I don't—"

"We won't run from him," Brad said. "Don't give him that satisfaction."

She straightened in the saddle and shot him a look of startled gratitude. "Of course. You're right. He doesn't mean anything to me now anyway."

He means something to me, Brad thought. *And I think you're fooling yourself. Looks to me like he's still the competition.* But he straightened his shoulders. He'd never been a man to run from a fight, and he wouldn't run from this one. Jenny meant too much to him.

Fido and Lady came bounding up, panting and frisking like a couple of pups. Suddenly Fido stopped frisking and faced toward the coming rider. He dropped to his haunches and growled, the fur on the back of his neck standing straight up.

"Fido," Jenny whispered. "No."

Brad shook his head in amazement. How the devil had the dog known that the horseman was Hugh? That Jenny was upset by him? Stupid question. Fido knew everything. He was beginning to think old Fido was Superdog. And to tell the truth, at the moment he was glad to have the dog there, glad for any help he could get.

Hugh came cantering up and slid to a grass-tearing stop, like some hotshot rodeo star. He was dressed like one, too, in jeans and one of those form-fitting western shirts with pearl snaps. Creamy Stetson and light-colored alligator-skin boots. The kind of stuff he'd be embarrassed to wear. But this guy could carry it off. He was a handsome man, with dark eyes and hair. And he sure could ride.

"Jenny," Hugh said. "I thought that was you. Good to see you again."

Good to see you! What a thing to say. The guy dumped the most wonderful girl in the world and then he had the unmitigated gall to tell her it was good to see her! Brad raised himself up in the stirrups. He'd like to jump down and punch this idiot in the nose. Of course, jumping down was completely out of the question. He wasn't sure he could even stand up straight after he hit the ground. And he'd never been good at boxing.

Jenny turned to him, a warning in her eyes. Hell, was she tuned in to his feelings the way Fido was to hers? Hey, maybe that wasn't such a bad idea. Brad settled down in the saddle again. What was he thinking of anyway? Jenny didn't need his help. She'd already made up her mind. Hugh was the one who was losing out here. The poor sucker didn't know what he was missing.

In front of Jenny's horse Fido eyed the man who'd hurt his human. The smell of Jenny's hurt and anger hung heavy in the air. Her mare danced around a little, smelling the tension but not understanding it. But the intruder—the man who'd hurt her—his scent didn't carry any discomfort at all. It carried only the sense of his own importance. Arrogant—that's what he was. And he needed to be brought down a peg or two.

Fido growled again. Yep, that Hugh human needed to be taught a lesson. And he was just the dog to do it. He tensed, ready to launch himself. He could probably jump high enough to get a good grip on the fellow's leg. That should spook his horse and—

"No," Jenny said. "Fido, sit." She said it so softly that at first he wasn't sure he'd heard her, but then he knew he'd better not do it. She wanted to handle this situation herself. And he'd have to let her. Sometimes humans had to solve their own problems. It was good for them, he supposed—helped them build their character—but it was hard on their dogs. He waited, watching. After all, she might change her mind and need him.

"Hello, Hugh," Jenny said. Good, that sounded natural enough. She wasn't going to let him upset her. She could do this. She could face him. He was just a man she used to know. He didn't mean anything to her now. She'd just make conversation. "How's Sunstroke doing?"

Hugh stroked the stallion's great neck. "He's fine. Like always."

"Good. I always thought he was a great horse."

Hugh eyed Brad. "Who's this?" Hugh asked. "He's not from around here."

He didn't have to act as though he owned the county. But she might as well get it over with. "Oh, this is Brad; Brad Ferris. Brad, this is Hugh Devon. He's our neighbor."

"Hello," Brad said. And he didn't smile. His chin had that granite look and his eyes were colder than she'd ever seen them.

She didn't mind. "Brad and I brought a pup for Sue's girls," she said.

She caught the flicker of surprise in Hugh's eyes. "Oh, that's nice."

"The girls think so. They love him." She left

that ambiguous on purpose. Let Hugh think it was Brad the girls loved. Anyway, they probably did.

Hugh looked at her horse. "Cinnamon looks like she could use a good run. Bet she misses you, way off there in Cleveland."

Her heart leaped. So he'd kept track of where she was. But wait—what did that matter? She didn't care what he felt about anything.

"Yes, sir," Hugh repeated. "A good run."

What was he after? "We've already—"

But he didn't wait for her to finish. He turned to Brad. "How about it, Ferris? You up to a good run?"

She opened her mouth.

"Sounds great," Brad said.

She closed her mouth. Men. Did they ever have any sense? Even if Brad had been a good rider—which he wasn't—Midnight wasn't up to a race with Hugh's stallion. He never had been. Anyone with any horse sense could have seen that. And Hugh certainly knew it. This race was a setup.

"Let's go," Hugh said. "Jenny can be the starter."

Chapter Twenty-two

This was stupid, Jenny thought. But if Hugh thought she was going to say so, he was wrong. She wouldn't demean Brad by trying to protect him. She'd seen the quick glance he'd thrown her when he'd agreed to this race. She hadn't needed it, of course, to know that Brad had his male pride and wouldn't like her interfering. And that male pride wouldn't let him back down from this race, even though he couldn't possibly win it. She just hoped his backside could stand all that bouncing up and down. He was already pretty sore.

What she wouldn't give to see Hugh beaten, though! He was so full of his own importance. It was hard to see how she could possibly have loved him, have actually thought he was a wonderful man, and wanted to be his wife. Well, she'd been young and foolish. She could admit that she'd been taken in by his sense of his own importance. But she wasn't foolish anymore. She wasn't going to be fooled by him again.

Hugh pulled Sunstroke to a halt. "This looks like a good place to start. We can finish over there by those two stumps."

Brad pulled up beside them. He sent her another look that plainly said *I know I won't win this race, but I'm not giving up anyway.*

Then Hugh turned to smile at her, that cocky smile he always got when he was going to humiliate someone, usually her. Funny how clearly she could see things now. And how stupid she'd been not to see them before.

"Ready?" Hugh asked.

"Ready," Brad said, his jaw thrusting out. For an instant she could feel that jaw beneath her fingers, could feel his mustache against—Enough of that. Get the stupid race over with. Then maybe Hugh would leave them alone.

"One. Two." She took in a deep breath. "Three!"

The horses took off. Sunstroke took the lead immediately—he'd always loved to race—but Midnight was running gamely, almost as though he'd sensed some of Brad's feelings about the thing. It looked like Brad had given him his head, too. That was smart of him. He was a fast learner.

She swallowed an anxious smile. Brad was bent low over the saddle. His cowboy movies had taught him something, anyway, though it could be it was just because he was trying not to fall off Midnight's back. She hoped he didn't let his pride get in the way of clutching the saddle horn. He didn't have the experience to hang on with his legs. "Come on, Brad," she whispered. "Come on." Beside her Fido and Lady barked encouragement. "Good dogs," she said. "Good dogs."

Fido reached up to lick Jenny's fingers. She was awfully worried. He could smell a lot of fear. He sniffed. But even through the fear he could smell her love for Brad. Good! She needed a human to love. Actually, she needed the Brad human. No one else would do.

And the man must need her. Why else would he agree to run a race he couldn't win? Fido glanced sideways at Lady. He knew about showing off to prove yourself. Sometimes a dog had to fight for his female. Humans just had different ways of doing it.

He could go out there and get in the way, maybe throw the bad guy's horse off stride. He could even send Lady. She'd like doing it. But Jenny didn't want them to interfere. She wanted to let her man show her what he could do, even if it was lose the race. Strange creatures, humans, but once they gave you their love, they could be really loyal. It wouldn't matter to Jenny if Brad lost this race. She expected him to lose it—the smell of her fear told him that. But she was proud of the man, too, just for trying.

The horses thundered on, Midnight right behind Sunstroke. Jenny bit her lip anxiously and raised up in the stirrups. He didn't need to win. She didn't care about that. If only he didn't get hurt. "Come on, Brad," she breathed. "Come on!"

And then Sunstroke veered to the right, suddenly and without any warning. Midnight's stride faltered and broke. And Brad flew from the saddle and hit the ground. It looked as though he had landed on his back.

"Brad! Oh, no!" She put her heels to Cinnamon's sides and raced forward. Fido and Lady got there first and started licking Brad's face. Midnight stood off to one side, patiently cropping grass. He was too well trained to run off.

As she jumped down, dropping Cinnamon's reins, the dogs sat back on their haunches. She dropped to her knees and shook his arm. "Brad! Speak to me. Brad, are you all right?"

He opened his eyes. They looked a little glazed, but she could tell he recognized her. "Ahhhh!" he moaned, trying to lift his head and falling back with a faint motion of one hand.

"Lie still," she told him, smoothing the hair back from his face. In his tumble his hair had come loose, and curls were clustering around his face. He looked so young and vulnerable. She wanted to gather him up like a little boy and comfort him. But it wasn't a good idea to move him yet. Besides, there was his pride. "Lie still," she repeated. "You'll get your wind back soon."

She stroked his forehead. "You just hit the ground hard." She hoped. She looked him over anxiously. "Does anything hurt?"

He waved his hand again and gulped air. "Don't—think—so."

Good. He was getting his air back. "Now. Move your arms and legs. One at a time. Slowly, now."

He did what she said, moving each limb slowly—and easily.

"Good," she said in relief. "Everything looks all right."

He pulled in another deep breath. "What—happened?"

"It looked like Midnight hit a swell in the ground. Sometimes they're hidden under the grass. He couldn't see it and broke stride. And when he did you lost your seat."

He chuckled weakly. "I thought I'd lost a lot more than that. For a few seconds there, I even wondered who was making those funny noises." He grinned. "Then I realized it was me."

"Can you sit up now?" she asked.

"Let's see." Slowly he pushed himself to a sitting position. "Guess so." He turned his neck slowly from side to side. "Nothing hurts."

Hugh's stallion came trotting up. "What's the matter?" Hugh asked. Couldn't he see?

"Nothing," Brad said, clambering to his feet. He swayed a little, but she knew better than to reach out to him. And then Fido was there, his nose in Brad's hand, steadying him. And Lady took up a position on the other side. Those two were really something.

"I took a spill, that's all," Brad said, his voice even, though maybe a little lower than usual. "Guess that means you win—the race."

A strange look flitted across Hugh's face. "I always win," he said.

Brad shrugged as though he couldn't care less. "Is that so?"

Hugh turned to Jenny. "Can I speak to you for a moment?"

She didn't really want to talk to him alone, but she didn't know how to get out of it. Hugh usually persisted till he got what he wanted. "I suppose so." What did he want now? He'd won the stupid race.

Cinnamon was still ground-tied beside the waiting Midnight. Jenny walked off to one side with Hugh, out of earshot of Brad, who had gotten down on his knees to pet Lady, and maybe because he was still too wobbly on his feet to risk standing for long.

Hugh didn't bother to get off Sunstroke to

talk to her. He just looked down on her like he was king of the world and said, "Where on earth did you pick *him* up?"

She eased a step backward so she could look up at him without getting a crick in her neck. "I didn't pick him up," she said, fighting to keep her tone level. He had no right to speak to her like that. Who did he think he was, anyway? "Brad and I are friends," she said. "*Good* friends."

Hugh shrugged. "If you say so. But he looks like a loser to me. What do you want with a man who can't even stay on a horse?" He sniffed. "A man who wears his hair in curls."

What nerve! There he was in a getup no decent cowboy would be seen dead in—and he was taking potshots at Brad! This, after he hadn't even apologized for pushing Brad into a race that should never have been run. But why was she surprised? Hugh had always been self-centered. The only person who mattered to Hugh was Hugh.

"I like hair that curls," she said, smiling and looking pointedly at his straight dark hair. "It gives a man character. Brad has many other good qualities, too. Now, if you'll excuse me . . ." Without waiting for Hugh to reply, she turned her back to him and went back to Brad, Fido right beside her.

She felt Fido's nose sliding into her fingers. Good old Fido. He knew she needed calming down. Venting her feelings at Hugh would only let the man know he'd reached her. She wouldn't give him that satisfaction. Especially since nothing she said to him would do any good.

Talking to Hugh was a lost cause. None of their breakup was his fault—at least, that's what he claimed. It was all because of *her* behavior that he had fallen in love with another woman, because she, Jenny, wasn't doing her duty as his woman. And to think that she'd believed that guff, let it make her feel less than worthwhile. How could she have been so gullible?

She heard the sound of receding hoofbeats as Sunstroke cantered away, but she didn't turn to look. Why should she care what Hugh thought about anything? He was a shallow, vain man—a manipulator. She wanted nothing more to do with him.

Brad looked up as Jenny came back toward him. He felt sort of silly sitting there on the grass, but it was better than keeling over while that pompous ass was watching. Hitting the ground so hard had really knocked the stuffing out of him, leaving him weak in the knees. He started to get to his feet again.

"No," Jenny said. "Sit still." She dropped down beside him in the grass, her brow furrowed in worry. "Are you sure—"

"I'm all right." He didn't like seeing her frown

like that. She had enough troubles without worrying about him. "Honest I am. I just had the breath knocked out of me."

She nodded. "I'm sorry about Hugh. I had no idea we'd run into him out here. He's even worse than I remembered. Such a conceited ass."

Brad grinned ruefully. "I knew he'd beat me." He rubbed his backside. "I just didn't know it'd be quite so painful a defeat."

Jenny peered at him. "If you knew he'd beat you, why did you agree to the race?"

Did she really not know? "Come on, Jenny. I'm a man. He offered me a challenge. I couldn't be lily-livered and turn it down. Not in front of the woman I—" Better not say that, even if it was true. "Not in front of you."

"But you couldn't win," she went on. "You knew you couldn't win."

He put on his solemnest face. "It isn't winning that counts, but how you play the game." Then he grinned. "Besides, when I saw you bending over me with that worried look on your beautiful face, it was worth it. I'd rather take a tumble, even if it means landing on my poor bruised backside, and have you worry about me, than be an Olympic equestrian."

He saw the laughter gathering in her eyes; then it reached her mouth and she laughed long and loud. The sound of it made him want to hug the world. He'd settle for hugging her.

"Lay down," she said, pushing on his nearest shoulder.

He stared at her. Had he heard right? "Lay—down? Here?"

"Yes. Lay down. Now. Here." Her eyes were full of mischief.

"Yes, ma'am." He eased himself down in the meadow grass, for the first time noticing its fresh, clean smell. He looked up at the bluest of skies, laced with white clouds. Then he stretched carefully. "Everything's still okay," he said, wondering what she had on her mind.

And then he knew. She burrowed into his arms and pressed herself against him. "Yes," she said, laughter still in her voice. "I think all your parts are still there. And still working."

"Definitely still working," he said, pulling her even closer, or trying to. It was so good to have her against him, to have that closeness with her.

She reached up to wrap one of his curls around her finger. "I love your hair," she said. "The color of it. And the way it curls."

What had brought that on? "I love yours, too," he said. "But why couldn't I have fallen off in the woods?"

She kissed his chin. "Doing it in the woods is very overrated."

"You've done it in the woods?" he asked, a surge of jealousy racing through him.

"No. No, I haven't." She kissed his neck. "But I know the woods. It has mosquitoes and ticks and brambles. Take my word for it; the barn is better."

"Or a bed," he said. "I'd vote for a bed."

"Yes." She sighed. "But we don't have either."

He ran a finger under her chin and tipped her mouth up toward him. "So I guess I'll have to settle for a kiss."

"Or two or three."

"Or a dozen."

She snuggled closer. "Who's counting?"

Chapter Twenty-three

It was almost dark when Jenny and Brad finally got back to the barn. Brad had suggested that he walk home instead of riding, but she'd had to tell him it was just too far to walk. So he'd heaved himself up on Midnight with only a few groans. They'd taken it slowly, so slowly that the dogs had run on ahead. Even so, Brad had said at least once that he wished he could ride home on his stomach, slung over the saddle the way they used to do it in the movies.

"I can't believe we're actually finally here," he said with a great sigh.

"I know," she told him. He must be miserable. "You must be awfully sore."

He moaned and made an exaggerated face. "Sore doesn't begin to describe it. I thought my backside was sore before. But now . . . I never knew anything could hurt like this."

"You poor thing," she said. "I'll have Pop break out the liniment."

Brad grinned. "Will you rub it in for me?"

Trust him to make a joke of this, though she knew he had to be hurting. The riding had been hard enough on his behind, but a fall like that was bound to make a person stiff and sore all over. "Afraid not," she said with a chuckle. "You'll have to manage that yourself."

He sighed. "Well, first I'll have to get off this animal." He rubbed Midnight's neck. "No insult intended, boy. You're a good horse."

"You just swing your right leg over the back," she said.

He made a face. "Just! I *know* what to do. Trouble is, I'm not sure I can do it."

He eased his right foot free of the stirrup and groaned. "How about looking the other way? This is going to be painful to watch. Almost as painful as doing it."

"I know," Jenny said. "But the best thing to do is get it over with. Just do it."

"Just do it," he repeated. He swung his right leg over Midnight's back and, loosening his left foot from the stirrup, slid down till his feet hit the ground. "Ahhh!"

She swung down and hurried to him, but she was too late. His knees had already buckled under him. But, fortunately, he'd hung on to the saddle skirts and not fallen on his poor abused backside. Instead he was on his knees, his forehead against Midnight's belly. And Midnight had stood firm. He wasn't easily spooked. "You're right," Brad said, grinning up at her. "Horses do smell good."

"Well, I'm not always right," she said. "But I do know about horses."

"Yes, you do."

She bent closer. "Can you stand up?"

"I'm not sure," he said. "But I guess I'd better. I don't want to spend the night out here. Besides, I don't want your father to think I'm a weakling."

"Pop's not like that. Besides, even the strongest men have bones in their behinds."

Brad frowned. "Not iron-man Hugh."

"Nonsense," she said. "You're a much better man than he is."

He stared up at her, his eyes round with surprise. It was strange having him on his knees like this. It made her feel funny in her stomach. Besides, it must be hard on his knees. She put his left hand on her shoulder. "Push on me and pull on the saddle. Okay?"

"Okay."

"Let's try it. One. Two. Three."

He bore down on her shoulder, as she'd told him to. He bore down hard. And he managed to get upright, where he could cling to the saddle horn. "Just let me stand here a minute," he said. "Get the old bones straightened out."

"Sure. You know, you're lucky. You could easily have broken something important."

"I know," he said ruefully. "I've been thinking about that all the way home. I did a real dumb thing. Guess I got overtaken by the macho image."

She smiled. "Well, you're not the first man that's happened to. And it ended all right."

"Yeah. If I can get my legs to working right."

She patted his shoulder. "Let's take the horses into the barn. You can sit down while I unsaddle them."

"Sit?" he cried, making a face. "How can you even suggest such a thing? I don't know if I'll ever want to sit again."

"Come on," she teased. "Where's the man who couldn't back down from a challenge?"

He made a face. "I think I left him out there in the meadow."

"Nonsense. Come on." She started into the barn, leading Cinnamon.

Brad managed to follow. She unsaddled Cinnamon first, leaving Midnight for Brad to hang on to. She put Cinnamon in her stall and turned back to Brad.

He was looking a little better. "You can let go now," she said. "Hang on to the post there, if you want."

He shook his head. "I'll wait over there in the corner. Think I'll lie down."

"Okay." She watched him go, step after careful step, to collapse, slowly, on the straw.

When she finished with Midnight, she went to kneel where Brad lay on his side in the straw. "Come on," she said. "We'll get you a hot bath. That'll make you feel better."

He looked up at her, mischief in his eyes. "I know what'll make me feel better."

She giggled. "What about your poor backside?"

He grinned. "I don't have to use it for what I have in mind."

"You're incorrigible," she said.

"I know. You told me that before. But it's not my fault. It's because of you. You do these wild things to my libido."

The barn door slammed open and Fanny and Ellen skipped in, Harry cavorting at their heels. Harry spied Brad and ran over to lick his face. "Harry," Brad said, defending himself with one hand. "Come on now. Enough's enough."

"Whatcha doing in the straw?" Fanny asked, scooping up the wiggling puppy and hugging him.

Ellen giggled. "Do you think they were kissing?"

Fanny shook her head. "Nah. Aunt Jenny's not blushing."

Jenny swallowed a laugh. The girls were impossible. "Brad took a tumble while we were riding. He's sore. He was resting while I unsaddled the horses."

"Oh," Fanny said. "I'm sorry." She tucked Harry under one arm and started for the tack room, Ellen at her heels. "We'll get Grampa's liniment. It works good."

"What's with all the questions about kissing?" Brad whispered, laughter in his eyes. "Are those two psychic?"

"Nope. They're just growing up. They're curious, that's all."

"I hope it's all," he said. "I thought I knew kids, but I guess I don't know as much as I thought. At least, none of the kids I've photographed have ever asked me questions like that."

By the time they reached the kitchen Brad was wishing he'd kept his mouth shut and done his suffering in silence. Now Fanny and Ellen wanted to know every particular of the ride—and the race. An irate father couldn't have done a better job of cross-examining him. Finally Sue said, "You girls scat now. Brad's tired of all your questions. He's going up and soak in a nice hot bath."

"Can we—" Fanny began. For a minute he actually thought they were going to ask if they could watch! He caught Jenny looking at him and saw the laughter in her eyes. Had she guessed what he'd been thinking?

"Can we walk down the lane for the mail?" Fanny finished.

"All right," Sue said. "But come right back. And don't let Harry cross the property line. He has to learn where he belongs."

"We know, Mommy."

Brad smiled to himself. Lucky Harry to belong here, with these loving people.

He picked up the liniment and started toward the stairs. Slowly.

"Dinner'll be ready in about an hour," Jenny's mom called after him. "Take your time."

Brad chuckled weakly. "I'm afraid I'll have to."

Five minutes later he sank into the tub of hot water with a sigh of relief. He'd have to get over this stiffness before tomorrow. He had to spend six hours on the road then, and another six the next day. And, so far as he knew, there was no way to drive without sitting down.

He leaned back in the old tub and let the water wash over him. If only there was some way to stay in Iowa longer. Maybe he could plead his bruised and battered backside. But no, that wouldn't be fair. If Jenny couldn't get back to that Simon Legree of a boss, she'd have her stomach tied up in knots. They had to leave on schedule.

But there hadn't been any schedule this afternoon out there on the prairie. Lying in each other's arms, he'd kissed her till he thought their lips would fall off. And she'd kissed him back. He couldn't believe the way she'd opened up to him. What was it she'd said that night after the storm? She thought maybe she'd been struck by lightning?

He just hoped it would last. He could see them in his house, or hers, or another one. The house didn't matter. He could see them waking up in the morning in the same bed, turning to each other with love on their faces. That would be so wonderful, so incredibly wonderful.

He sank lower in the water and let himself remember the feel of her against him, the love in her eyes. Oh, yes, please God, let it last.

Chapter Twenty-four

Sunday morning came far too soon. Following Sue and the girls into the family pew, Jenny couldn't believe time had passed so quickly. Thank goodness Brad had nearly recovered from his fall. He moved a little slowly sometimes, and he sat down even slower, but otherwise he was all right. And a good thing, too—they had to leave for home this afternoon.

She didn't want to. She wanted to stay here forever. She didn't want to go back to Cleveland, to Morris and all that trouble.

It hardly seemed possible that time had passed so quickly. Two and a half days gone already. She and Brad had spent hours walking and talking. Sometimes Fido and Lady had gone with them; sometimes they'd ranged by themselves. But always at dark the dogs were back at the farmhouse, ready to eat and settle down for the night. Pop's suggestion had worked. Worked real well.

Sue's girls had gone crazy over Harry, dressing him in their doll clothes, putting ribbons on his collar, playing with him till he fell asleep in their arms. And Harry soaked up all the attention they could give him. So that had worked out, too.

And the hours she'd spent alone with Brad, in the barn making love—their roll in the hay, he called it—and out in the meadow after the race, just lying there in his arms, kissing. It was hard to believe that just kissing could be that good. But it was. She could have kissed him for a whole day.

She glanced sideways at him sitting in the pew beside her. This was the first time she'd seen him dressed up, wearing a suit and a white shirt and a tie. He looked great, like an advertisement for a men's magazine. He had his hair pulled back in a ponytail, of course. Not that anyone here would care. Iowa wasn't the end of the world, after all. But she'd rather see him in jeans, in the kind of clothes he wore when they walked the dogs. That was the Brad she was coming to love.

These days with Brad had worked so well. She felt relaxed and happy. Happier than she'd ever felt before. Maybe she wouldn't need the time she'd asked him for. Surely she could trust him. He would never hurt her. She could believe in him.

Pastor Schmidt always preached a good sermon, but though she tried to listen, Jenny was having trouble getting his words to register. All she could think about this morning was that she didn't want to leave Iowa. And as soon as they shared the dinner that Mom had left cooking in the oven, they would have to leave. She and Brad would have to head for Cleveland. She didn't want to go back. She didn't want to go to work again. Morris & Pleasant seemed like another world, a world she didn't even want to think about, let alone go back to. But she had to. There was reality, after all, and she had to bow to it. At least until May. After that she'd have enough saved to look for other work.

And then church was over. With Brad behind her and the family behind him, Jenny followed Sue to the front door. Suddenly Sue stopped. She turned, her face pale. "I really didn't think—" she began.

But Jenny had already seen. They were there by the front door: Hugh and Melodie. Hugh looked as good as always, rock-star handsome in his expensive silk suit and fancy leather loafers. But she'd seen through him yesterday, and though she'd examined her feelings toward him again, she couldn't find even the littlest smidgen of pain or regret that they weren't still together.

She didn't feel anything except indifference for him. And disgust at the way he'd treated Brad.

And Melodie . . . Melodie was dripping diamonds, as usual, wearing what was obviously a designer outfit. Expensive and beautiful. And she was stunning in it. Naturally.

"There's—" Jenny began, turning to Brad. And her words died in her throat. He was staring at Melodie, really staring. Jenny swallowed and tried again. "There's Melodie," she managed to get out. "Hugh's wife."

Brad nodded, but he didn't look at her. He couldn't seem to tear his eyes away from Melodie. Jenny felt the bottom drop out of her stomach and pain hit, pain as she'd never known it before. Her stomach seemed to flip clear over and send out wave after wave of sickness. *Don't,* she wanted to scream. *Brad, don't you be taken with Melodie, too! Not you.*

"Let's go," Pop said from behind her. There was subtle warning in his voice, and she straightened up when she heard it. She knew what he meant. A Carruthers had pride. He wanted her to remember that. She wouldn't let on if her heart was breaking. She didn't want Hugh to see. He was so conceited anyway, he'd think her being upset was about *him.* And Melodie didn't need to know either. She had enough men panting after her.

Jenny took a deep breath, raised her face to Brad's, and smiled. It was a false smile, but no one would know that. At least she hoped not. She put her arm through his. "Come on," she said. "You've already met Hugh. Now you should meet Melodie."

Brad gave her a funny look, as though he was wondering what was wrong with her, so maybe the smile didn't fool him, but he came along anyway.

"Hello, Hugh," she said, proud of her calm, level voice. "Hello, Melodie."

"Good morning, Jennifer," Melodie said in cultured tones. She turned a smoldering glance on Brad. "And who is this good-looking fellow?"

"This is Brad," Jenny said, willing herself to keep the smile on her face. "Brad Ferris. He's a friend of mine from Cleveland."

Melodie wrinkled her perfect nose and sent Brad another smoldering glance. "Cleveland? Dreadful place, don't you think? At least I've heard so. No culture to speak of. I much prefer New York City."

"I like Cleveland myself," Brad said, shaking the hand Melodie offered him and dropping it quickly. "It has a lot of advantages people don't ordinarily hear about." And he turned and smiled right down into Jenny's eyes—in a way that could only mean one thing. Or should.

She felt her face flushing, but she smiled back. Let them think she and Brad were in love. Even though they weren't. Even though he was so taken with Melodie's beauty that he could hardly stop looking at her. It wouldn't hurt Hugh to think someone loved her. Wouldn't hurt him to know that someone wanted what he'd thrown away. If he wasn't too dense to see what was right under his nose.

"Well," Pop said, "you tell your folks hello for us, Hugh. We've got to get along now. Sarah's got dinner cooking in the oven. Wouldn't want it to burn." And he ushered them out.

Back at the farm Jenny changed out of her rose-colored suit and into her traveling clothes. She carried her suitcase down to the front door and went to the kitchen to help with dinner while Brad loaded the car and got it ready for them to leave. "That Melodie," Sue said. "She's such a—"

"Now, now." Mom took the roast out of the oven and turned to place it on the counter. "Let's not be uncharitable about the girl."

"But she just lords it over everyone," Sue complained, making a nasty face and plunking the loaf of bread on the cutting board as if she wished it was Melodie she was getting ready to slice. "Her and her expensive outfits. And those flashy diamonds. Does she have to wear them all at once?"

"But," Mom said, "we should feel compassion for the poor girl."

"Compassion?" Jenny echoed, almost dropping the pan of corn in surprise.

"Poor girl?" Sue stopped, the bread knife in midair, to stare.

"Yes," Mom said with a sweet smile. "After all, isn't she married to Hugh?"

Sue broke into laughter, and Jenny laughed, too, but she wasn't really amused. They could say all the nasty things they wanted to about Hugh. She didn't care about him at all. His dumping her had been a blessing in disguise, and seeing him hadn't hurt the least bit.

But seeing Melodie—or rather, seeing Brad look at Melodie—*had* hurt. A lot. Were all men like that? Was that all they cared about—a woman's looks? If that was true, she might as well give up now. She couldn't compete with a woman like Melodie.

"So, Jenny," Mom said, a big smile on her face as she carved the roast, "when can we expect our invitations?"

Jenny put down the bowl of salad she'd just taken out of the fridge. She swallowed hard. Now what was Mom talking about? "Invitations to what?"

"The wedding, silly."

"Whose wedding?"

Sue giggled. "Come on, Jen, we've got eyes. We can see what's going on. Brad's really in love with you."

Jenny sighed. Yesterday she would have agreed with them. Wholeheartedly. But now, with the memory of Brad staring at Melodie fresh in her mind, she couldn't be sure of anything. "I don't know if I want to get married. I mean, I've got lots of time yet."

Sue put down the bread knife and shook a finger at her. "Jennifer Marie Carruthers! If you let Brad get away, you should have your head examined."

"But men are so—different," Jenny said. "I mean, Hugh told me he loved me. He told me that for years. And I believed him. Then look what he did to me. And look at what Peter did to you—you were married to him and he ran off with someone else. And Mr. Morris," she lowered her voice. "Don't tell Pop, please. I don't want him to know about it. But Mr. Morris has been stealing my designs, taking credit for them himself."

"Jenny," Mom said, her smile turning to a worried frown, "that's wrong. That's real wrong."

"I know, Mom." She should have kept that to herself. Why had she ever mentioned Mr. Morris to Mom? She might have known that would make her upset. "But that's what I'm saying here. You want me to trust a man. And how can I do that when all around me I see men cheating and lying and stealing?"

Mom shook her head. "Jenny, Jenny. All men aren't alike. No more than all women are alike. Or all horses. Or all dogs."

"That's right," Sue said, giving Jenny a hug.

"Think about this a while. We're not like Melodie, are we?"

Jenny made a face. "I should hope not!"

"Well, then," Sue went on, "you've got to judge each person on his or her own merits."

Jenny supposed that made sense. "Well, I guess I can try."

Chapter Twenty-five

"I can't believe the weekend is over," Brad said, heading the wagon out the lane. "I'd give anything to make it last longer. I just don't want it to be over."

"Me neither," Jenny said, leaning back in her seat with a big sigh. "I hate going back to Morris and Pleasant. I just hate it. The new project waiting for me, the same old rat race. And Morris just as nasty as always."

"I wish you didn't have to go back there ever again," Brad said. "You really ought to get out of that place."

"Let's not talk about it."

He turned to look at her. Good grief! She seemed to have wilted already. Leaving her family had taken the glow out of her face just like that. Or wasn't it leaving that had done it? Was it having seen Hugh this morning? She'd been awfully quiet on the way home from church. And she'd hardly said a word through the monstrous lunch her mother had laid out for them.

Yesterday she'd said Hugh didn't mean anything to her anymore. And he'd believed her, though he didn't know what the guy had said to her before he rode away. But this morning she'd gotten all dressed up—in that gorgeous rose-colored suit and high heels. Until this morning he'd never seen her in anything but jeans. But she was gorgeous either way. Even more gorgeous without a stitch on. Or covered in mud, as she'd been that first night. He'd never seen anything more beautiful than her mud-covered face when she came into his arms that night. Never.

But the stricken way she'd looked at Hugh this morning . . . His stomach hit the floor just remembering it, the sickening feeling that had swept over him when he saw her face. He'd had to fight hard to keep from dragging her right out of there, away from that bastard. It was hard to understand how she could look at the guy that way after his rude behavior yesterday. But some women were turned on by rudeness. Or so he'd heard.

Still, that didn't seem like Jenny. She was so kind-hearted, so caring. But love was a powerful thing. Who could say why a person loved someone? Or why they went on loving him even when they weren't loved in return?

He swallowed a sigh. Hugh was a real scumbag, hurting her as he had. How could anyone leave Jenny for a plastic clotheshorse wife? Melodie; it didn't even sound like a person's name. How could anyone love such a mannequin? For all her so-called beauty, Melodie couldn't hold a candle to Jenny. Not in looks. And certainly not in character.

But maybe he was just borrowing trouble. Maybe it was just heading back toward Cleveland and that lousy job that had gotten Jenny so depressed again. Working for Morris must be a real drag.

"Shall we plan on stopping at Joliet tonight?" he asked, hoping to get a smile out of her. "Maybe we can get our old room again."

She gave him a funny look. "The dog show must be over by now. We can get two rooms."

His heart dropped again. Now he was sure. Something was definitely wrong. "I guess so," he said, not knowing what else to say. He couldn't push her. "I was only kidding." Why did she look at him like that, like he'd suddenly become a stranger to her? He'd have sworn she was softening toward him, that the trip was accomplishing what he'd hoped it would, that maybe now she'd be able to love him.

Hadn't they made love twice? And both times

it'd been her idea. Well, she'd been the first one to mention it, at least. But now it looked as if the last few days might as well not have happened. And all because of Hugh. He wished he'd tangled with the guy when he'd had the chance. Though he'd probably have lost the fight, and looked even stupider than he had flat on his back on the grass. But there was no way a man who'd never been on a horse could win a race against one who'd ridden all his life. And Hugh knew that. For sure he knew it.

Brad sighed. Looked like vacation was over. He'd known he'd have to get back to reality again. He just hadn't been expecting to have to do it so soon.

He must have sighed really loud, because Jenny leaned over to pat his hand. She gave him a sad little smile, and said, "Sorry, Brad. I'm kind of down today. I'm not very good company, I'm afraid."

"It's okay," he said, and tried hard to mean it. "I'll keep quiet and give you some peace."

She gave him a grateful glance and turned to gaze out the window again.

He'd keep quiet, all right. What else could he do when she had that haunted look in her eyes again? But keeping quiet wasn't what he wanted to do. He wanted to stop the car and pull her into his arms. He wanted to hold her and kiss her until she forgot all about that so-and-so Hugh.

According to Jenny, Hugh was a guy who always got his way. Well, if yesterday was any example, he was a first-class manipulator. Brad frowned. Manipulating wasn't *his* style. He had to respect Jenny's wishes, whether he agreed with her or not.

He turned to look at her again and, in spite of his sadness, he had to smile. Fido was peering over the seat at her. While Brad watched, the dog leaned over and licked her ear. She reached up a hand to ruffle his ears, but she didn't look at him.

Brad turned back to the road. The trip had been a great success. Until this morning. Until she saw Hugh. What he wouldn't give to get that guy in a dark alley alone! Well, he couldn't. So he might as well concentrate on driving, getting them home safely. He could do that for her, at least.

Fido licked Jenny's ear again. What on earth was wrong with her? Everything had been going so well, Jenny and Brad communicating as they should. And now this had to happen. Why were humans so difficult to train? But he didn't have time for philosophical questions now. Clearly something had gone wrong between those two. He licked Jenny's ear to comfort her again and then curled up beside Lady.

Let's see now. Jenny'd been fine when she got up this morning. She'd come downstairs humming a happy tune under her breath. She'd smiled through breakfast, laughing and joking with her family, and she'd held Brad's hand on their way out to his car. So whatever had changed her had happened after that. While they were away from the house.

He sighed and snuggled closer to Lady. She opened one eye and licked his nose sleepily, then settled back down again. Whatever had happened to Jenny must have had something to do with that human on the sun-colored horse, that human who thought he owned the world. Well, he didn't own Jenny, and he wasn't going to either. He, Fido, was going to make sure of that. He'd get this thing straightened out yet.

They reached Joliet about dark, after a long, silent ride that seemed to Brad to take days instead of hours. He didn't ask Jenny about the rooms again, just went and registered for two, next-door to each other. While she took care of the dogs, he carried in the suitcases. At her door she smiled at him, but the haunted look was still in her eyes, as though something was giving her awful pain, something deep inside her where he couldn't reach.

He didn't know whether to try to kiss her good night or not. Last night he'd kissed her automatically, after checking up and down the hall to make sure her nieces weren't watching. But today . . . The way she'd been behaving since this morning, she might not want him to kiss her. But if he didn't, he'd be losing all the ground he'd gained and . . . Why did things have to be so darned complicated? Why couldn't she just love him the way he loved her?

"Good night, Brad," she said. "I'll see you in the morning."

He took a step toward her, one little step. Might as well risk a kiss. But before he could take that last step, before he could get his hands on her and pull her into his arms as he wanted to, she turned her back on him and went inside the room, Fido right behind her. And he was left facing a closed door.

"Well, Lady," he said, his spirits falling, "guess we might as well go to bed."

Inside the room, Jenny stood looking at the bed, tears in her eyes. Brad had turned down the covers for her, making it as inviting as he could. And to one side, on the low chest of drawers, he'd put her suitcase. It wasn't the same room they'd had before—it was on the opposite side of the parking lot—but it looked the same.

And the bed looked so empty. If she closed her eyes, she could almost see Brad lying there, waiting for her. She could see his chest covered with golden fuzz, and his long muscular legs, and the loose hair curling around his dear face.

The tears she'd been holding back since that

morning came rushing out, and she turned to the bathroom. She'd just take a shower and go to bed.

But though she stood in the shower and let the tears flow, even let herself sob out loud while the sound of the shower would hide it, it didn't really help. She came out of the shower cleaner but no nearer sleep. Still, she did all her usual bedtime chores, climbed into bed, and turned out the light.

Then she stared up into the darkness. Yesterday she'd been so happy, sure that she was going to make a future with Brad. Even seeing Hugh hadn't bothered her. But now that was all gone. Now Melodie had managed to ruin her life again.

"A person's responsible for her own life. Can't put the blame on anyone else." She could hear Pop saying it, as he'd said it so many times when she was growing up. And she'd always believed him. Until that mess with Hugh, at least. Having your fiancé walk out on you just a month before the wedding was bound to leave a girl a basket case. Eventually she'd pulled herself together, graduated from college, and got a job. Gone on with her life. Or thought she had.

But doing that had been easy compared to this. She'd been so close to finally letting herself love Brad, to wanting to spend the rest of her life with him. And now all that seemed impossible. How could she trust him after the way he'd looked at Melodie?

Well, she didn't have to think of Brad as a potential husband. She never should have done that in the first place, never should have forgotten her no-men rule. He was still a good friend. Look at how patient he'd been today. Not talking when she didn't want to talk. Not getting all pouty and bent out of shape because he couldn't have what he wanted tonight. Hugh would have had some pretty sharp things to say about that. He'd have made her feel so guilty that she'd have given him anything he wanted, whether she felt like it or not.

She swallowed a sob. Brad had turned down the bed for her when he knew she was going to sleep in it without him. He was a good man.

It had even looked as though he meant to kiss her good night after the distant way she'd treated him today. But she couldn't handle kissing him. Not tonight. She'd been afraid she'd burst into tears. If she started crying, Brad would keep after her to explain why. So she'd come inside, away from him, though that wasn't what she really wanted to do either.

What she really wanted was to go back in time, back to before this morning. She pulled the other pillow over so she could wrap her arm around it, as she'd wrapped her arm around him, those times they'd been together. But this wasn't the time to think about that. It was time to go to sleep. And tomorrow she'd be a better companion. After all, they could be friends, even if they couldn't be anything else. Lucky thing she'd insisted on there being no strings attached to their making love. Lucky, sure.

In the room next door Lady paced from one side to the other. Back and forth, back and forth. "Why don't you go to sleep?" Brad asked. "You can't pace like that all night."

But she didn't pay the least bit of attention to him, just kept on pacing back and forth, back and forth. Hell, he didn't feel like sleeping either. He wanted Jenny. He wanted her here in the bed with him. He wanted to kiss her, and undress her, and make love to her. And lay beside her all night, feeling her softness against him.

But he wasn't going to get to do that. He might never get to do it again. No! He slammed one fist into the other palm. He wouldn't believe that. He loved Jenny. He loved her and he wouldn't give up. No matter what.

Leaving Lady still pacing, he stripped off his clothes and went to take a cold shower. He had to get through the night somehow. There was a lot of driving to do tomorrow.

Chapter Twenty-six

Around the middle of Monday afternoon Brad turned into Jenny's driveway. She'd been different today, talking and laughing. But not the way she'd been on the farm. He had a funny kind of feeling that she wasn't really there, that some vital part of her was missing, left behind in Iowa, maybe. With that bastard Hugh. Still, today had been better than the silence of yesterday. Anything was better than that.

He turned off the engine. "Here we are. Home at last."

"Yes," she said. "Now, before I go in, I want you to tell me what I owe you for Harry. I want to reimburse you for him."

"No." The word came out harder and flatter than he meant it to. "I mean, that's not necessary. After all, I stayed at your folks' place for the whole weekend." He managed a chuckle. "And I ate enough food to feed an army."

She frowned. "But there was the expense of the motel and our food, too. And gas."

"It was worth it to me," he said. "Where could I get a vacation like that for so little? And I got a home for Harry at the same time." He managed a little laugh. "Besides, the whole trip didn't cost me as much as one night of Harry on a chewing rampage."

That got her. He could see her thinking about it, about the damage Harry could do, damage that could run into hundreds of dollars. That was no exaggeration, either.

"Well . . ." She hesitated. "I guess it's all right, if you put it that way. But thank you for taking me. Us." In the backseat Fido sat up and eyed the tailgate.

"You're welcome," Brad said. He wished he could say what was really on his mind, ask her why she still loved a man like Hugh Devon. But love was a really weird thing. She probably couldn't help loving Hugh, any more than Brad could help loving her. "I just wish coming home hadn't been such a downer for you."

She shrugged. "Oh, don't worry about it. I guess seeing the folks makes me miss them even more."

"Yeah." That wasn't all of it, but he wasn't going to challenge her. He was walking on eggshells here. If he said the wrong thing, she might tell him to get lost. Permanently. And then he wouldn't even have a chance with her. Better to be her friend than nothing at all.

He opened the door and went to take her stuff out of the tailgate. There was only her suitcase and the bag with Fido's blankets and bowls. She'd left most of the dog food for Harry, and the rest the dogs had eaten on the way home.

Fido jumped out and Lady tried to follow him. But he'd put her on the leash again when they started traveling and tied it to the seat. She gave him a disgusted look. "Sorry," he told her, "we've got to go home."

He passed Jenny the bag of Fido's stuff and picked up her suitcase.

"I can carry that," she said, sticking out her hand.

"I know." But he didn't hand it over. "Just following our usual routine. You handle the dogs, I handle the luggage."

She gave him a bewildered look, as though her mind wasn't really on what they were saying. Probably it wasn't. Probably she was thinking about Hugh, wishing she could be back in Iowa with him.

"Oh," she said and went ahead of him up the steps.

Brad put the suitcase down by the back door. "Well, I guess that's it. I'd better get home and get ready for work tomorrow. Got a big day at the studio, lots of appointments."

She nodded. "Me, too. Tomorrow it's back to the grindstone. I've got to get started on that new project."

He couldn't help himself. He said, "I hope you didn't bring it home."

She shook her head. "I didn't. I don't even know what the project is. I left it in my office. So I have one more night of freedom."

"Good." He didn't quite know how to say good-bye to her. Actually, he didn't want to leave her. He never wanted to leave her. But what he wanted didn't matter here. It was what she wanted that counted. "Well, see you."

"See you," she said, her eyes glazing over with the sadness he'd seen in them so often, the sadness he'd thought he'd driven away until she saw Hugh again.

He turned away. If he didn't get out of there soon, he was going to kiss her. And from the look on her face that would be a big mistake.

Jenny watched him go. Some part of her wanted to call after him, to tell him not to leave her, that she loved him, but she swallowed the words without saying them. She couldn't love him. She couldn't love any man. It hurt too much.

She carried her stuff inside and took off her coat. Dumping Fido's blanket in its usual place, she looked around. She didn't want to be here. She didn't want to be alone. Most of all, she didn't want to think.

She took her suitcase into the bedroom and, while Fido watched, put her stuff away. Clean things in the closet and drawers, soiled things in the hamper. Slippers under the bed. Toiletries in the bathroom. Everything in its place. But that only took a few minutes. And it was still the middle of the afternoon. The whole evening stretched before her, with nothing to do but think about Brad and what might have been.

"I can't do this," she said aloud and headed back to the kitchen and her coat. "Come on, Fido. Let's go see if Clara's home."

Clara *was* home and eager to hear all about the trip. She stood aside for Fido and motioned Jenny into the kitchen. Fido crossed the linoleum to sniff noses with Duchess, and Clara bustled about, putting on the kettle and setting out teacups and the inevitable plate of cookies. "Do tell me, dear. Did the little girls like Harry?"

Jenny smiled. "Oh, Clara, yes. They loved him. You should have seen them, dressing him in doll clothes. And he liked it, too. He just ate it up, the little stinker."

Clara laughed. "I hope he didn't *eat* the doll clothes. I never saw a dog could chew like that one."

Jenny chuckled. "Well, he's met his match with Sue's girls. They'll keep him so busy, he won't have time to chew on anything!"

She looked around the sunny, cheerful kitchen. "I'm glad to see your house seems to be back to normal. Are things going all right now?"

"Oh, yes." Clara smoothed her apron. "Duchess is just wonderful. She's such good company and she never makes a mess. You did a fine job picking her out."

Jenny looked down at the tabletop. "Not me. Brad's the one who picked her out."

Clara beamed. "Well, I'm sure you helped."

"Actually, I didn't. You see, I feel the way you do about the shelter. If I went there and couldn't bring them all home, I'd feel haunted by the ones I'd left behind. And Brad saw that. So he offered to go there alone."

"He's a dear boy," Clara said, turning as the kettle started to whistle. "You're lucky to have him."

"I guess so." That didn't sound right, but she just couldn't get enthusiastic about the man now, not when she kept thinking about yesterday, about him looking at Melodie like that.

Clara turned back with the teapot and peered at her. "Why, my dear, why do you sound so sad? What's gone wrong between you?"

"N-n-othing," Jenny said, but the word wasn't very convincing, especially when it ended in a wail.

"Now, now." Clara poured a cup of tea and set it in front of Jenny. "You just have a nice cup of tea and tell me all about it."

And to her surprise, Jenny did—all about Hugh and those years in high school and college when she'd tried so hard to be everything he wanted her to be, and gotten dumped anyway when gorgeous, rich Melodie came along. About Sue's husband leaving her and the girls for a younger, prettier woman. About Mr. Morris and the way he refused to give Jenny credit for her designs.

Clara stirred sugar into her tea. "That's terrible, dear, but what has all that got to do with Brad? He seems like such a nice boy. And he likes you, I can tell. I thought you'd have a nice weekend together."

"It *was* nice," Jenny said. "Real nice. Until Sunday morning. Until we went to church. Hugh was there, you see. Hugh and his wife, Melodie."

Clara looked puzzled. "But I thought you were over this Hugh. You said you were lucky he dumped you."

"I was," Jenny said. "Seeing him didn't even hurt. I don't care about him anymore. But Melodie was there and—"

Clara looked even more puzzled. "But if *he* doesn't mean anything to you, why should she?"

A big sob threatened to choke Jenny. She swallowed it down and went on. "Because of the way Brad looked at her! Like she was something so special, so wonderful. It was like the whole thing happening all over again. I wasn't anybody compared to her."

Clara's eyebrows shot up. "Don't tell me Brad Ferris ever said such a thing to you!"

"Of course not. He's too nice for that. But I could tell. He couldn't keep his eyes off her. And after that nothing seemed right anymore."

"Dear, dear." Clara sipped her tea and stared thoughtfully into the distance.

Jenny sipped, too. Well, she'd made a real idiot of herself, blubbering all over Clara this way. The woman would think she was crazy. But she did feel a little better. Just talking to someone had helped.

Clara put her cup back down on its delicate saucer. "You know, dear, I can't help thinking you're wrong about this. Even if Brad *did* look at this woman, that doesn't mean anything. Men like to look, you know. It's part of their nature. But I've seen the way Brad acts with you. And I truly believe he cares for you."

"I thought so," Jenny said, looking down at her cup. "And I wanted to care for him. It's hard, after Hugh. After being hurt that way it's really hard to trust. But I was getting there, I was letting down my guard, and now this happened." She stared into her teacup. "I can't help it. I just want to run away and hide."

"Running away never works," Clara said,

shaking her head. "I learned that just lately." She smiled. "In fact, I learned it from the two of you."

Jenny looked up in surprise. "You did?"

"Yes. Before I met you I was a lonely old lady who never left her house, not even to get groceries. Now I go out every day. Duchess and I walk to the grocery or the drug store. We see people and we talk. I even go to church on Sunday. I've made a lot of new friends there. And I'm entertaining company. Other company, besides the two of you."

That *was* good news. It was great to see Clara looking so happy, just beaming over her teacup. "Clara, that's marvelous! But we didn't do it. You did."

"Maybe so, but it all started when you came into my life. You helped me. And I want to help you. So, I'm telling you, I wouldn't run away and hide. Hiding doesn't work. It just leaves you lonely and more miserable. I know. If I were you, I'd give Brad another chance."

"But it's hard to do that," Jenny said. "It's hard to trust after you've been hurt so bad."

Clara nodded. "I know. But—" The doorbell rang. "I'll be right back," she said. "Have another cookie."

it out? And then she smiled at him, and he decided he couldn't leave yet, not when he could be with her.

"Hi, Brad," Jenny said. "Guess you decided to see how Clara was doing, too."

"Yeah." That reason would do as well as any. He couldn't very well tell her that he'd been going crazy at home, that he missed her like the very devil and had come here to get away from memories of her. Memories of her lying on him in the mud with the rain pouring down on them, of being in the shower and washing her, of their making love in the hay, of those wonderful hours of kissing in the meadow the day he'd taken his fall. Memories of walking hand-in-hand around the farm, seeing the places where she'd grown up. Memories of standing by the graves of her dead animal friends while she mourned their passing. And, worst of all, the memory of the look on her face when she saw that bastard Hugh in his Italian silk suit. He'd never hated anyone before, not even his parents, but with Hugh it'd sure been easy.

"Sit down," Clara said, bustling about the kitchen. "I'll just get out another cup. And I have some more cookies in the cupboard. I was hoping you'd come to see me soon."

He sank into the chair across from Jenny and took Lady off her leash. She went right to Fido, of course—no problems for those two. Brad swallowed a sigh. Maybe it was a good thing he'd come to Clara's. Looked as if he needed a good dose of sugar. He sure needed something. The cookies didn't look that tasty to him, but maybe that was because he'd been off his feed since things had gone wrong with Jenny. Besides, he'd eaten enough over the weekend to last him a month.

Clara was smiling at him and putting a cup of tea in front of him. He swallowed another sigh and reached for a cookie. If he didn't eat some, she'd have her feelings hurt. And she was too nice a person for that.

"It's good to see you both," Clara said, settling into her own chair again and picking up her cup. "It's been a lonely time with you gone."

Jenny started to say something but, at a look from Clara, drank tea instead.

"But I'm doing better," Clara went on. "I have more friends now. And I walk Duchess every day. But I still miss you two. You were my first new friends."

"I'm glad things have worked out for you," he said. "I owe you a lot for taking care of Lady."

Clara smiled. "Well, that's all right. You brought me Duchess. She's a great friend." She motioned toward the corner where Duchess lay beside Fido and Lady, who were sniffing noses. Then she grinned. "Jenny tells me her sister's girls liked Harry."

He chuckled. "Boy, did they! They loved him to pieces. Those two are about as hyper as

Harry. They'll keep him busy, I can tell you."

Clara laughed. "I'm just glad it's them chasing him, not me. Duchess is more my speed."

Jenny laughed, too. Brad looked at her in surprise. He hadn't heard her laugh since early yesterday morning. What had happened to make her feel better? Well, he wasn't likely to find that out, but he sure could appreciate it. He settled down and reached for another cookie, smiling at Clara. "Tell me about these new friends."

More than a hour later Jenny looked out the window at the fading light. Time to get home. She put down her cup. "It's going to be dark soon. I've got to get going."

Brad straightened up, his face looking strained. "Me, too. I didn't see your car outside." He hesitated, almost as if he was afraid to say what he really wanted to say. But finally he got the words out. "I'm walking, too. Shall I walk you home?"

Clara was looking at her encouragingly. She winked, and Jenny knew what she thinking—give Brad another chance. Well, she could do that much. And she *did* want to keep him as a friend. "Okay."

Clara beamed. "Listen, you two. I know it's early yet, with Thanksgiving just over and all, but I want to get my invitation in before you get any others."

"Invitation?" Brad asked.

"Yes. I'm going to have a party on Christmas Eve. My first party since—since Horace passed on. I want you both to be there. It won't be right if you're not." She twisted her apron and looked at them anxiously. "Please say you'll come. Please."

Jenny looked at Brad. He probably had something else going on. After all, his job didn't take his evenings, too, the way hers did. He might have all kinds of social opportunities. He might even have a girlfriend. Well, that was stretching it. He'd spent too much time with her lately to be having a girlfriend, and if he did, he wouldn't have been sleeping—

"That'd be great," Brad said enthusiastically. "I don't have any plans at all."

Jenny let out her breath slowly, carefully. Did that mean he was hoping—

"You do now," Clara said, and turned to Jenny. "You'll come, too, won't you, Jenny? You aren't going home for the holidays, are you?"

"No." She wished she was, except that going home would be so different now. The old place would be full of memories of Brad and the time they'd spent together. "I'm not going home. I don't like to make the trip in winter. Driving in bad weather makes me nervous." She looked at Brad. "I was lucky to have Brad take me home for Thanksgiving. It was great seeing my family."

"You'll come to my party then?" Clara said. "Please?"

"Yes," Jenny said, giving in to the inevitable. "I'll come. What can I bring?"

"Oh, don't bring anything!" Clara shook her head. "Just bring yourself. It's my party. I'm looking forward to getting ready for it. I haven't had a real dress-up party for a long, long time."

"All right," Jenny said. "But you be sure to tell me if there's anything I can do to help. It sounds like fun." It would certainly beat last Christmas Eve, a terrible night that she'd spent alone, remembering Hugh and the way he'd betrayed her.

Fido came over and put his head in her lap. She smiled. "Looks like Fido's ready to go, too." She got to her feet.

Brad chuckled. "I'd swear he knows what you're thinking. That dog has got to be the smartest animal around."

"He is," she said. "He's smarter than most people I know."

They were at Jenny's back door all too soon. Brad stood there tongue-tied. He wanted so much to tell her how he was feeling, how much he missed her, how much he needed her, but he didn't dare. He could still remember telling his mother, "I love you," and waiting to hear her say in response, "I love you, too." He knew other kids got that answer. He'd seen it on TV—parents told their kids they loved them. But he'd waited in vain. He never wanted to feel that way again, so empty, so useless, so worthless. By the time he was ten he'd learned his lesson so well that he'd stopped saying the words, stopped even hoping his parents would love him. He'd kept his love for Tuffy, with a little left over for Mrs. Vincent, the closest thing to a grandmother he'd ever known.

It had taken him years away from his parents to find the self-esteem they'd denied him. He had it now, but he was still afraid sometimes, afraid that he'd be rejected and have to suffer that pain again. Besides, Jenny had been so strange these last couple of days. She must still be pining after her Hugh. It was better to give her a little time to forget about him. Hard as it might be. There was no sense in making a wrong step and having her push him out of her life altogether.

Jenny turned to face him, her face shadowy in the light of the porch lamp. "Thanks for walking us home."

"It's all right," he said, glancing down at Fido. "I know it wasn't necessary. Fido'd take good care of you." He managed a little chuckle, though it sounded artificial to him. "But I needed the exercise. I bet I gained five pounds while we were gone."

That got him a smile, faint as it was. "Me, too. I'd ask you in for some coffee, but—"

"I know. You've got to get up in the morning. Face Simon Legree. Besides, I'm pretty well water-logged already."

She nodded. "Me, too. When she wants you to eat or drink Clara can hardly be resisted."

He made a face. "Don't I know it! I wonder what kind of food she'll put out for her party."

"Lots of goodies, I bet. Full of sugar. You should be happy."

"Yeah," he said. "I guess I should be." He hesitated. Well, ask her idiot, he told himself. "I heard you say you don't care much for winter driving. Shall I plan to pick you up that night?"

"I—" He could almost see the wheels turning in her mind. Too bad he couldn't tell what she was thinking. "I suppose so," she said finally. "Unless you want to take someone else."

What the hell was she talking about? Take someone else? Not much chance! Couldn't she see he was wacko about her? "No," he said, fighting to keep his voice calm. "I don't want to take someone else. I want to take you."

He studied her face, but its expression didn't tell him anything. "Well, then," she said, "I guess you can pick me up."

She hadn't sent him away! He wanted to throw his hat in the air and yell hurrah. He settled for grinning like an idiot. "Great."

Maybe he shouldn't push his luck, but . . . "And don't forget, you said you'd come down to the studio and watch me in action."

She nodded. Her expression didn't change. "I did, didn't I?"

"Yes, you did. When will you come?" He didn't want to push, but he had to be sure of having some time with her before Christmas.

"I'll think about it," she said. "But I've got to get the new project off the ground first."

"Okay." Still he stood there, waiting, wanting her so desperately. He wanted to touch her, needed to touch her. "Jenny?"

She gave him a quizzical look. "Yes, Brad?"

"Could I—Would you do me a favor?"

Her eyes glittered in the lamplight. "What is it?"

"Would you—Would you kiss me good night?" He didn't know where he'd found the guts. Maybe because his need was so great. He tried for humor. "It's that addiction of mine, you know."

She didn't smile. "Well . . ."

Could that be amusement in her eyes?

"Please?" He wasn't used to wheedling, but he didn't mind doing it for her.

And then she laughed. She actually laughed and his world grew brighter. "Oh, all right. Come here."

She put her arms around his neck and raised her lips to his. "But don't make me do all the work."

He kissed her then, kissed her long and hard, with all the longing that had been building up in him since yesterday morning. When he finally released her a great sigh escaped him. "Thank you," he said. "Good night. Sleep well."

And then he tore himself away, before he grabbed her again and made a fool of himself.

Jenny closed the door behind her. What a kiss! Had she made a mistake telling him she'd kiss him good night? He'd looked so sad, and she'd wanted to make him feel better. He had been good to her, after all. And in spite of the way she'd treated him the last couple of days he'd been patient and kind.

But she hadn't counted on the kiss getting so intense that she didn't want him to stop. For a second there she'd wished he wasn't so polite, that he'd pick her up and carry her inside. That was foolishness, of course. She was inviting heartache to keep sleeping with him before she knew for sure that he was *the* man for her. And she wasn't sure about that. Not now. At the farm, she'd been sure, but she wasn't anymore. Still, Clara had been right: Brad deserved another chance. You didn't ditch a friend just because he liked to look at women.

She dropped into a chair and Fido came to put his head in her lap. "I'm a mess, aren't I, boy? First I love him, then I hate him, then I love him again. A basket case, that's what I am! Between Brad and old man Morris I'm losing my mind!"

From under a fringe of tangled hair Fido's dark eyes gazed into hers. She scratched behind his ears, in the place she knew he liked best. "Can men really be trusted?" she asked him. Fido's tail brushed the floor. "Well, I trust you, of course, but I'm still not sure about Brad. How can he kiss me like that after the way he looked at Melodie yesterday? Oh, Fido, I don't want to love him and I do want to love him." She ruffled his ears. "What am I going to do?"

For the millionth time Fido wished he could talk. But at least now he knew what was going on, what had made Jenny so upset yesterday. Something to do with another female, and with Brad looking at her. He didn't understand why that should upset Jenny. Males always noticed females. It was their nature. And Brad would never love another female the way he loved Jenny. Fido could see that. Clara Kelly could see that. Anyone could see it—anyone but Jenny.

Of course, dogs did have some advantages. They could tell things through their sense of smell. If Jenny could smell, as he could, she'd know the smell of longing was strong on Brad—longing and worry hung all around him. He was afraid, afraid Jenny was going to send him away.

And so was Fido sometimes. If only he could get her to stop this stubborn silliness. Brad was the human for her. And Jenny was the human

Chapter Twenty-eight

It was almost a week before Jenny could arrange to visit Brad at the studio while he worked. The new project Morris had given her was almost as bad as the Viking one, and as usual he hadn't given her enough time to do a really good job on it. But she settled in, working long hours again, her only social outlet the evening walks with Brad and their visits to Clara on weekends.

Brad showed up every evening, even after the ground was covered with snow, to insist that she get out for a walk, although it would be just a short one. They walked the dogs and talked, and every night when they got back and said good-bye outside her back door he asked her for a good-night kiss. Since she'd given him the first one, it seemed a little weird to refuse him others. And besides, she was getting used to having that kiss herself, needing it as the warm ending to their walks. And every day she felt a little more the way she had in Iowa, thought a little more about a future with possibilities, a future that included Brad.

"I'm glad you brought Fido," Brad said, opening the studio door for her that sunny Saturday morning. "Come on in. Let me show you around."

"Sure." Brad looked really good in his working clothes of faded jeans and white shirt, the sleeves rolled halfway up so she could see his arms. Of course, he looked good in anything.

"This is the waiting room," he said, gesturing around.

She looked at the desk where the phone sat. "Your receptionist doesn't work Saturdays?"

He shook his head. "I don't have one. I have a good answering machine and I keep regular hours." He grinned. "I'm a man who likes to live simply. I save my money for important things." He chuckled. "Like houses—and dogs."

She grinned, too. "I know what you mean." She looked around the waiting room. Comfortable-looking washable chairs lined two walls. One corner had a child-sized table-and-chair set and books in a small bookcase. An open toy chest revealed toys waiting to be played with. But what caught her eye most was an entire wall covered with photos, mostly of babies. And all of them smiling or laughing.

She stopped to admire them, then turned to him. "Brad," she said enthusiastically, "these are really great. I'm so glad you asked me over."

He looked a little sheepish. "Thanks. I enjoy being with the kids. And it's a job."

"It's more than that," she said. "Anyone can see you really put your heart into it."

The doorbell rang. "That must be Mrs. Cooper," Brad said. "She has the next appointment." He motioned to a door at one end of the room. "The studio's in there. Why don't you go in and sit down? There's a chair in the corner for visitors. Take Fido along if you want."

"Okay." She went in and settled into the chair. Fido sank down at her feet, his head on his paws. She was glad to have him along. Funny how much comfort a dog could be.

A woman came in carrying a baby, a cute little fellow, probably seven or eight months old. His mother had him dressed up, of course, but his clothes seemed awfully fancy even for picture-taking.

"Mrs. Cooper," Brad said, "this is Miss Carruthers. She's come to observe today."

Mrs. Cooper looked at her and Jenny's stomach clenched into a knot the size of Pittsburgh. Mrs. Cooper looked—like Melodie! The same smooth-skin veneer, every hair in its place, not a wrinkle in any piece of clothing. And worst of all she had a body guaranteed to heat a man's blood and expensive clothes designed to show off every curve of it.

Jenny swallowed hard. *Stop it!* she told herself. How ridiculous to be thinking about Melodie now. Mrs. Cooper had a baby. She probably had a husband, too. Someone had to pay for those clothes, and a working woman wouldn't dress that way anyhow.

"Hello," Jenny forced herself to say. "I'm pleased to meet you."

Mrs. Cooper gave her one disinterested glance. "Hello." Then she shrugged and turned away.

She didn't need to be so cold and distant. After all, she had all the advantages. The looks, and the money, and even a husband.

"Okay," Brad said, crossing to his camera. "Now, Mrs. Cooper, if you'll set Johnny on the table there by the wall. Maybe give him that stuffed horse to play with. Then stand to one side, not too far away. So you can get to him if he moves."

Mrs. Cooper crossed the room to put the baby on the table and then smiled at Brad, the same kind of seductive invitation that Melodie issued to any attractive man within reach. Jenny's stomach did flip-flops, and for a minute she thought she was actually going to be sick to her stomach. But she wouldn't. She wouldn't give in to such silliness. There was more than one woman like Melodie in the world. Jenny didn't have to like it, but it seemed she'd have to get used to it.

Mrs. Cooper smiled again, and Brad smiled back. "Move him a little to the right," he said, leaving the camera and going over to the table to help her. "That's it. Good. Now turn him a little. Like this."

Mrs. Cooper turned the baby, all right, and in the process managed to brush against Brad. Jenny couldn't see his face, but she could see that he took his time moving away, adjusting the baby again before going back to the camera. That must mean he liked having the woman come on to him.

Jenny's hands tightened into fists. It wasn't just Melodie. Women like her, women like Mrs. Cooper—women who were always after other women's men—made her so mad she could scream. But it wouldn't do Brad's business any good to have a crazy woman go screaming around his studio. And anyway, Brad wasn't *her* man. She'd better remember that. She'd told him no strings, and she'd *meant* no strings.

A cold nose pushed against the fist she'd clenched in her lap. And there was Fido, looking up at her. He had sensed her feelings and gotten up to console her. Good old Fido. He always knew what she needed. Too bad she couldn't find a man as trustworthy as Fido. She could love a man like that.

She rubbed Fido's head, smoothing the soft hair away from his eyes, eyes that seemed to say, "It's all right, Jenny. I'm here for you." Thank goodness she still had Fido, that she hadn't been able to scare him away that first day. She could hardly imagine what her life would be like without him. How lonely and empty it would be.

Mrs. Cooper smiled up at Brad. "Mr. Ferris, Brad . . ." she began, moving toward him in a way that definitely wasn't motherly.

Fido let his head stay in Jenny's lap. She liked to stroke his fur. It seemed to calm her. He liked it, too, of course, but it probably did more for her than it did for him. After all, he was no pup. He'd been around for a while. Still, pup or not, everyone needed strokes. Speaking of which, he wished Brad had let Lady into the studio, too. He'd like to be out in the kitchen with her, but it smelled like Jenny needed him in here.

He'd already smelled her anger, and her fear, both of them directed at the woman with the baby. Strange that Jenny should be this angry at a woman she'd never met before. But he didn't care much for the looks of the woman himself. She didn't look like the sort to be a good mother. Mothers were supposed to be tousled and rumpled. They should be too busy taking care of their litters to be all fancied up like this one.

Brad stuck a funny hat on his head and made faces at the baby, coaxing him to smile. Jenny laughed. The baby laughed, too. Brad took one shot and then another.

"Ah, Brad," Mrs. Cooper began, leaving her post by the side of the table and moving toward him.

The baby leaned toward his mother, toward the sound of her voice, reaching out for her with chubby little hands. But the woman wasn't watching the baby. Not at all. She was too busy looking at Brad. Humans and dogs might do it differently, but it was easy to see that the woman was in heat.

The baby rolled to his hands and knees and looked around, his bright little eyes following his mother as she moved away from him.

"Brad," Jenny said.

But Brad was too far away. And so was that excuse for a mother. Fido didn't wait. He jumped, just as the baby's hand went off the table. The rest of the baby followed his hand as he slid over the edge toward the floor.

Jenny cried out. Then Fido couldn't hear much but the baby wailing, and his mother screaming. But Fido couldn't let that bother him. He'd reached the table just in time to get a mouthful of the baby's pants. And there he stood, a screaming, kicking baby hanging from his jaws, suspended just inches above the floor.

That one's pups wouldn't live long if she didn't do a better job of mothering.

"Good boy," Brad said, rushing over. He took the baby under his flailing arms. With a sigh of relief Fido let go. That baby was heavy. "Easy there, little fellow," Brad said. "I've got you. It's all right now."

Fido came back to Jenny. "Good dog," she crooned, scratching behind his ears. "Good, good dog." He sighed in satisfaction. At least Jenny and Brad appreciated him. They knew it was a good thing someone was around here to watch out for that baby. If most mothers were like that Mrs. Cooper, humans wouldn't get a chance to grow up and cause each other trouble. But Jenny wouldn't be like that. Jenny had heart. She'd be a good mother. The best.

Jenny sat there, almost in shock, absently petting Fido. Fido had saved the baby from a bad fall, a really bad fall. Good old Fido. He always knew just what to do.

Brad hefted the baby to his shoulder and patted his back. The baby's screams turned to sniffles. "Maybe you'd better take Johnny," Brad said to Mrs. Cooper. "He's still a little scared."

"Of course he's scared," she said, giving Fido a dirty look. "That dog had him in his mouth! Now, now, honey. That nasty dog won't hurt Mommy's snookums."

Jenny stiffened. Nasty! How dare she! Another one of those people who never took responsibility for their own actions, who always blamed someone else for what went wrong. Talk about ingratitude! If Mrs. Cooper hadn't been so busy playing up to Brad, her little boy wouldn't have fallen off the table. And for her to call Fido a nasty dog—after he'd saved Johnny from a bad fall, a fall that was her own fault—that was going way too far. Someone ought to—"Listen here—"

"I don't think we're going to have much success today," Brad interrupted smoothly, giving her a warning look and easing himself between her and Mrs. Cooper. "Not with Johnny so upset. Maybe you should make another appointment for him. Some day next week."

"Of course. What a good idea." And Mrs. Cooper flashed another blinding smile in Brad's direction. What a fake the woman was! Poor baby, growing up with a mother like that.

Brad escorted her and the sniffling baby out the door. Five minutes later he came back to the studio, heaving a big sigh. "See what I mean? Some of these mothers will drive you crazy!"

Jenny heaved a sigh herself. Maybe she'd been mistaken about his reaction to Mrs. Cooper. After all, he was running a business here. He had to be polite to the customers. "Well," she ventured, "she didn't seem very motherly."

He raised an eyebrow. "No kidding! Women like that shouldn't be allowed to have kids. Kids need mothers who're real. Mothers who care about them." A pained look crossed his face. "Still, I guess she does love him."

Jenny wasn't so sure about that, but she didn't want to argue about it. Who could say about love anyway? And there was no sense in reminding him of his sad childhood, or the parents he said hadn't cared about him.

He hadn't liked Mrs. Cooper, then. Or at least he wanted her to think he hadn't. *Stop this,* she told herself. *He's not Hugh. Just because some woman came on to him doesn't mean you should suspect him of anything. You don't have to let Hugh ruin the rest of your life.* She tried for a smile. "So who's coming next?" Maybe the next appointment would be easier to stomach.

Brad consulted the book he'd carried back in with him. "Mrs. Ruether was supposed to come in with Tansy. She's a little doll. Two years old and all curls and dimples. But right now she's also all measles. Her mother called and canceled. And she was the only other appointment for today. So, that means I have the rest of the day free." He grinned. "Can I talk you into doing something with me?"

Jenny hesitated. She didn't want to go home and work on the new project. She was sick of it already, and she had to have some time off, give her mind a rest.

"Will you at least think about it?" he asked, his grin starting to fade when she didn't answer.

"Well, maybe. What do you have in mind?"

His grin came back. "We could walk the dogs."

She had to laugh. "We must have the healthiest hearts in town, given the amount of walking we've done lately. Some kind of record, too."

"And after that," he went on, closing the appointment book with a snap, "maybe we could take in a movie."

She tried to remember the last movie she'd seen. It hardly seemed possible, but she hadn't seen one since she'd moved to Cleveland, over a year ago. A movie might be a good idea, something to take her mind off Morris and his stupid project. "What's playing? I've been so busy, I haven't any idea what's out there."

A strange look crossed his face and was gone. She couldn't tell what it meant. Probably he was thinking about what an empty life she led. No recreation.

"Do you like science fiction, or action, or love stories?" he asked.

She shrugged. "It doesn't matter. Going was your idea. You pick the movie."

He shook his head. "But I want you to enjoy it."

"You pick it," she repeated, "and I will."

"Well, there's one about a dragon-killer just out. I've been wanting to see it."

"Okay. But I'll have to take Fido home first."

"How about if I pick you up around noon? We

could have lunch first and then take in the movie."

Lunch. They'd never gone out to eat together. Unless she counted those fast-food drive-throughs on the way to Iowa. "No fast food," she warned him.

He grinned. "Promise. I know a Chinese restaurant that makes the best cashew chicken in town. Do you like Chinese?"

She shrugged. "Let's find out."

A couple hours later, walking into the movie theater with Jenny beside him, Brad breathed a sigh of relief. The cashew chicken had been excellent and she'd seemed to enjoy it. He was still trying to believe that she'd said yes, that after all these weeks they had finally gone out to eat together. It was almost like a real date, even if it was only lunch in jeans and sneakers.

He'd like to see her dressed up again. He remembered that rose-colored suit she'd worn to church in Iowa—and how great she'd looked in it. But he hadn't wanted to suggest dressing up. That made it sound too much like a date. And she didn't date. Besides, she'd been wearing the suit the last time she saw Hugh, and it might make her think of him. Not a good idea. It'd be better if she never thought of Hugh again. Lots better.

He helped her off with her coat, settling it around her shoulders, wishing he had the guts to put his arm around her. Was he being too careful? But if he scared her, he might ruin all he'd accomplished so far. With a sigh he shrugged out of his own coat. *Watch the movie,* he told himself. *Just have fun.*

Halfway through the show, she tugged at his sleeve and leaned over to whisper, "Look at that dragon! It looks so real. I wonder how they do it."

"I don't know. Some kind of computer technology, I think."

She shook her head. "I should have known that. Probably like the programs I use at work."

He shrugged. "Couldn't prove it by me. I'm not into computers yet." He didn't tell her that computers seemed cold to him, that what he wanted was a real live person, right there in front of him, to speak to, to touch—to love.

The idea flashed into his head, crystal clear. "Maybe you could teach me about computers."

"Maybe," she said, her shoulder touching his. "We'll see."

Could he? Should he? What the hell! Nothing ventured, nothing gained. Isn't that what they said? He shifted a little, easing his arm around her shoulder. And she didn't move away! Instead, she gave a little sigh and leaned closer. Yes! He felt like leaping to his feet and shouting. Instead, he sat there, almost afraid to breathe, drinking in the scent of her hair, of the soap she used, and thanking his lucky stars that things had worked out like this.

If there was just some way he could make her love him. *You ought to know better than that, Brad Ferris. You can't make anyone love you. Didn't your parents teach you that—from bitter experience? Love is a gift, a gift you can't earn.*

Chapter Twenty-nine

The next Friday afternoon Jenny sat at her desk, her drooping head propped in her hands. What a day! She wished she had a couch in her office. She'd read somewhere that when something wouldn't work for Einstein he just took a nap. And then he'd get what he needed from his unconscious while he slept.

Yeah. Right. She could just see Morris's face if she asked him for a couch. The old man would probably throw a fit and pound his fist on that huge desk of his. She doubted that anyone had ever asked him for anything. She looked around the dinky office. Well, no matter. There wasn't room to squeeze another chair in here, let alone a couch.

You're getting off the track again, she told herself. *Relax. Give yourself time and the thing will solve itself.* She leaned back in her chair. It had always been that way—give it time and her unconscious would come through with whatever she needed.

She sat up straight again and glared at the wall. That was the rub, though, for she didn't *have* time. Morris was breathing down her neck all the time. In fact, he was expecting an update today. And he wasn't going to be happy with what she had to report.

A timid rap sounded on the door. With a sigh, she turned toward it. "Come in."

Phil opened the door, just wide enough to slip through, as usual. You'd think someone was after him. He shut it softly behind him. "How's it going?" he asked.

She shrugged. "So-so. I guess."

A frown wrinkled Phil's pale forehead. "Mr. Morris expects a report on the new job today."

"I know that!" She shook her head. "Sorry, I shouldn't have snapped at you. It's just—I don't work well under so much pressure."

Phil nodded. "I know. But you can't persuade Morris of that. He thinks pressure makes us work harder." He looked at his watch anxiously. "You're supposed to see him at two, right?"

"Right." She stared at him. "Phil, tell me something?"

"Sure."

"Why does everyone around here kowtow to Morris the way they do?"

Phil's eyes widened in surprise. "He's the boss."

She swallowed her distaste. There was no point in blaming Phil for what he was. "I know that, Phil. But not every boss thinks he's God. Or acts like it."

Phil's face turned even more pale. "Don't talk like that," he whispered. "He might hear you."

"Phil, the man never leaves his office. How could he hear me? Unless he's got the place bugged."

She'd meant it as a joke, but Phil didn't laugh.

"I don't think he has anything bugged," he whispered, lower still. "But he knows what we say to each other."

Jenny straightened, a chill shivering down her back. "You mean—you think there's a spy among us?" It sounded so melodramatic, said that way.

She had to lean forward to hear his whispered "Yes." And she didn't feel melodramatic then—she felt mad, spitting mad. "Who would do that?"

"I don't know. But someone is telling him things. Because he knows everything."

She shook her head in disgust. "You're a good architect. Why do you let him treat you like dirt? Why do you stay here?"

Phil looked at her as if she'd lost her mind.

"Come on, Jenny. I have a wife, five kids. I can't lose my job."

"Surely you could find another one."

He shook his head, his expression disbelieving. "I did that once before. It took me months. I can't put my family through it again."

She gave up. There was no getting through to him.

He looked at his watch again. "I'd better get out of here and give you a chance to get ready. Just wanted to say good luck."

"Thanks."

She stared at the door as he closed it after him. Poor Phil. He was scared to death of Morris. It wasn't right to live like that. It just wasn't right.

But she could hardly fault him. She didn't have anyone to support . . . well, except Fido; and she was going to put up with Morris until May, until she could get enough stashed away in her savings account to live comfortably while she hunted for another job.

She gathered her material and stood up. Time to face the ogre.

When Fido met Jenny at the door that night he didn't like what he saw. She looked worse than a lost dog. She was getting those dark circles under her eyes again. Looking almost as bad as she had before their trip to Iowa. She needed to get away from that boss of hers.

Every night she came home muttering about her work. But she was too proud to quit and go back to her family. He didn't want her to do that, of course, didn't want her to go away from Brad—or from Lady.

Yes, Jenny was proud. She had to take care of herself. But why couldn't she see that Brad loved her? Loving didn't have to keep her from being independent. Loving just made life more comfortable, gave you someone to share with, to curl up beside on cold nights. He'd learned that being with Lady. He sighed. Well, she was *his* human, so if she couldn't see what was under her nose, it was up to him to *make* her see it.

"Hello, Fido," she said, scratching behind his ears in the exact place he loved. She'd learned that real well. "How was your day? Mine was lousy."

He barked once and nosed her hand. Then he was out the door. Some things couldn't wait, even for Jenny.

When he came back inside she had put a glass of milk and an apple on the table. What she needed was a piece of good red meat to chomp on. How could she get any energy out of an apple?

She hadn't even taken off her workclothes, just kicked her heels into the corner. She ought to—

He straightened up and sniffed the air. That

was Brad coming down the street. Lady, too. Time to go into action. He limped over to his dish and sniffed at it.

But Jenny didn't notice. She didn't hear anyone coming, of course. Or smell them. They were still too far away for human senses. She sank into her chair and picked up the glass of milk, staring at it as though she didn't know what to do with it.

He turned as footsteps came up the walk. Then, waiting till he was sure she was watching him, he gave his best limp toward the door.

"Fido," she said. "What's—"

Brad knocked.

"Stay right there." She went to open the door.

"Hello," Brad said. "Ready for our walk?"

She shook her head. "I just got home. Haven't changed clothes yet."

"We'll wait."

"I don't think we can walk tonight," Jenny said. "Something seems to be wrong with Fido's paw. He's limping."

"Let me look at him." Brad stepped inside and slipped off his boots. "Maybe he's got a thorn in it or something."

Jenny shut the door.

So far so good, Fido thought. They were inside. He stood there, holding up one paw, trying to look as pitiful as he could. The things he did for his human!

"Come on, boy," Brad said. "Let me see your paw."

Fido limped over to where Brad knelt, pausing only long enough to sniff noses with Lady. She was with him on this. If they could just get these two stubborn humans together, there'd be two dogs who wouldn't have to spend their nights alone anymore.

He let Brad look at his paw, whining when he touched it, like something was wrong.

"I can't see anything," Brad said with a worried frown, "but something's hurting him. Maybe you'll have to take him to the vet."

Jenny nodded. "The vet's closed tonight. But if Fido's not better, I'll call in the morning."

Brad got to his feet. "Well, I guess that means no walk for us tonight."

"I'm sorry," Jenny said.

Come on, Fido thought. *Look at the man. He needs you.*

"It's all right," Brad said in a voice that said it wasn't all right at all. "I'll just go on home."

Good, Fido thought. *Make her feel sorry for you. That's the way to go.*

Jenny looked at Brad sharply. He didn't sound as though he was all right. And he looked about as bad as she felt. "Is something wrong?" she asked.

Brad sighed. "Oh, it was just one of those days. Nothing went right. Nothing at all. And to top it off I got a letter from my mother."

"Oh." What on earth had the woman said to make him look that awful?

"I was really eager for our walk," Brad said. "I wanted to have someone to talk to about—" He hesitated, looking over her shoulder.

"About what?" she asked. Something must have upset him a lot. He had that lost look in his eyes.

"Oh, just some stuff my mother said in the letter," he admitted, his face tensing. "I don't believe it, not really, but—" He turned toward the door. "Never mind. You've got your own problems."

She did. More problems than he knew. But she couldn't let him go off feeling so bad. "Wait." She took Lady's leash from his hand and unhooked her. "You're not going anywhere till you talk to me, tell me what's wrong." She grabbed his hand. "Come on in the living room."

She led him in and pushed him down on the couch. Then she settled sideways beside him, tucking one leg under her. He looked so lost and alone that she reached out and took his hand in hers. "I'm your friend," she said. She looked into his eyes. "You believe that, don't you?"

He looked back at her, his eyes dark with sorrow. "Yes. I believe it."

"Then tell me about this letter. I've never seen

you look so down. What on earth did your mother say to you?"

With a sigh, Brad looked into her beautiful, caring face. He wanted to hold her, to feel her against him. Not for sex, for comfort. For a while there, reading Mother's letter, he'd gone zipping back to the past, to the lonely, unloved little boy he'd once been. That little boy had had no friends, no one to turn to. But it wasn't that way now. He had a friend. He had Jenny.

"Tell me," she repeated, as the dogs came in and settled at their feet. "What did she say?"

He didn't need any more urging. "She said that she's disappointed in me. She said I've chosen to waste my life on a job that's meaningless. That I should have done something useful with my life." He repeated the words in the flat, mocking tone he used when talking about his mother and father. To use any other tone would be to reveal how much they could still hurt him. And he didn't want to do that—not even to Jenny.

Jenny's face darkened. He could see the indignation kindling in her eyes. It warmed him to think that she cared that much for him.

"Useful?" she repeated.

"Yes. Like being a doctor or a lawyer. A professional, she calls it."

"But you *are*," Jenny cried. "Photography *is* a profession. A good one."

He shrugged. "Tell that to my parents." He

reached in his pocket and pulled out the offending letter. "Here, you can read it for yourself. If you want to."

She took the letter from him, holding it up to the light to read. He watched her face, her beautiful, mobile face, as the emotions chased across it. Indignation, disbelief, and finally anger. Anger for him. Seeing that anger made him feel a hundred percent better.

"This is awful," she said. "Just awful. If I hadn't seen it with my own eyes, I wouldn't have believed it." She raised her hand to his cheek, touching it tenderly. "Oh, Brad, I'm so sorry. What can I do to help?"

"You're helping already," he said. "Just by letting me sit here. Just by letting me talk to you. That reassures me that I'm not the failure they say."

"You're *not*," she cried, and tears stood in her eyes. Imagine, tears for him. The pain of the letter was almost worth it to see Jenny standing up for him. For him!

But he didn't like to see her worried about him. She had enough worries of her own. "I'm sorry," he said. "I shouldn't have unloaded all that stuff on you."

"It's all right," she said. "Maybe—" She looked over his shoulder, her face closing down.

"Maybe what?" he urged.

"I don't want to make you feel worse."

He took her face gently between his palms.

Her cheeks were warm, her skin so soft, reminding him of that time in the barn. He pushed the memory far back in his mind. He couldn't think of that now. "Jenny Carruthers, are we friends or not?"

She smiled. "Yes. We are."

"Then tell me what's wrong." He traced the line of her chin with his thumb. "Something at work?"

She nodded, and tears filled her eyes. "Morris called me on the carpet today. I'm behind on the new project and he let me know it in no uncertain terms. But I don't work well under pressure. I need more time. And he won't give it to me."

"I'm sorry," he said. "I wish you could get away from him."

"I will. In May." She shuddered. "But May seems like an awful long time off." She took his hands from her face and held them in her own. "I'm sorry. I shouldn't have burdened you with this. There's nothing you can do about it."

"I can listen," he said. "The way you listened to me."

She smiled at him. "That's what friends are for, isn't it? To help each other."

He couldn't stop himself. He thought about their first night together, about the rainstorm that had thrown them into each other's arms and the way they'd talked about friends then, about helping each other through the night. But he didn't dare mention that. He didn't want her to think that he was playing on her sympathy. He would never do that. He loved her too much.

From his place on the floor Fido listened carefully. This was better than he'd expected. He'd meant to keep them inside by pretending a limp, hoping something would come of it, but he hadn't counted on Brad having something to say to Jenny, something that would make her feel so tender toward him. Or Jenny talking to Brad about her troubles at work. That was really good.

But why did she just sit there holding Brad's hand when she should be moving into his arms? This was the perfect time for it. Humans! They were so stubborn, so hard to teach. Well, he'd give her another minute or two. Then he'd have to do something himself.

Jenny blinked back her tears. She shouldn't be feeling sorry for herself. No matter how badly Morris treated her, she had her family behind her. But poor Brad—he had to face the world alone. She couldn't imagine parents acting the way his had. But she'd read the letter, seen the actual words. Brad must be hurting real bad. And there wasn't much she could do to help him. He did look a little better, though, since he'd—

Suddenly Fido jumped up beside her, hitting

her with his shoulder and knocking her sideways into Brad. Brad's arm went out to enclose her, and she ended up against his chest. She didn't move away. She could stay there for a minute or two, at least. It felt good to be close to him again. So good. "Sorry," she said. "I guess Fido lost his balance. It must be his sore paw."

"I don't mind," Brad said, his voice going husky. "I don't mind at all. I *wanted* to hold you. Maybe old Superdog knew."

She turned to look at him. A mistake because it put his mouth so close to hers, and she discovered she wanted to kiss it. Instead she asked, "Superdog?"

Brad chuckled a little. "That's how I think of Fido sometimes. He seems so smart. As if he knows things we don't." He gave her a funny look. "I never told you, but that night we got caught in the rainstorm, I'd have sworn that he got in the way of the door deliberately—so I couldn't shut it and keep Lady in."

She chuckled, too. "He's smart, but not that smart."

"Maybe not," Brad said, gathering her closer. "But I'm not all that sure."

He leaned back against the cushions, taking her with him. She could feel the tension easing out of him as bit by bit his body relaxed. She let her head rest against his shoulder, feeling his warmth, letting go of her tension, too.

"This is good," he said finally. "This is really good. I feel lots better."

She snuggled closer to him. "Me, too."

They stayed there in silence for a couple of minutes. Somehow her hand had gotten on his chest. She could feel his heart beating under her spread fingers. It seemed to be beating so fast, just as hers was.

Iowa seemed so long ago—two weeks that seemed like years. Had their lovemaking really been as good as she remembered it?

"Jenny?" Brad whispered into her hair.

She didn't think about evading his question. "I was thinking about Iowa. And how long ago it seems."

"Ages and ages," he said. There was longing in his voice. Was he thinking about the same thing she was?

"Brad?" she whispered.

"Yes?"

"Remember what we talked about that night—before we made love?"

"No strings," he said, his voice strange. "You said no strings."

She waited, but he didn't go on. "Remember anything else?" she asked finally.

"I remember every precious second," he said. "Which part are you talking about? Falling in the mud? Or washing you? Or making love? Or watching you sleep? Or waking beside you in the morning?"

"Actually," she said, "I was thinking of the song we talked about."

" 'Help Me Make It Through the Night'?"

She let the sigh escape her. He did remember. "Yes."

"Why are you thinking about that?" he asked, his voice deeper again.

"Because—" She hesitated. She could do this. She wanted to do this. And it wasn't just for him; it was for her, too. He needed comfort, but so did she. They could close out the world—his unloving parents and her tyrannical boss. For a little while they could make a new world, a beautiful new world just for the two of them. "Because I thought—maybe—maybe we could help each other through—*this* night." There, she'd said it. And she wasn't sorry.

His arms tightened around her. "You mean—" His voice cracked. "You mean the way we—did that night?"

"Yes," she whispered against his chest. "The way we did that night. If you want to."

"Oh, I want to," he said, longing in his voice. "I definitely want to."

"Then," she said, getting to her feet, "let's go into my bedroom."

He gave her a weak grin. "No straw and horse blankets this time?"

"No," she said. "Just a bed."

"That's all I need," he said. "A bed. And you."

* * *

Yes! Now they were definitely getting somewhere. What was it Brad had called him? Superdog? Fido grinned. He liked that. Not that he was conceited or anything, but he was pretty good at managing humans. He curled up around Lady and licked her ear. It shouldn't be long now.

Chapter Thirty

Jenny closed the bedroom door behind them.

Brad slid his arm around her waist. "Better pinch me," he said, "so I know I'm not dreaming."

Obligingly, she reached a hand around to pinch his behind.

"Ouch! That hurt." He rubbed his backside and grinned. "Well, I guess I'm not dreaming."

She had a sudden fit of the giggles. He stared at her in surprise. "I'm sorry," she managed finally. "I just—feel like giggling."

He grinned. "Why?"

"I don't know." She turned into his arms. "I guess because I feel so good."

"I'm glad." He smiled down at her.

She giggled again. "Remember that first time,

when we showered and you wanted to carry me to bed all wet and soapy?"

His grin broadened. "How could I ever forget it? I think about it almost all the time."

"Well, I have lots of sheets, and it's been a long, hard day, and the shower's over there and—"

"I can't believe it!" he cried. "Even with that pinch I can't believe we're going to be together again." He pulled her to him and kissed her; then he held her off and looked into her eyes. "I don't know what to do first—whether to rip off my clothes or rip off *your* clothes, or kiss you or—"

She laughed. "Well, why don't we just take our time? I mean, it's not as though we're in a hurry." A little niggle of doubt tiptoed into her mind. "Unless you have somewhere to go tonight."

He stared at her. "Are you kidding? This is where I want to be. Here with you."

He kissed her again, kissed her till she had to hold on to him to keep standing. Yes, she'd made the right decision. She *did* love him. Reading those awful things his mother had written had made her want to go and tear into the woman. But this was better. She could make him forget his mother and all those awful things she'd written. She knew she could.

She took him by the hand. "Come over here," she said. "By the bed."

"Sure."

"I want to undress you first. If that's all right?"

"Can't think of anything I'd like better," he said, his eyes gleaming. "Except maybe undressing you. I do get to undress you, don't I?"

"Right."

"I'm all yours."

"You know," she said, slowly unbuttoning his flannel shirt. "You know what I like best about you?"

He laughed. "My sterling character?"

She looked up into his face, his happy face. "Well, I like your character, of course. You make a wonderful friend. But I was thinking of something else."

"Tell me."

"That first day, when I brought Fido to your door and you laughed—"

He frowned. "I still feel bad about that. It was really a rude thing to do, laughing at you like that."

"Don't. You ran after me and apologized. Well, that day, when you pulled me up off the sidewalk, my hands accidentally touched your chest. Your bare chest, because you just grabbed a jacket to come after me."

She had his shirt unbuttoned now and she smoothed her palm slowly over his chest, running a finger around his nipple.

"I remember," he said, his voice husky. "I

could feel your hands on me for days afterwards."

She looked up in surprise. "You could?"

"Sure." He raised an eyebrow. "What do you think? I have women putting their hands on my bare chest all the time?"

She kissed one nipple, then the other. "I hope not."

"Me, too." He smiled. "After your hands I don't want anyone else's there. Now is it my turn?"

"I'm not done yet." She reached for his belt buckle.

"I mean, is it my turn to tell you what I first liked about you?"

"Sure. Go ahead." She slid his jeans down over his hips, let them fall around his feet.

"Well, let's see. First I noticed your eyes. You were so indignant. And then your mouth. I wanted to kiss it even then. And then when you flounced away I saw the rest of you, and—"

She felt the heat rising toward her face. "One thing," she said. "You were only supposed to think of one thing."

He shrugged. "Why? I could go on all night about your many charms." His jockey shorts fell to the floor. "But as soon as I get my feet untangled, I'm going to have my turn undressing you."

Seconds later he eased her out of her suit jacket. Then he was unbuttoning her blouse and putting it aside. He grinned. "No pink satin tonight."

"No. I wear serviceable white to work."

He unhooked her bra and tossed it after the blouse. "No matter. It's what's *in* the package that counts, not how it's wrapped."

He unzipped her skirt and slid it over her hips, pulling her half slip after it. "Panty hose," he said. "I never could figure them out."

She grinned. "It's easy. You just peel them down."

"If you say so."

His hands were warm against her skin, warm and tender. And then she was as naked as he was. He drew in a great, deep breath. "You're so beautiful. So very beautiful."

He pulled her into his arms. "Sorry, I can't wait. I need to feel you against me now. Right now. I can't think of anything that feels better than your skin against mine."

"I still think a horse's nose is softer than my skin."

He broke into laughter. "I don't think I want to go naked around a horse's nose. They've got teeth, too, you know."

The picture his words made sent her off into peals of laughter. "No, I guess not."

He held her off and looked at her again.

"I need a shower," she said, to cover her embarrassment. No one had ever looked at her the way he did, with such tenderness, with such longing.

"That's easily fixed," he said. "Just lead the way."

She led him into the shower. The familiar bathroom would never be the same to her. The memory of him in it, of him washing her back, of him holding her when they were all wet and soapy, of his deep laughter echoing off the tiles—those memories would stay in her mind forever. Like her memories from the room in Joliet, and from the barn at home. Had she made a mistake letting him so far into her life? But she hadn't made any promises to him. And she wouldn't, not until she was sure. Absolutely sure.

When they had finished washing each other he stepped out. "Now I get to carry you to the bed, soapsuds and all."

She grinned. "I'm game."

"You're also slippery," he said, swinging her up into his arms. "So hang on tight. We don't want to end up on the floor."

She wrapped her arms around his neck, and another giggle came bubbling out of her. "But we've never made love on the floor."

He laughed and held her closer. "Another time, maybe. Floors are hard, and tonight I've got my heart set on a nice soft bed."

He set her down on the bed and then he stood there, his eyes dark with longing.

She raised her arms to him. "What are you waiting for?"

"I just like to look at you," he said. "I have a picture of you in my mind. And I'm checking it against the reality."

She reached up and pulled at his hands till he came down on the bed beside her, till she could feel his body against hers. "Ahh, that's better. So, how do I stack up against reality?"

He broke into laughter again and raised up on one elbow. "You *stack up* just great," he said, kissing one nipple and then the other.

"I didn't mean—"

"I know." He fell back on the bed and pulled her close to him. "Oh, Jenny, this is so great. I've missed you so much."

"Missed me?" she said against his chest. "How could you have missed me? You've seen me every night."

"You know what I mean." He put a hand under her chin and tilted her face so she was looking at him. "I've missed feeling close to you and—"

The giggle came again. "Can't get much closer than this."

He laughed. "No. But we can try." And he kissed her.

Some time later Brad stretched and sighed luxuriantly. "I'm afraid it's illegal to feel so good."

Jenny smiled. "Then we'd better not leave the bedroom. Someone might see us and guess what we've been up to."

He kissed her nose, her sweet little nose. "I vote for that, but there's the little matter of food. We've burned up a lot of calories in the last hour."

She kissed his chest. "Hmmmm. And in such a nice way."

He grinned. "And we really ought to replenish ourselves."

She moved against him. "I thought we'd just done that."

He laughed. He couldn't believe the way she was acting tonight. The way she had after the rainstorm and in the barn. So open and loving. Did this mean that that Jenny was back? Would she go on being this way to him? Or would she be a stranger again tomorrow? But he wouldn't think about that. He had tonight. Best to just enjoy it.

He smoothed the hair from her forehead and looked down into her dark eyes. "Now who's being incorrigible?" he asked.

She laughed. "Me. And it feels really good. But if you insist, I guess we could go have an apple and a glass of milk."

He raised an eyebrow. "No pie or cake?"

She ran a hand over his stomach and dropped a kiss on it, making him forget all about food. "Not in this house," she said. "And if you don't lay off Clara's cookies, you're going to lose that washboard stomach."

He traced a line down her thigh. "And if you don't start eating better, you're going to waste away to skin and bones." He kissed the nipple closest to him. "Then you won't be stacked anymore."

"Don't worry about it. I'm developing a voracious appetite."

"For—" he started to ask, but her hand closed around him and he no longer had to ask. This was the closest he'd ever come to heaven. He lay back and enjoyed it.

And then he had to laugh.

"What's so funny?" she asked, bending over to kiss his chin.

"I just got a mental picture of my parents."

Jenny stared at him. "And you laughed?"

"Yeah. 'Cause I realized they can't touch me now. I don't care what they think. I only care what you think."

"In that case," Jenny said, with a wide smile, "you're going to get a swelled head, because I think you're the most wonderful man around. But if you don't kiss me again, I'm going to get right out of this bed and go eat apples."

Chapter Thirty-one

One week passed, and then another. The day before Christmas finally arrived. Jenny had been terribly busy at work, and exhausted when she got home, but somehow she'd managed to get her green velvet dress brushed, find her good shoes, and set out her good jewelry. Through the long working days she'd often thought about the party, about getting really dressed up and having fun with Brad—the kind of fun people could have in public. That always raised her spirits.

They'd *helped* each other several times since the night she'd read his mother's letter. Sometimes she thought their being together this way was all that got her through the long, miserable days—that and their nightly walks. Work was getting worse every day, Morris more and more demanding. But she kept herself going by looking forward to the holidays, to getting at least a brief respite from his tantrums *and* having more time with Brad.

But on the day before Christmas she came storming home from work, madder than a wet hen. Fido was there to welcome her, as always, but even his greeting couldn't calm her as it usually did. "That Morris!" she sputtered, slamming the door. "He's such a pig! Imagine him changing the deadline on me like that. First he says the end of January. Now he tells me he wants it all done by the second. The second! The man's impossible! Just impossible!"

She tossed her coat and scarf over a chair and kicked off her boots. "I suppose he expects me to work through the holidays. Well, I won't! I just won't! I've been looking forward to having some time off. And I deserve it!" She went to the refrigerator to get a glass of milk. Milk was supposed to be calming, wasn't it?

Fido barked twice. He must be hungry. "Sorry," she said, turning to him. "I—"

She stared at him in surprise. "Fido! I didn't know you could do that! When did you learn to sit up and beg?"

He held the position a little longer; then, with another funny look at her, he stood on his hind legs and did a dance. Then he laid down and rolled over to play dead.

"Fido! I can't believe it. What's with you? Where'd you learn all this stuff?"

He came to stick his nose in her hand and look at her quizzically with his dark eyes.

He looked so funny that she burst into laughter. "All right, all right. I get the message. Forget Morris. Enjoy the party."

At last, Fido thought. If he had to perform one more stupid trick, he was going to be sick. A dog of his quality shouldn't be forced into such silly antics. But he'd do anything for Jenny. And he didn't want her to be upset for this party.

This was a special party, a special night for her. He could smell her sense of anticipation. That was good. And maybe this was the night she and Brad would finally settle things. He certainly hoped so. This dog was getting tired of sleeping alone. He wanted the human thing settled so he could be with Lady.

An hour later Jenny opened the back door to Brad. He looked marvelous in a dark suit, a white shirt, and a green Christmas tie. A little blond curl had escaped his ponytail and lay against the collar of his shirt, making her fingers itch to touch it. He stood there, staring at her with his mouth open.

"Come in. Don't just stand there."

"Sorry," he said, shaking his head. "It's just—you took my breath away. You look gorgeous."

"Thanks. You don't look so bad yourself." Warmth rose from deep within her. This was how things were supposed to be between a man and a woman; this joy, this love. Being with him was wonderful, just being with him. More and more she was thinking that Mom and Sue were right about Brad; she *could* trust him. Brad *was* the man for her.

He stepped into the kitchen. "What a dress!"

It wasn't that sexy a dress. The scoop neckline wasn't low cut and the skirt wasn't short. But it did make her feel good, like someone special. Someone really special. And the look in his eyes told her Brad thought so, too.

Some hours later they stood at Clara's front door, the party still going strong behind them. "I'm sorry, Clara," Jenny said, "but I'm out on my feet." She was awfully tired, but more than that she wanted to get home, to ask Brad in and—

"I'm just glad you could come," Clara said. "But before you go I want to ask the two of you to stop around tomorrow. All my friends have family coming in." She sighed. "But my children can't get away this year. So I thought maybe you'd come over and keep me company. For a little while, at least." She looked at Brad and smiled. "There'll be lots of cookies left. I made extra on purpose."

Jenny looked at Brad, too. She did that a lot

lately, she realized; she looked to him before she answered questions. Was that some kind of sign that she trusted him now?

"I'm sorry," he said to Clara. "I can't make it tomorrow. I'm—"

Jenny swallowed. Weren't they spending tomorrow together? Christmas was a day for family—and lovers. He looked away, avoiding her gaze. What was wrong with him?

"I'm having company," he said to Clara. That explained it, then. But who could be coming to his house? He hadn't mentioned any close friends. And he was an only child.

"Company?" Clara asked, obviously surprised, too.

"Yes," Brad said, looking sheepish. "My—my parents decided to come for a visit. To see my house."

Jenny swallowed again. His parents? Why hadn't he told her they were coming? Maybe they'd called just before he left for the party, and then it had slipped his mind. Or maybe he didn't want to spoil the party for her. Probably he meant to tell her about it on the way home, tell her what time to come over tomorrow. She didn't look forward to meeting his folks, of course. How could she? After what she'd heard about them, after reading that hurtful letter, nobody would. But they *were* his parents.

"Well, of course," Clara said, smiling at Brad. "But what about you, Jenny? You'll come, won't you? Any time of the day. And bring Fido, of course. We wouldn't want to leave him alone on the holiday. Duchess'll be glad of the company."

"Okay," Jenny said. "I guess we can make it sometime tomorrow." She could visit with Brad's folks and then come over to Clara's. That would give her a chance to get away from them, not have to stay too long in their company. "And thank you."

"Yes," Brad said. "The party was great. I'm glad you've made so many friends."

Outside, Jenny huddled down in her coat and tied her scarf tighter around her head. The wind was really blowing up. She put her arm through Brad's. Now he'd tell her what time he wanted her to come and meet his parents.

"Let me see," he said. "The car's down this way. Nice party, wasn't it?"

"Yes. It was good to see Clara so happy. She's made a lot of new friends, hasn't she?" Why didn't he say something about tomorrow? Maybe he was waiting for her to bring it up. She took a deep breath. "I didn't know your parents were coming for Christmas."

"I didn't either," he said, his voice flat. "Not till they called this morning."

"Kind of late notice," she said. She'd thought they'd spend Christmas together, just the two of them. But that was out now. Well, she could share him with his parents. After all, they didn't get to see him often.

But he didn't ask her to join them. He just talked about little unimportant things. He talked while he walked her to the car, while he helped her in, while he drove to her house.

By the time they reached it her stomach was acting like a roller coaster, and she was having trouble thinking straight. He wasn't going to ask her over tomorrow. He wasn't going to have her meet his parents at all. What had made her think she'd finally found the right man? These last weeks hadn't meant what she thought. It was pretty obvious he didn't think he'd found the right woman. She'd fooled herself again.

She got out of the car and started for the back door. She just wanted to get inside, get away from him. But she wasn't fast enough. He was right there beside her. "I'm sorry about tomorrow," he said, looking really sad. "I'd hoped we could spend the day together. But they called this morning." His voice was bitter. "I didn't have the guts to tell them not to come."

She heard the pain in his voice, but she was hurting, too. "You can't tell your parents not to visit you on Christmas."

"I guess not," he said ruefully, "but I'd sure like to."

She put her key in the lock. "I've got to go in. Thanks for giving me a ride to the party."

He gave her a funny look. "Jenny, I—"

He didn't think he was going to come in! Not after treating her like some stranger. "Good night." She opened the door and went in, closing it behind her before he could say anything more, before she could burst into tears. She stood there for a minute, leaning her head against the door, wishing he'd pound on it, wishing he'd holler, "Jenny, Jenny, wait! You didn't let me tell you. I want you to come over tomorrow."

But there was no sound from outside the door. And then she heard his car pull away. She stood there a minute longer, blinking back the tears. Finally she straightened up. Crying wasn't going to do any good. It was late and she was tired. She might as well go to bed. At least asleep she wouldn't be able to think.

Fido stuck his nose into her hand. "I know, I know," she said. "You have to go out. And you're probably hungry. Come on."

Brad drove away in a haze of misery. He'd let them do it again. He'd let his blasted parents ruin this special evening. Because of them, he wasn't in there with Jenny in his arms. Because of them, Jenny had pulled away from him again. He could see the pain in her eyes, hear it in her voice. And that coldness, that lonely coldness that meant she'd withdrawn from him, that the Jenny he loved had disappeared. He'd never hear her say, "I love you," now. It'd be just like it was when he was a little boy. He'd wait and wait, and there'd be no one to say it.

She'd been happy enough at the party, until she found out his parents were coming. She was probably upset because he hadn't asked her over to meet them tomorrow. But that was really a kindness to her.

And anyway, what kind of a masochist did she think he was? He didn't want her to be there while they told him what a failure he was. And they *would* tell him; they would tell him through the whole visit. He could be sure of that.

Why did they have to come *now*, now when Jenny was finally letting him into her heart again? Why hadn't he told them not to come? Because, like a fool, he was still hoping against hope for the love they'd never given him, hoping for a real family.

He slammed a hand against the steering wheel. He was a fool, all right, wishing for the impossible. And now he'd gone and lost Jenny again. She'd become a stranger to him, cool and distant, like before. Only this time he wasn't sure he'd be able to get her back.

Jenny went to bed—she even went to sleep. But not for long. At 4 A.M. she was wide awake again, staring up at the ceiling. Another mistake. She'd made another mistake—thinking that Brad loved her. He didn't. He couldn't. If she meant anything special to him, he'd have asked her to meet his parents. Wouldn't he?

That's what people did when they cared about someone—invited them to meet their parents.

But Brad hadn't. Instead, he'd hemmed and hawed and left her to spend Christmas alone. The most important holiday of the year and she had to spend it alone.

She turned on her side, punching the pillow into shape. What was wrong with her that she let men treat her this way? Like she was a thing they could use. Just put her on the shelf when they didn't want her around and take her off again when they did. Cheat her and take credit for what she did. Treat her like dirt.

Enough! She punched the pillow again and rolled the other way. She was sick and tired of men and the rotten way they treated her. It was time to do something about it. Past time.

On the floor Fido put his head down on Jenny's slippers and sighed. The way she was tossing and turning, he couldn't sleep either. Something had her really upset, something to do with Brad and Christmas Day. He'd expected her to bring Brad in with her tonight, but instead she'd come stomping in alone, looking as though her world had come to an end. And just when things had been going along so well. Why, he'd been expecting them to make the final move any day now. He was really getting tired of spending his nights alone. So was Lady. She'd told him so.

Chapter Thirty-two

Jenny woke at first light on Christmas morning. "Yes," she said aloud, "I'm going to do it. I've had enough and I'm definitely going to do it."

She threw back the covers and swung her legs over the edge of the bed. Fido sat up. "Merry Christmas," she told him.

He got up to put his head in her lap. "I'm really lucky to have you," she said. "And guess what, I got you the biggest rawhide chew in the store. It ought to keep you busy for a while. Come on, let's go get some breakfast."

While Fido was outside, she fixed tea and a bagel. After she let him in she took her breakfast into the living room, switching on the lights on the little tree. Brad's present was still under it. She'd meant to give it to him today. It wasn't a boyfriend present, exactly; more like a best friend present.

She stared at the tree. If she didn't feel he was her boyfriend, what *did* she feel? And why was she upset that he hadn't asked her over to meet his parents? Maybe because he'd met her folks, and turnabout—

No. She'd better be honest with herself. Trying to hide from what she felt wouldn't help any. She'd been feeling the way she had in Iowa, only more so, feeling that Brad was a man she could love, could spend her life with. Not just *a* man, but *the* man. "And now look," she said to Fido, who was happily gnawing on his gigantic rawhide chew. "I've goofed again. I guess I was right. I should swear off men. Where they're concerned I'm not a good judge of character."

Fido dropped the chew and came to put his head in her lap again. "I'm good at choosing dogs," she said, "but not men." He nosed her hand so she'd pet him. "Well, okay, actually I didn't choose Torrie. And I didn't choose you either. You chose me. But I am lucky with dogs."

She rubbed behind his ears and looked at the clock. "Eight-thirty. Well, at ten I make my call." She glanced down at him. "You'd better make that chew last. I'm not sure when you'll be getting another one."

* * *

At ten o'clock Jenny picked up the phone. It might be better to wait till she could see Morris face-to-face, but she didn't want to wait. She wanted to get this over with. Finished. And get on with her life.

She might have known—an answering machine. Well, even Morris wasn't in on Christmas. But, she was going to do it anyway. And she was going to do it *now*. She pulled in a deep breath.

"Mr. Morris, this is Jenny Carruthers. I'm quitting. I'm giving you my two weeks' notice, as of now, today, December twenty-fifth."

She needed another breath to finish. "I'll do my best to finish my current project, but in two weeks I'm leaving. Whether it's finished or not." She put the phone back gently. No need to slam it now. She'd had her say.

She turned to Fido. "Well, I've done it," she said, rubbing his ears. "I've burned my bridges behind me. So we'll have to be careful till we—I—find another job. But don't worry, we'll manage."

Fido licked her hand and plopped down again. He wasn't worried. At least, not about having enough to eat. He was glad she'd told her boss she was through. She should have gotten out of that place a long time ago. Working there upset her, and life was too short for that. But there was still that smell of determination about her. Determination—and anger. And he didn't like it.

She was still angry with Brad. Something about the people who'd whelped him. Humans were an odd lot. Any sensible dog knew that once a pup was weaned you were supposed to teach him how to make his own way. And when he was grown you didn't come back and start telling him what to do. If you did, you were apt to be growled at, or even bitten. And you'd deserve it.

Jenny leaned back in the chair, staring at the little tree. They'd had such fun putting it up last week, she and Brad, laughing over the placement of each ornament. And then sitting on the couch together to watch Jimmy Stewart in *It's a Wonderful Life.* She'd ended up crying, and Brad hadn't laughed at her. In fact, his eyes had been suspiciously damp. And Fido and Lady had curled up together. The two of them got along as well as she and Brad did. Or had till last night.

This thing about his parents had really thrown her. He hadn't actually said he'd see her on Christmas Day, not specifically, but she'd felt he would, expected he would. After all, she'd seen him every day since they came back from Iowa. And every day, or every night, since the night he found Lady.

She sighed. How could she have been so mistaken about the man? Was she like one of those poor, frantic women who could be taken in by any smooth-talking man who came along? Did she want to be loved so much that she'd lost all her common sense?

No! She wasn't going through that again. She looked once more at the brightly wrapped presents under the tree. The dog pin for Clara, chews for Lady and Duchess, and the small box that held Brad's gift—a lapel pin shaped like a camera and a gift certificate for the camera shop, to go toward that new camera he'd been saving for.

The day stretched before her, a long, lonely day. Well, she wasn't going to sit there. She still had some options. She could call the folks. But they knew her voice too well. They'd know something was wrong. Better let them have their happy holiday first.

She could go visit Clara. But it was awfully early for that. She couldn't stay there all day. And after she left what could she do? Come home and feel bad again?

The light reflecting off the presents seemed to mock her. Some Christmas. Some holiday.

She got to her feet and headed for the bedroom. Enough sitting around feeling bad. She'd bought presents and she was going to deliver them.

At noon Jenny approached Brad's house, Fido beside her. She had the presents in a plastic bag. That was her excuse for being there. But she knew what she was going to do. She was tired of this roller-coaster thing with Brad. She was going to tell him what she thought. Give him his present and tell him good-bye. Tell him she didn't need any more men in her life, especially one who treated her so poorly.

She raised her hand to knock. Just a couple of months ago she'd stood here like this with Fido beside her. Then she hadn't had a dog or a man. Well, she had a dog now. A good dog. Too bad Brad wasn't as good a man.

She brought her knuckles down on the door, maybe a little harder than she needed to. But now that she was here, she wanted to get it over with. Otherwise she might lose her nerve.

The door opened. "J—Jenny!" Brad said.

She stared at him. He was wearing a suit, a white shirt, and a tie, and shining black shoes. His hair was slicked back in a ponytail. Who got dressed up like that for his parents? Her heart threatened to somersault right out of her mouth. Had her suspicions been legitimate? Was Brad cheating on her, too?

His mouth worked a couple of times. Finally he got out, "What are you doing here?"

She kept her voice calm, level. It wasn't easy, but she did it. "It's Christmas. I brought your present." She peered over his shoulder. "And I wanted to meet your parents." She gave him a hard look. "Even if you didn't invite me."

"I—ah—" He looked as though he was wishing for a hole to crawl into. But of course there wasn't any. Why couldn't he have just come out and told her the truth? Why couldn't he have said they were just friends instead of letting her think they were something else, something special?

Well, she was going to see for herself. She was here and she was going to see this other woman. She took a step forward. For a second he held his ground, and then he gave way, getting out of her path. "Ah—I meant to—"

She didn't wait for the rest of his explanation. She just stepped on in. She was going to see the woman. He owed her that much. "Where are *they?*"

"In—in the living room," he stammered. "But, Jenn—"

"Fine." She shoved his present into his hands and pushed past him. Might as well get it over with. Might as well—

In Brad's living room two startled people looked up. The man, who had a bald head and bifocals perched on the end of his nose, was reading the paper—from the size of it, *The New York Times.* The woman in the designer clothes and the bright red fingernails was freshening her makeup.

"Mother, Father," Brad said from behind her. "This is Jenny. I met her when Lady was lost."

"We told you not to get a dog," Brad's father

said with a dirty look at Fido. "Nasty things, full of germs." He patted the sheet that swathed his chair. "Why, in this house I have to cover the furniture before I can sit down. I told him, you don't want a dog. Nasty things. But he didn't listen. He never listens."

Jenny stood there, flabbergasted. This was worse than Brad had said. Not even a hello. Just right into the complaints. Right into tearing Brad down.

The woman shook her head, and not a hair on it moved. "The whole house is a pigpen. I don't think Bradley ever cleans a thing."

Jenny felt the hair on the back of her neck bristle. This was the woman who'd hurt Brad so badly, who'd made that little boy think he wasn't loved. And she looked like—Good grief, she looked like Melodie! This woman was Melodie to a tee, Melodie thirty years from now.

Well, that was it! It was time someone told Brad's mother how mistaken she had been. Jenny straightened her shoulders. "I think Brad keeps a very clean house," she said sharply. "I like his place just the way he keeps it. And besides, too much neatness destroys creativity. Makes a person into a martinet."

She heard his deep intake of breath, but she didn't turn to look at him. She didn't dare, not when she was thinking about the little boy who'd had to grow up with these awful people for parents. She didn't want to cry in front of these pitiful specimens, people who'd let a little boy hurt like that and didn't even care, didn't even seem to know.

She turned to Brad's father. "I'm sorry, sir, that you don't understand what fine friends dogs can be. They can make people into kinder human beings. And some people really need that."

Whoops! She might have overdone it. But who did they think they were, treating Brad like some kind of second-class citizen?

Good for you, Jenny, Fido thought. Maybe he should get into the act. That fellow in the chair—he definitely needed shaking up. Fido trotted over and plopped his head in the man's lap.

Brad's father jerked the paper aside, waving it at him. "Get! Bad dog! Get away!"

Bad dog, indeed! For a minute Fido wished he still had fleas. He'd like to give this guy a good dose of them. Or maybe a nice nip on the leg. But no, Jenny wouldn't approve of that. And dogs that bit could get into a lot of trouble. This guy wasn't worth it.

He looked to Jenny. She didn't call him back. She wasn't smiling, but she was amused. He could smell it.

"If you'd just give him a chance," she said. "Try to get to know—"

He stuck his nose into the man's hand.

"Ugh!" The man wiped his hand on his pants. "Filthy beast! Why should I want to know an animal? They can't think."

Can't think! That was the final slander. Fido considered relieving himself on the man's shoe. But no—that would be too embarrassing for Jenny. Better hold off, let her handle it.

He went back to Jenny. At least she was caring about Brad again. She was defending him. But imagine humans turning their backs on dogs—not the way Jenny had, because of the pain, but out of pure stupidity, because they didn't know the value of a friend. Thank goodness most people had more sense than that.

Jenny turned to Brad. His face was red, probably with embarrassment, but his eyes were bright. She looked around. "Where's Lady?"

"She's in the kitchen," Brad said with a look at his father. "Why?"

"I think she needs to take a walk."

Brad stared at her as if she'd lost her mind. "Walk?" he repeated.

"Yes," she said. "She needs to take a walk. Now." She turned to his parents. "You'll excuse us, won't you?"

Mr. Ferris had already gone back to his paper. It was obvious he couldn't care less what they did.

"Good-bye," Mrs. Ferris said, waving a red-nailed hand and opening her compact again.

Jenny pulled Brad toward the entry hall. "Get your coat and call Lady. Come with me. Please."

He looked at her numbly, but he shrugged into his coat, wrapped his scarf around his neck, and called for Lady.

Minutes later they were out on the sidewalk. Brad still looked stunned, but he walked along at her side, silent. And the dogs paced beside them.

Halfway down the block, Jenny stopped and turned toward him, putting a mittened hand on his arm. "Brad, stop please. I want to apologize to you."

His eyes widened. "To me? No, I need—"

"Just listen. I need to say this. All of it. I know I've been acting really funny today. Last night, too. I thought—" She swallowed. She had to say this, had to get it out, hard as it was. "I thought you were lying to me. I thought you had—another woman in there."

"Another wom—" he gulped, and stared at her. "Jenny, I—"

"I'm sorry," she went on. "But after Iowa, after the way you looked at Melodie, I thought—"

"After the way I looked—I was wondering how that creep Hugh could ever have preferred that clotheshorse to you. She was so artificial-looking. And she reminded me of my mother."

What he said made perfect sense, now. But she'd twisted it all around, let what Hugh had done to her creep back in to taint her life. Talk about stupid. She laughed out loud.

"What's so funny?" he demanded.

"Me. I thought you were so taken with her that you couldn't look away."

His eyes widened. "You mean, *that* was why you acted so strange on the way home?"

"Yes." She might as well tell him the whole thing. "Hugh—Hugh's leaving me hurt a lot. It was only a month before the wedding, you know. It made me suspicious of men, afraid to trust, afraid of being hurt. But I'm sorry I was suspicious of you. You've always been a good friend to me. I should have known better."

He patted her arm. "I'm sorry, too. I knew you were upset last night when I didn't invite you to meet my parents, but I couldn't do it. Jenny, you saw them. You saw what they're like."

She couldn't help sighing. "Yes, I saw them. But you'd already told me about them. And I'd read your mother's letter."

He snorted. "Telling isn't the half of it. And you can put a letter away and forget it." He grinned. "Especially if you have a friend to help you through the night." His grin faded. "But you saw how they are, how they talk. Nothing pleases them—and I mean nothing. I'm used to it, but I didn't want to subject you to it." He sighed. "They aren't like your folks. And besides, it's humiliating to be treated like a seven-year-old. A naughty seven-year-old."

"I know," she said, moving closer to him. "But it's all right now. I understand."

"Not quite," he went on, staring down into her eyes. "I haven't told you all of it. I didn't want you to meet them because—because I was afraid you'd say no."

What was he talking about? "No to what?"

He took both her mittened hands in his. "I wanted to ask you to marry me. I know you said 'no strings,' but these last weeks—everything has been so good between us. And I thought—I wanted to ask you to marry me."

The breath had left her lungs in one great whoosh. She hung on to his hands to keep from falling over. "Marry you?" she repeated.

"Yes. You see, I was afraid if you met them, if you actually heard the way they talk to me, you wouldn't want to marry me." He shook his head. "I had my proposal all planned. Until they called. I was going to ask you last night after Clara's party." He patted his pocket. "I even had the ring with me. But then I lost my chance. I couldn't ask you when I knew you were upset. And I couldn't bear to have you meet my parents."

Her heart was pounding like crazy. "Marry you?" she repeated, her throat gone dry.

"Yes. I know we haven't had a conventional courtship." He grinned ruefully. "We've never been out to dinner together. Only once to lunch and the movies. But we've walked a lot. And we've talked a lot. And we've helped each other through the night." He pulled her closer. "And I love you. I love you so much. So awfully much. I thought—I hoped—you loved me too." His warm, gray-green eyes eyes pleaded with her. "I know you're still hurting from Hugh, and—"

She didn't want him to think that. It wasn't true. "No, no, Hugh doesn't mean anything to me. When I saw him I knew it was all over. I already loved you. That's why, when I saw you looking at Melodie I went kind of crazy. I started thinking all men were alike. Like Hugh."

"We're not," he said, "any more than all women are alike. But you haven't given me an answer." His forehead wrinkled in a frown. "Will you? Will you marry me?"

"Yes." She threw herself into his arms. "Oh, yes." She didn't have a doubt now. This was the man she loved, the man she wanted to spend the rest of her life with.

He kissed her then, right there on the sidewalk. At about the same spot where she'd fallen and bruised her dignity that first day. Maybe they should put a marker up. This would always be a special spot.

Then he held her off a little and looked into her eyes. "You're sure? My parents aren't easy to get along with, you know. You saw them. Saw how they behave. They'll treat you the same way. Nothing anyone else does is right. And I mean *nothing*."

He smiled, a smile that warmed her through her whole body. "It was marvelous the way you stuck up for me," he said. "Nobody has ever done that before. It made me feel real good."

"Well, of course I stuck up for you." She looked into his eyes. "I love you," she said, emphasizing each word. "I love you and no one's going to trash you when I'm around. I don't care who they are. That's the way it's supposed to be, you know. We're friends. We stick up for each other. We help each other through the night."

He laughed and hugged her tight. "You're right." He frowned. "But that means I have the right to stick up for you, too. And I have to tell you, I don't intend to let Morris treat you the way he has been. It's just not right. And I'm going to tell him so. As soon as the Christmas holidays are over."

Laughter bubbled out of her and she kissed his chin. "You won't have to tell him. I quit this morning. Left a message on his answering machine. Gave my two weeks' notice."

He grabbed her and whirled her around and around. "That's great! That's just great!"

Finally he set her on her feet. "You said yes! You actually said yes!"

"There's just one thing," she said.

His face went serious. "Anything. Anything you want."

"Well, it's about the wedding. We've got to find a place to hold it, a place that allows dogs.

Fido and Lady have to be there. They brought us together. And Clara and Duchess." She laughed. "I suppose the girls will want to bring Harry."

"Of course," Brad said, pulling her into his arms again. "But I don't want to wait till spring, till we can have a garden wedding. I need you now. As soon as we can manage it." His voice turned anxious. "If that's all right with you."

She kissed him fiercely, right there in the street. "All right? It's more than all right. It's great." She leaned back in his arms. "But what about your folks? How are they going to take our getting married?"

"We could just not tell them," he said sheepishly. "Do the deed and send them an announcement afterwards."

It was a good idea. Too bad they couldn't do it. "Brad, we can't do that! My folks would never understand."

He sighed. "I suppose not. But it sure is tempting."

"Listen, we'll be all right. We've got each other. And Fido and Lady. And my family. And Clara and Duchess. We'll make it just fine."

"Your family's great," he said. "Do you really think they'll be happy about us?"

"Of course. Pop told me you were a keeper the first time he saw you, and when we left, Mom and Sue were already making wedding plans. I was the one who wasn't sure. But I'm sure now. Real sure."

"Good. Let's go tell my folks." He kissed her again. "Before you lose your nerve. And we can call yours."

"And Clara, we have to call Clara. Maybe I'll ask her to be part of the wedding party. She'd like that."

"Good idea," Brad said. And he kissed her yet again.

At last, Fido thought. Jenny had done it. And this time she hadn't even needed his help. Of course, there were still Brad's parents to deal with. He selected a tree and relieved himself. Those two were a challenge even for Superdog. But he was up to it. In fact, he already had a couple of ideas.

STOBIE PIEL

"An exciting new voice!" ***—Romantic Times***

Sheep, sheep, sheep. Ach! The bumbling boobs are everywhere, and as far as Molly is concerned, the stupid beasts are better off mutton. But Molly is a sheepdog, a Scottish Border collie, and unless she finds some other means of livelihood for her lovely mistress, Miren, she'll be doomed to chase after the frustrating flock forever. That's why she is tickled pink when handsome Nathan MacCallum comes into Miren's life. Sure, Nathan seems to have issues of his own to resolve—although why people are so concerned about righting family wrongs is beyond Molly—but she knows from his scent he'll be a good catch. And she knows from Miren's pink cheeks and distracted gaze that his hot kisses are something special. Now she'll simply have to herd the spirited Scottish lass and brooding American together, and show the silly humans that true love—and a faithful house pet—are all they'll ever need.

_52193-8 $5.99 US/$6.99 CAN

Dorchester Publishing Co., Inc.
65 Commerce Road
Stamford, CT 06902

Please add $1.75 for shipping and handling for the first book and $.50 for each book thereafter. NY, NYC, PA and CT residents, please add appropriate sales tax. No cash, stamps, or C.O.D.s. All orders shipped within 6 weeks via postal service book rate. Canadian orders require $2.00 extra postage and must be paid in U.S. dollars through a U.S. banking facility.

Name____
Address______________________________________
City ________________________ State______Zip______
I have enclosed $______in payment for the checked book(s).
Payment <u>must</u> accompany all orders.☐ Please send a free catalog.